THE CALM VOICE

ROBERT E KREIG

THE CALM VOICE

WHITEKEEP BOOKS

For Shonny

ANTELOGIUM

A question that sometimes drives me hazy:
am I or are the others crazy?

ALBERT EINSTEIN

ANTIQUUM

THE KILLARNEY FACTOR
SATURDAY MAY 13 2017

___

The room was lit more brightly than he had believed it to be. It looked a lot darker when he watched the show on his television at home. The set appeared simple, consisting of two black chairs upon a raised platform. Between them was a glass coffee table with a pitcher of water and two freshly filled glasses.

The backdrop was a large black curtain with the words THE KILLARNEY FACTOR, hanging from a drop-down sign attached to something far above them. The studio lights, shining from directly above, out in front and off to each side, were blinding. He didn't know how people on television did this every day without eventually losing their eyesight.

Perhaps they did.

Sitting in the chair left of the screen, he squirmed nervously as he reached for the glass closest to him. He took a quick sip, wishing it was something stronger.

"Take your time," Bill Killarney, the gracious host, told him.

His eyes moved across the three cameras with their lenses directed towards the two men on the platform.

Placing the glass gingerly on the table, he cleared his throat and moved his gaze back to the other man.

"I'm sorry," he said. "I'm a little nervous. First time on TV."

"It's all right," Killarney replied. "This isn't live. We'll edit this pretty tight for time's sake. I know that doesn't sit well, considering the context. It should be me apologizing to you for making you relive this."

"The wife thinks it might help if I was to talk about it," the man replied. "I was thinking more along the lines of a therapist or someone like that."

"I can recommend one I've used from time to time after my time reporting from war zones," the other suggested. "It seems stupid, but they do really help."

"I might take you up on that."

"Are you ready to continue, Mister Ramus?"

The man nodded. "I think so."

"Okay," Killarney fixed his tie. "Mister Ramus, in your time as Chief Inspector for the Texas Forensics Science Commission, have you encountered a crime scene in any way similar to that which was found at Edwards Hill State High School?"

"Never," Ramus replied, taking a deep breath afterwards.

"Could you elaborate?"

"You need to understand that this is an ongoing investigation," he answered. "To all involved, it would appear an open and shut case. But life isn't that simple. And what we saw in there was anything but a simple homicide or mass shooting for that matter."

"You're still referring to this case as a 'mass shooting'?" Killarney wrote something on a clipboard that was positioned on his lap.

"We don't know what to call this," the other said, shaking his head. "Many of the victims were shot. Some were..."

"Are you all right?" Killarney glanced at someone behind the cameras. "Do you want to stop?"

"No," Ramus replied instantly. "I'd like to continue, please."

"You were saying?" The host nodded.

"I was saying that most were shot, but there were others who were murdered in more creative ways." He took another deep breath as he considered the words he had just spoken. "*Creative* isn't the right word. But it's the most appropriate that I can think of at the moment."

"Talk us through what you encountered," Killarney suggested. "Keeping in mind that this is an ongoing case."

"Well," Ramus reached for the glass of water again. After taking a long sip and swallowing hard, he placed the glass back on the table. It clunked a little loudly. "Sorry."

"It's all right," the other assured him. "Please continue."

"We arrived after everything had unfolded," he said. "It was roughly seven-thirty and already quite dark. Someone had placed a couple of floodlights hooked up to generators around the outside of the building on the front lawn and had them pointing towards the ground. There were two bodies out there. I guess someone watched too many cop shows and decided they needed the lights for our team or something."

"Where should they have been?"

"We didn't need them at all," answered Ramus. "We always bring our own equipment. I mean, it didn't matter. The power was on and most of the external and internal lights were still working, even after the sprinkler system had been triggered. They weren't necessary. But, being a small town, maybe someone got a bit zealous and decided to get all the toys out. I don't know."

"So you went inside?"

"Yes. We entered at the side of the building through the emergency exit from the school cafeteria. We then split the team up and took different sections of the building. We hoped to process the scene a little quicker by doing this. As I said, it all appeared as an open and shut case."

"How many were in your team?"

"We had a large team," Ramus replied. "Eighteen. We were told that there were a lot of victims and that we would need numbers to process the scene."

"What would a usual number on a forensics team be?"

"Well, that depends upon the scene," he answered. "I would usually work with a team of three to five. But there have been times when I've worked with as many as twenty-five. The truth of the matter is that eighteen was all we could fit into the vehicles with the equipment we brought with us. That, and not too many wanted to go for a ride all the way from Houston to Edwards Hill."

"What happened next?"

"We split into sub-teams of three. My sub-team moved upstairs, where we took the center hallway. The first victims were murdered there. I think it's safe to say that we found three youths and five adults, all with fatal gunshot wounds. One was a police officer and four were teachers employed at the school."

"Safe to say?" Killarney interjected.

"Sorry?" Ramus moved his eyes to the presenter. His expression appeared as if he didn't understand the question.

"You said, 'safe to say'. What do you mean by that?"

"I was referring to the fact that this is still an open case," Ramus replied. "I know I can't give names for the time being. I may not be able to discuss gender either. But so much has already been announced in the media, including the victims' identities, that I feel I must give some clarification. That's why I said that I think it's safe to say these things."

"Of course." The host nodded, jotting something else down on his clipboard. "Please."

"Well, we processed the scene. Put tags down. Took photos and video. Measured what blood spatter hadn't been washed away by the sprinklers, distances of shell casings from the deceased. Nothing all that exciting.

"We then moved into the northern corridor and what we saw were bodies piled upon bodies. It was a complete and utter bloodbath. We spent nearly two hours in that hallway with the assistance of three other sub-teams.

"That was where the bulk of the massacre occurred." He took another sip of water. Hs eyes were glistening with moisture. "I had seen blood before. But not that much. Even then, something inside of me told me I wasn't going to walk away from this one without some scarring inside my psyche. But there was more.

"It was when we returned downstairs and were summoned by our colleagues to see what was in the gymnasium that caused my stomach to turn. I've never seen anything like it in my life and never want to see anything like it ever again."

"You're referring to the burnt bodies?"

"Burnt?" George Ramus, resigned Chief Inspector for the Texas Forensics Science Commission, felt his throat tighten. His eyes welled with tears. "They were children. Little children that were no older than fourteen at best. I mean, the vast majority of victims were only kids. But I've seen nothing like that. Not in my whole thirty-eight years in service with the Forensics Science Commission."

"And this is what sparked your resignation?" Killarney queried. "It was too much? You didn't want to see anything like that again?"

"She took their innards," Ramus blurted. "She arranged their guts along the floor to form a message."

"What message?" Killarney sat forward, intrigued. He flipped through the papers on his clipboard for notes about such a thing, but found nothing. This information was new.

"Jesus," Ramus cried. "What sort of person does that?"

"What was the message, Mister Ramus?"

"You wouldn't have guessed that someone like her would be capable of doing such things. She killed seventy-three in that school and took the time to leave a message."

"What was the message she left?"

Ramus didn't seem to hear the interviewer. The words dribbled out of him as he became more and more upset.

"She looked like any other normal kid. But she ripped their stomachs open and took their intestines out." He was a blubbering mess. His cheeks were wet. His nose was running over his lips in thick strips of mucus.

"Mister Ramus?"

"They were only burnt on the outside, you see," he explained. "But inside was still raw. Still raw."

"What message, Mister Ramus?" Killarney pressed.

"I think that's enough," called a voice from behind the cameras.

"Mister Ramus..." Killarney reached over and put his hand on George Ramus' knee. "What was the message she left?"

Ramus started hyperventilating. His breathing became erratic and snot sprayed across the floor at his feet.

"Cut!" the voice from the darkness called. "Cut. The interview is over, Bill."

"Mister Ramus," Killarney stood to his feet and placed his hand on Ramus' shoulder. "I apologize for pushing. Mister Ramus?"

The resigned chief inspector lowered his head towards his knees.

"Oh God," he wheezed. "Oh God. Oh, God."

PUELLA : THE GIRL

Sanity is a madness put to good uses.

GEORGE SANTAYANA

I

It was still dark.

The white Buick Somerset pulled into the driveway that stretched along the southern edge of the large building. For a moment, the headlights flared over the façade of the structure, illuminating the bold letters attached to the wall just above the main entrance.

EDWARDS HILL STATE HIGH SCHOOL.

Two bare flagpoles stood on either side of the door, reminding the driver of yet another task he needed to perform before the rest of the staff arrived.

He drove past the lawn, covered with neatly mowed grass and several large trees that provided shade through the day. Oaks and mesquites with their wide branches stretched across the yard.

The Buick moved by the southern wall of the school, passing a few windows with metal grilles over their faces, before pulling sharply to the right to enter a car park. A small sign on a long pole, posted on the ground where the vehicle turned.

STAFF PARKING ONLY.

The driver moved by the spaces, each with a bright yellow number painted in the center and two lines on either side to show to others where to park their cars.

Carefully, he backed the Buick into his allotted space, switched the headlights off, and killed the engine. He reached across to the passenger seat, lifted a gym bag that was resting there, and exited the vehicle.

Using his key, he locked the door and made his way across the car park, towards the front of the school.

He dressed in a uniform of sorts; dark green work pants and steel-capped boots. His work shirt, adorned with a name tag that read *Lionel Jenkins* above the right breast pocket, matched the color of the trousers.

Pushing his thick spectacles up his nose, he crossed the driveway and found a thin cement path that stretched along the front of the building, leading towards a raised platform in front of the main doors.

As he made his way along the path, he picked through his keys with his thumb and finger. With skillful dexterity, he placed the Buick's key into the palm of his hand, flipped his house key over the ring so that it sidled up to the one belonging to the car. Next was his post box key. Two more and he would have the one he was seeking, the key to the front door of the school.

By the time Jenkins reached the steps leading up to the platform, he had the key ready. He stopped before the doors and placed his gym bag on the ground. With his left hand, he took the padlock attached to a thick chain woven through the handles of the doors. With a twist of the key, the lock came undone.

Jenkins pulled the chain free of the door, causing it to rattle loudly. He then reattached the padlock to the two end links, making a loop, and placed it over his head like a heavy necklace.

With the same key that he had used for the padlock, he unlocked the main doors with a soft click. Crouching by his bag, he unzipped a side pocket and retrieved a canvas bag with the school's emblem on it. The words *Edwards Hill State High School Library* were printed in bold letters across the top.

He pulled one door open as he lifted his gym bag from the ground and stepped inside the school. Immediately, Jenkins moved to the left of the foyer and pressed the combination on an electronic keypad positioned on the wall.

It signaled the alarm release with two beeps.

Beside the alarm console were several switches. He flicked them all, turning on all the lights in the hallways of the lower level of the building.

Jenkins moved on into the building, passing a door with RE-CEPTION printed on it. There was a small window beside it, closed shut with a steel roller panel, similar to those found on some garage doors.

A long corridor stretched on ahead of him to the eastern end of the structure, intersected by another that ran from the northern end to the south. He turned left here and made his way to the northern end of the school.

Following the passageway, he eventually came to a corner that turned right. This corridor would lead him towards the eastern end of the building, linking up with another that stretched from the northern end to the southern end.

Halfway along the northern hallway, a passage that was slightly narrower than the main access ways, took him between boys' and girls' bathrooms to an emergency door that led outside to the student car park.

The padlock, threaded through a hole just under the release mechanism of the door, still had the key sitting in it.

Jenkins turned the key to open the lock and removed it from the door. He closed the lock again and dropped it into his canvas library bag.

Turning, he retraced his steps back to the main passageway and turned left, continuing to the eastern end of the building.

The cafeteria was his next stop. It was on his left, through a large open doorway. The area was vast, filled with tables and chairs.

There was one emergency door to the southern end of the eatery area, which he needed to unlock. The other was at the rear of the kitchen along a passage to the north-eastern edge of the room.

After placing both locks, with their keys still plugged in the keyholes into his library bag, he moved out of the cafeteria to the next intersection, where the passageway turned to the right. He passed a stairwell on his right and the open doors to the gymnasium on his left.

There were more doors that had padlocks on them inside. He considered retrieving them, but decided against it. After all, it was Monday and the track area to the rear of the building was closed to students and classes for small maintenance work at the beginning of the week. Friday sport, or Fucking Friday Funtime as Jenkins called it, usually saw patches of turf lifted and damaged. He usually spent a sizable portion of his Mondays repairing the ground for the next barrage of heel divots, crash tackles, and nonsensical destruction from students and physical education teachers alike.

He made his way to his office, just a little farther along the eastern corridor. Passing the girls' change rooms, then the boys', he stopped at a door with the word *MAINTENANCE* stenciled on it. He entered the tiny room and switched on the light.

A long florescent globe flickered to life noisily as he dropped his gym bag on a desk that sat flush against the right wall. Instinctively, he turned on the computer and television resting on the table's surface before grabbing the two flags that sat on his high-backed swivel chair.

Slinging the library bag over his shoulder, Jenkins carried the flags under his arm and moved back into the corridor. He still had two more locks to retrieve from the southern hallway.

After that, he would erect Old Glory into place on one flag pole, followed by the Texas state flag on the other.

By then, the cleaners would start their rounds, the kitchen staff would fire up the grill and the morning deliveries would be arriving.

Then it would be time to make himself a hot cup of joe.

II

Dark, ominous storm clouds swam around and around inside her head. Streaks of lightning clawed from deep inside them and scraped against the edges of her mind. Yawning gorges formed in her thoughts, dredged wide open, keeping the pain at the surface.

Keeping the hurt alive.

Her eyes flickered open, an attempt to stop the burning sensation she experienced against her eyelids. Tears blurred her vision, but she could still see the flashing lightning in her mind and feel the swirling tempest deep within.

It breathed.

It moved.

It edged its way to the surface, ready to escape.

Balling her fists against her temples, resting her elbows against her knees as she pressed her back against her bedroom door, she cried.

Above her, pinned to the wall nearby, a poster of a kitten peered down to her with deep blue eyes as it clung on to a clothesline for dear life, the words "Hang in There" displayed along the bottom.

She was trying to.

But *hanging in there* was proving to be impossible.

The damage had been done.

It had been done a long time ago.

She could hear the thunder rolling over again and again in her head.

Over and over.

The flash.

The thunder.

It wanted her to let go.

She wanted to.

But the struggle inside of her became a battle between falling prisoner to her guilt or submitting to the will of the storm.

She closed her eyes and made a guttural cry as she bawled again.

The clouds churned and changed from shades of gray and black to crimson red. They spread and stretched like puddles that grew in the rain, reaching across slight depressions to link with others of its own kind.

Crimson.

Red.

She couldn't stand it.

Opening her eyes again, she cried out loud, just as she had when she was a little girl.

Her mother would come running then. Gentle arms would wrap around her. Wrapped with love.

But not anymore.

No one came.

No one would come.

Not anymore.

Sliding to the floor, still naked and wet, she pulled her knees to her chest and placed her own arms around her legs.

Deep within the clouds, the faces of her parents formed in the shadows.

She pictured their smiles as they doted on her, their only child.

Loving, caring.

All they had ever done was for her.

So, she thought, *why did I do that to them?*

Her inner voice invoked more pain. Her stomach tightened and her throat ached as she continued to cry.

Her skin still felt unclean, even after the long, hot shower she had only moments ago.

Focus, the calm voice told her. *You should dry yourself. You should get dressed before you catch a cold.*

Wiping her eyes with the heel of her hand, she pushed herself from the floor and picked the towel up she had dropped by the door.

As she dried herself, she envisioned her parents' faces in the crimson clouds, smiling and laughing. Then they changed.

Their upturned mouths dropped as their eyes widened in fear.

The look of confusion unveiled on both of them before she completed the first step of the plan.

It had to start with them.

It just had to.

After all, they were to blame just as much as the others.

After pulling on jeans and a t-shirt, socks and sneakers, she used a hair dryer and brush to dry her scalp before making a ponytail with a black hairband.

She checked herself in the mirror.

She was pretty.

The all-American girl next door.

Blond, blue eyes and boobs that attracted the eyes of grown men and boys her own age. Usually, that would make her feel confident, knowing she could turn heads without even trying.

But not today.

Not for a long time.

Not even one of them had ever approached her, asked her out, barely said hello. They looked. They ogled. They ate her with their hungry eyes.

Talk in the boys' circles about how they would like to *do her* had reached her ears. It repulsed her and made her feel curious at the same time.

There were a few girls who were worse.

They spoke about her, called her names that insinuated that she slept around, and gave her sideways glances that made her feel less than welcome in their world.

But she was none of those things that they said.

She had thought she was normal.

She had believed she behaved like any other sixteen-year-old girl.

Yes, she felt confused about certain changes she was going through. And, yes, she had strange thoughts about boys in her classes, certain male teachers who looked as though they were just out of school and other men that she had encountered. But she had only ever given herself to them in her mind.

But was that so strange?

Didn't other girls do that too?

Never had she taken her clothes off for a man. Not even her father had seen her naked. Not since she needed her diapers changed.

So why would they say such nasty, hurtful words about her?

Because she was different?

Because she wasn't like them?

Because she was strange?

They were the ones who frequented parties at places where parents supplied the booze. They were the girls who dressed like *skanks* and *sluts*, *whores* and *tramps*.

Their hands were all over the jocks, the band members, even some of the library nerds copped a feel of those *fucking* bitches.

She packed her bag, a small backpack made of canvas and decorated with hearts, as she thought of the party that she was not allowed to attend. She was never allowed to attend any of them.

She was never allowed to do anything.

Her mom had told her it was for her protection. That things happen at those parties and they would not be acting like responsible parents if they had let her go.

Her dad said boys who go to these kinds of things only have one thing on their minds. That all they will want to do is try to *get with her*.

She had argued that she could say, no. Secretly, internally, she had told him she wanted to *get with them*, sometimes.

Moving to her desk, she placed a large notebook into her bag and her diary. It was pink with a picture of a kitten playing with a yellow ball of wool on the cover. She had scribbled her name on the front with a marker.

Kirstin Matthews.

Underneath, a small piece of graffiti read, "I [heart] JB."

I love Justin Bieber.

She didn't really love the singer. She'd written on the cover of her diary because other girls her age had said that they believed he was *hot*. She couldn't see it. But wanting to fit in, she wrote the brief message on her diary to appear as one of her peers.

Opening the bedroom door, she stepped into the hallway and walked past two doors. The first was the bathroom that she had been in not too long before. The second was her parents' bedroom.

Across the hall from there was another door to a spare room her father had made into a home office. She entered and crossed the room to his desk that was pushed against the windowsill.

After rummaging through the drawers, she found what she was looking for.

Two boxes of nine millimeter bullets and one magazine for her father's ninety-two compact that took seventeen rounds. She opened a box and started loading the clip, filling it to the top.

She slipped the magazine and the unopened box of bullets into the front pocket of her backpack. Keeping the other box in her hand, she moved out of the room and descended the stairs at the end of the hallway to the lower level of the house.

The gun was still resting on the kitchen floor, where she had dropped it.

Retrieving it, she pressed the magazine release and pulled the clip from the base of the handle. She placed the handgun on the kitchen bench, and carefully reloaded the magazine with four more bullets, replacing the ones she had used.

She placed the clip back into the revolver and pulled back on the slide, placing a bullet into the chamber. With her thumb, she switched the safety on before slipping the pistol into her bag.

Her eyes moved to the floor.

Her mother was lying on the tiles near the stove. Blood had spilt onto the clean, white floor as her mom drained fluid from two holes in her body. One in her chest, the other in her neck.

"Bye Mom," Kirstin said, holding back the tears.

She moved through the dining room, past a large mahogany table and chair set and into the living room where her father sat in front of the television on the sofa. His face turned towards the news. There Matt Lauer discussed the opening of some important film about something with a director about whom no one truly gave a shit.

The holes in her father's chest and in the cheekbone just below his right eye were the only sign that he was not watching the program. That and the cup of coffee that had stained the carpet by his feet.

"Bye Dad." She frowned, turning towards the foyer and making her way to the front door.

Walking down the long driveway, leaving the door open behind her, she peered at the silver Escape parked by the house. The Texan plates stabbed her eyes, causing tears to well up again as she ventured farther from the front door, passing under the morning shade of a large maple that grew in the front yard.

She knew there was no coming back from this now.

She was committed.

Texans didn't take kindly to the sort of thing she had already done, and what she was about to do.

The gravel crunched beneath her shoes as she started along the road towards the bus stop in the distance. She could see three others milling about as they waited for the yellow vehicle that would eventually come to take them to their place of incarceration for their daily dose of punishment and torture dished out by so-called educators. Coffee addicted, chain smoking, middle-aged, under-sexed dorks who got off by talking to one another about the latest episode of *Game of Thrones* or *The Walking Dead* before grumbling as the bell rang, calling them back to their sentry duty for another period or two.

She hated them.

She hated all adults.

They were the ones who prevented her from doing all the amusing things those others her own age did.

Over-protective parents.

Self-righteous teachers.

The maintenance man who stared at her chest as she passed by. He always looked at the girls, trying to see what they hid under short skirts or down blouses.

Fucking creep.

Three girls near to her age and one boy, who was in the last of his high school years, stood at the side of the road, at the end of another long driveway, where the bus collected them every day.

There were several two-story houses, spaced far apart, separated by wide yards and plots of land with horses or sheep.

She recalled a time when she would walk in the fields behind the houses with the other girls, talking about all manner of things that young girls did at the ages of twelve and thirteen. What music were they listening to, what was happening on their favorite TV show were favorite subjects; things that truly mattered and helped the world continue to turn.

But as they grew older, they drifted apart more and more. Partly because Kirstin had always preferred the company of herself, but the overriding factor was because she wasn't allowed to join in their adventures any more.

"...and then I threw up all over his pants," she heard one girl say as she drew nearer.

"Hey, Steph." She smiled, hiding the pain, calming the storm.

"Don't talk to me, slut," the girl replied.

Kirstin felt the verbal stab penetrate deep through her heart and stomach.

Why do you hate me so much?

The boy had been watching her approach the whole time, listening to the other tell her tale, but not really listening.

"How are you, Kirstin?" he asked, his eyes showing concern. He could see that something wasn't quite right about the girl standing in front of him.

"I'm fine," she told him.

"What are you doing tonight?" he asked her.

She moved her eyes to his.

Is he asking me out? She wondered. *I'm sixteen and he's almost eighteen.*

Steph and the other girl moved their gazes between the boy and the girl. This was unusual and unacceptable. Steph was clearly annoyed at the exchange between the two.

"Probably homework," she replied. "Like always."

"What if I came over?" he questioned further.

What's with the interrogation?

Steph's jaw dropped.

"I don't think my parents would allow that, Donny," she replied, picturing the two corpses in her house.

"I just mean to hang out," he told her. "I mean, I haven't seen your folks for a while either. Only to wave to as they drive past, you know."

He knows, the calm voice inside of her said. *He knows what you did.*

"I'll need to check with them," she said. "Can I call you back after school, when I get home?"

"Sure." He smiled, a slight dimple forming on his left cheek as he fixed his backpack over his shoulder. His eyes moved to a spot farther along the road behind her.

Turning, she could see the small yellow school bus was rising over the crest in the road, making its way towards them.

As it pulled up beside them, the two girls that had been waiting longest stepped on board and raced to the back seat. Donny stepped back to let Kirstin climb aboard, as he always did.

He does like me;; she thought.

But it's too late to turn back now.

It has already started, reminded the calm voice. *You need to focus.*

She peered around the bus and saw a few other students chatting across the aisle, occupying most of the seats except for the dreaded position directly behind the driver.

Sitting in the space that she seemed to always sit, she quietly placed her backpack on her lap and watched Donny pass by.

He gave her another smile and a wink, before moving further into the bus to sit with one of his friends a couple of seats behind her.

"How are you today, honey?" the bus driver, an elderly lady, asked her.

"I'm well, thank you, Missus Walker," she replied, masking her true feelings as she reached into her bag. Her hand brushed past the cold metal of the Beretta. "How are you?"

"I'm still breathing," the old lady answered as she moved the stick to drive. "Guess that means I'm okay."

Kirstin pulled her diary from the backpack and opened it, flicking through the pages until she landed on the next blank leaf. After retrieving a pen from the front pocket of her bag, she applied it to the paper and wrote her last entry.

III

Sipping her coffee slowly, she stared at the framed photograph of her husband, two children and herself, positioned on her desk by the computer that kept flashing reminders for her to check the messages that continued to flood in. Her much valued office receptionist, Mavis, used to filter the messages that entered the system. But she was gone now, retired at the ripe age of sixty-seven, hanging in an extra few years because she simply loved the place.

Instead, two extremely young women, not much older than the students enrolled in the school of which she was principal, sat in the front office deciding what color nail polish to wear as they discussed how much Sambuca they downed over the weekend.

God, how she disliked them, with their over-energetic enthusiasm, wearing their low-cut tops, skin-tight skirts and high-heeled shoes.

The photograph on her desk showed her husband and children posing for their most recent family portrait. She sat in front of her husband, Frederick, with his hands awkwardly placed on her shoulders. His face held an expression telling everyone that saw the picture that he didn't feel comfortable.

The tie around his neck was too short, and his shirt appeared way too loose around the waist. He told her after seeing it for the first time that he should have worn his jacket.

Andrew, her six-year-old son, looked a natural in the shot. Like her, he was photogenic and knew how to hold himself in front of the lens. Her four-year-old daughter, Terri, was like her father. She attempted to smile, but it looked more like an evil grimace instead.

Smiling as she peered at the photograph, draining the remains of her morning coffee, she wished she could be home with them all the time, or at least for one day. But the work of a principal wouldn't wait for her.

Edwards Hill State High School was a small school, but it had all the problems of the larger ones. She moved her eyes to the computer screen and read through the subject list of her emails.

Several were from parents regarding the overload of assignments and homework or the lack of it. Others came from students regarding yearbook content, the upcoming prom and track finals. Then there were the messages from staff members regarding state policies, changes to the curriculum, extracurricular programs and general complaints ranging from broken ceiling fans to toilet paper being out of stock.

She didn't want to know about most of it, but as a principal, it was her responsibility to keep the school running as smoothly as possible.

Giggles from the front office, the reception area, drew her attention away from the screen. Rising from her chair, she moved around the desk and opened the door to her office.

To the side of the room, a brunette woman, not much more than a girl, was bent over as she fussed through a filing cabinet against the wall. Her tight, black mini-skirt hitched so high she exposed her red panties that rode up into her butt crack.

If that skirt was any smaller, the principal thought, *it would be a belt.*

There was a boy no older than seventeen leaning over the service counter as he talked with the other office assistant sitting nearby. He rested on his elbows, smiling at the young woman as his eyes kept moving to her blouse with the top buttons undone, exposing her buxom cleavage.

The secretary was giggling at a remark made by the boy as she fingered a pendant that hung low around her neck. The boy's eyes transfixed, his smile growing wider.

The principal checked the clock on the wall.

Eight-o-five.

"You're a little early," she started. The boy shot upright and the secretary quickly turned to her desk. "Aren't you Mister Morris?"

"I ran to school today, Missus Richardson," he replied. "You know, getting ready for the track finals."

"And did you shower afterwards?" she questioned him.

"Of course," he answered.

"Then why are you sweating?" She kept her gaze on him. "Is it because I caught you looking at Miss Pearlman's breasts again?"

"I...I...I..."

"Go to the cafeteria, Mister Morris," she instructed him. "Stay there until the library opens at eight thirty."

"Yes, Missus Richardson." He quickly disappeared down the corridor and out of view.

"Miss Pearlman and Miss Childers," she addressed the two women in the room with her. "If you see Mister Jenkins, tell him I need to see him in my office as soon as possible. We have a few maintenance issues that require his immediate attention."

She turned away to enter her office.

"Oh, and Miss Pearlman..." She stopped by her door.

"Yes, Missus Richardson?" the junior secretary answered.

"I have never reprimanded either of you about your chosen attire," she said. "The exposure of the amount of skin that the two of you have on display is a little unsettling considering that you work in a school where we have many young boys with impressionable minds. I would be in my right to lodge a report with the state department for unprofessionalism. However, I'm not one to pick on a person regarding their clothing.

"But if I catch you flirting with a seventeen-year-old boy again, you can expect there to be consequences. Understand?"

"Yes, Missus Richardson." The girl lowered her head in shame.

Richardson returned to her office, closing the door behind her before moving around her desk to sit down. She stopped herself as she moved her eyes to her empty mug resting beside a pile of paperwork she was yet to get to.

Lifting the vessel from the table, she moved back to the door and entered the front office again. Both young women were engaged in tapping on keyboards as they completed financial reports, paid for expenses online using the school's account, and kept the facilities functioning by shifting funds from one place to another.

Richardson had to admit both girls were good at their job. They were efficient and fulfilled the duties their roles entailed.

But they were nothing like Mavis.

Mavis was an old warhorse who always went above and beyond her duties. She knew every student by name, something Richardson wasn't able to match.

If the principal required a meeting with a particular pupil, Mavis would have the individual's records on her desk waiting for her. Now, she would need to ask for every specific thing she required.

But Mavis was gone. She had moved away to Florida to soak up rays from the sun for the rest of her days.

Lucky girl.

She couldn't blame the two young women for such inadequacies, as they were still satisfying the work requirements. If Richardson asked either of them for anything, they did it within moments.

So why do I dislike them so much?

Smiling at them, she moved through the small space that was filled mostly with three desks, one remaining empty after Mavis' retirement, and the front counter which sat neatly under the reception window. Richardson, carrying her mug, opened a door to the side of the reception window that led to the corridor and crossed the area to the staff common room.

She guessed her reasoning for her dislike towards the young receptionists was nothing more than middle-aged jealousy. They were both attractive and intelligent. At times, they acted a little ditzy, but they were only a couple of years out of high school.

As she poured coffee into her mug, she tried to remember back to when she was their age. It seemed so long ago.

She recalled having a tremendous figure at the age of twenty. In fact, she still had a great body for someone of forty-two. Yes, some places had become a little bouncier with age, but the treadmill had maintained her muscle tone and she could honestly say she had abs.

The corners of her mouth rose a little as she considered others her age that had let themselves go after one child. She had produced two and kept trim without the help of surgery.

Many a time, she had patrolled the corridors of Edwards Hill State High School and heard the students refer to her in whispers as a MILF. As much as she scowled angrily at the boys and girls who had said it a little too loudly, she secretly relished the term as it gave her a little pep up after a long day of shuffling paper.

She discovered, as she poured cream into her cup, that her hand had moved to the pendant that rested on her buttoned shirt. She was running her finger over it habitually when she realized she had been a little hard on Miss Pearlman.

Yes, she dressed almost provocatively, but like most women, she was being flattered by the words of a well-built young man. Her fingers had moved to the jewelry around her neck as well.

An impulse, perhaps. Not an act of flirtation, but a reaction to the alluring words of an adolescent Cyrano de Bergerac or Giacomo Girolamo Casanova.

Richardson placed the cream back into the refrigerator and carried her steaming mug past the empty chairs in the teachers' lounge. Most of her staff wouldn't have arrived yet. Those who had were working in their classrooms, preparing the day's lessons.

She crossed the corridor and entered the small receptionist area, pausing in front of the two girls who were still tapping away on their computers.

"Ladies," she said. "I want to apologize for my little outburst."

The two secretaries stopped typing and looked up at her.

"What outburst, Missus Richardson?" Childers asked.

"About your attire," she replied. "I still stand by policy and will remind you of the professional dress code. But I implied that there was some flirtatious behavior towards a young man and I don't believe that I know the full story."

"I didn't think I was flirting, Missus Richardson," Pearlman told the principal.

"No," she acknowledged. "But I think he was flirting with you, and I think you might have liked it. And if I was sitting where you are, I think I might have been a little flattered, too. All I ask is that you be careful about the way you respond to them, because one of them will surely try again."

"Sure thing, Missus Richardson." Pearlman smiled. "Save it for Friday night at the club."

"That-a-girl." The principal nodded, returned to her office, and closed the door behind her. She moved around her desk and sat in the high-backed chair facing her computer, which continued to pile email upon email into her inbox.

Breathing a deep sigh, she moved her mouse to click the cursor onto the mail list. Starting from the top, she worked her way through the messages, trashing those of insignificance and responding to those which held some importance.

"Hey ladies," a voice called from beyond her door.

"Hi Mister Thompson," replied Pearlman.

"Hey Mister Thompson," Childers called back soon after. "Did you have a great weekend?"

"Can't complain," the man answered. "Is the boss in?"

"Sure," Childers told him. "I'll just see if she's available."

"It's okay, Karly," Richardson called out from behind her desk. "Mister Thompson can come on in."

"Well..." Childers giggled. "I guess you can go on in, Mister Thompson."

"Harry," he replied. "Please. I'm not your teacher anymore. We're work colleagues. I'm only Mister Thompson to the students."

"Okay," Childers replied, "Harry."

The door swung open and in walked a tall man wearing a cheap navy suit and red tie.

"Hey Boss," he said as he removed a brown leather satchel from his shoulder. He placed it upon the principal's desk before opening it and reaching inside.

"Morning, Harry." She smiled, looking up from her computer screen. "They should really call you Mister Thompson. One of them was your student only two years ago."

"Less than that," he said, pulling a jar containing a thick purple substance. "She was here, what... the year before last. Right?"

"Miss Pearlman graduated not last year or the year before, but the year before that." Richardson moved her eyes to the jar. "What's this?"

"I'm getting old." He shook his head, thinking about the years that kept sliding by unnoticed. "This is nectar of the gods. The plum tree in the yard has been producing a lot of fruit. Too much to eat. So, Wendy made jam. I brought you some. Hope you like it."

"Thanks, Harry," she said, opening the lid a little before lifting it to her nose and breathing in the aroma. It was sweet to the senses. "I didn't think it was plum season."

"You're welcome to come over and try to tell the tree that," he smiled. "I don't even think they're meant to grow out here. One thing I know is that you're gonna love it. I can tell from the look on your face."

She replaced the lid and put the jar gently on her desk.

"Well," he said, returning to the door, "I'll leave you to it and I'll get to work. Talk later." He waved as he entered the front office.

"See you, Harry," she said, and smiled.

"Bye, Mister Thompson," the two receptionists chorused.

"Harry, ladies!" He shook his head. "Come on. I'm not that old, am I?"

Childers tilted her head and wore an expression as if to say he may be older than he believed.

"Oh," he retorted with a smile. "Thanks a lot."

As his footfalls drifted away down the long corridor, Pearlman rose from her chair to close the principal's door.

"Thank you, Miss Pearlman," Richardson said as she returned to her computer.

"Quite all right, Missus Richardson," she replied. "Holler if you need anything."

"Will do," the principal told her as the door clicked shut.

She sipped her coffee slowly, savoring it before swallowing. After placing her mug on the table, she reached into the top drawer of her desk for a small tin of breath mints. This being her third cup this morning, she knew the inevitable trips to the bathroom would come later in the day, but she needed the breath mints now.

Her eyes moved to the framed photograph again. She was finding it difficult to focus her much-needed attention on the many things that required her consideration. A scheduled visit from district inspectors during the week to check electrical fittings and devices. Another group of maintenance officers expected to come out to the school to check thermostats and the boiler room.

Her own maintenance officer would show the visitors around to the various locations they needed to be, but all the communication to and from the different sections of the district office went through her email.

She started forwarding the messages to Lionel Jenkins, hoping he would have time to check them before the end of the day. Right now, at eight twenty, he was probably cleaning the cafeteria tables.

She sipped her coffee again, peering at her family for what seemed a long time. She didn't understand why she felt such a powerful urge to be with them, but it was almost overwhelming.

Richardson smiled as she moved her eyes over her husband's awkward hands, her son's photogenic smile and her daughter's evil grimace.

How she would give anything to be home.

IV

The spaces between the yards grew smaller. The number of houses within her view increased. The bus had crossed the imaginary line that encircled the town of Edwards Hill.

She had put her diary back into her bag and plugged her earphones in, turning up the volume and silently mouthing the words to the song playing on her mix. A slow, heavy acoustic guitar strumming away as one of her favorite singers waxed melodic.

The main street storefronts flashed by the window as the bus bounced over a few speed bumps, placed along the road to stop young hooligans from racing their cars up and down the long, straight stretch that moved from one edge of the town to the other. Kirstin wondered if Missus Walker had even noticed they existed as she believed the bus was airborne after hitting one of the speed bumps hard, bouncing back to the ground with a jolt.

The younger students from the elementary school laughed and cheered with each lunge and lurch as they hastened through the main street. Some urged the old lady to hit the gas. Others, mostly the older passengers, gripped the rails on the backs of the seats in front of them so tightly that their knuckles turned white.

After spinning to the right, the yellow school bus rattled along another straight stretch of road. Missus Walker slowed the bus down almost to a crawl as she drew near to the town's two schools. Ahead, on the right, was the local elementary school where the bus would make its last stop for the morning. There, the students destined for both educational establishments would all disembark the vehicle and separate from each other.

The younger passengers would walk straight into their school gate near to where the bus stopped. The high school students would need to cross the street to their place of daily penance, directly across the road from the elementary campus.

Kirstin waited until all the small kids were off the bus before pulling her earphones out of her ears and wrapping the cable around her iPod. She then dropped the player into a pocket inside her bag and waited for all the larger people to clear the transport.

"You okay, honey?" Missus Walker asked her as Donny stepped off the bus. He looked back to Kirstin, smiling at her as his friends called him away.

"I'm fine," she answered, rising to her feet and swinging her backpack over her shoulder.

"I've just noticed you are quieter than usual," Walker pressed. "Everything all right at home?"

My mom has two holes in her from the bullets I gave her, she thought. *My dad's watching TV with a dead stare. Sure, everything is all right.*

"Just a little tired," she lied.

"Well..." The old woman gave the girl a concerned look. "You take care of yourself. Okay? If you ever need to talk, you can always talk to me."

"Thanks Missus Walker." Kirstin smiled half-heartedly as she stepped off the bus. "Have a nice day."

She moved to the rear of the bus and looked both ways before crossing the road. Milling about, outside the high school's entrance, people met up with friends and talked about their weekend, catching up on gossip and gloating, lying about how debauchedly they had behaved.

Kirstin could feel eyes upon her as she walked along the long path to the steps that led to the large doors of Edwards Hill State High School. The stars and stripes waved lazily in the clear air near to the entrance to the building.

Donny was there, standing on the lawn under a tree in a circle of other well-built young men and scantily clad girls from his grade. One girl with braids in her hair and wearing next to nothing twiddled a pencil in her fingers, biting on its end seductively, hoping to gain his attention.

He didn't notice, or at least pretended not to, choosing to follow Kirstin with his stare as she moved by. She glanced towards him quickly, locking eyes with him for a moment before turning them away, embarrassed.

She then felt the leers, the silent jeers that stabbed her like knives in the back. These came from the other girls like Steph, Nancy and Angie, who spat spiteful words to one another about her as they leant against the guardrails at the side of the school's wide platform at the top of the stairs.

We were friends once.

Kirstin lowered her eyes as she moved by them, hastening her pace as she neared the door.

"Slut," she heard one of them say. She pulled the door open and moved through the foyer, past the administration office, where she heard tapping computer keys, and along the corridor towards the bathroom.

The door squeaked loudly as she stepped into the bathroom. The dank smell of dampness and undertone of bleach wafted throughout the room as she moved into a stall and closed the door.

After the bus ride, with constant jostling and jiggling, she had found it was best to come straight to the restroom before engaging in the day's activities. Lately, she had been using the visit to the facilities for a moment of recollection and emotional relief.

She didn't understand why they hated her so much.

There was once a time when she and Stephanie were the closest of friends. Since reaching a certain age, their relationship had simply ceased to be.

She was no longer worthy of being Steph's friend.

She was no longer worthy of being a part of them.

She was simply no longer worthy.

Donny was the only one who ever showed her kindness of late. But that had just made things worse between the other girls and herself.

Why can't he see that?

Why can't they see I have done nothing with him?

Why do they hate me so much?

She felt alone, isolated.

If only she had been allowed to join them at their weekend parties. Then they would see she wasn't any of the things they thought she was.

Too late now, she thought. *It will all be over soon.*

She grabbed some tissue from the dispenser beside her and wiped her eyes and nose, dropping it into the toilet and flushing it away.

She opened the door to the stall and stepped out to wash her hands, only to be confronted by the three girls that had ridden on the bus all the way with her.

"What do you think you're doing, bitch?" Steph stepped within an inch from her face, stabbing her finger into Kirstin's breast.

It hurt as the other girl poked her several times hard. Kirstin stepped backwards, bumping into the partition between stalls.

Angela and Nancy leant against the wash basins behind Steph as the rant continued.

"What are you trying to do?" Steph went on. "Are you trying to steal my man from me? I want Donny and I'm gonna make him want me."

"I haven't done anything," Kirstin whimpered.

"Bull fucking shit," the other barked. "Why does he keep looking at you like he does? Look at me and look at you."

Kirstin noticed the other's apparel. Short cutoff jeans with ass cheek sticking out the bottom. A tiny white tank top with her nipples almost poking through the material.

"How can he keep looking at you, wearing this inbred, redneck shit and not even notice me?" Steph growled, scowling.

"Maybe she's fucking him?" Nancy suggested.

"Is that it, slut?" Steph questioned, pushing Kirstin against the stall wall. The doors rattled as her head banged against the partition. "Are you fucking my man?"

"I haven't..." A lump formed in her throat as she fought back the tears that welled in her eyes.

"What?" Angie laughed. "You're a virgin? No way. No one who looks like you is a virgin."

Kirstin didn't know whether to take the comment as a compliment or to be offended.

The weight of her backpack felt heavy, as if she needed to unpack one particular item. She suddenly felt the need to feel the grip in her hand, the cold metal against her skin.

Not yet.

"I don't care what you think of me," she spat back. "I don't care about you or Donny. You're all shit!"

She pushed Steph out of her way, knocking her towards the other two girls before leaving the restroom.

Bitches.

She stormed along the corridor, hearing the bathroom door open behind her and footfalls on the linoleum floor following.

Your time will come.

Ignoring the three pursuers, she made her way towards the library, her first place to appear on her schedule.

Soon.

After pushing the door open, she moved into a large room where shelves of books stretched along the walls, reaching from the floor to the ceiling. She paused, peering out through the glass doors to watch the three girls strut by, glaring at her.

As they moved away, under the watchful eye of every adolescent boy in the corridor, Kirstin turned to move on into the library, finding a desk to sit at as she waited for the bell to ring. A quick glance at the clock told her she still had five minutes to wait for Mister Redman, her homeroom teacher, to enter the room.

She reached into her backpack for her iPod and plugged her earphones back into her ears. After turning the device on, she pressed play and sat back as the next song on her playlist started.

Her heart was still pounding hard and fast, and her breath was rapid and uneasy. The experience with the girls in the bathroom had shaken her.

This was why she had to do what needed to be done.

This kind of thing happened to her every day.

She tried to slow her breathing and force her heart back into her chest. Her hand moved to the place where Steph had jabbed her with her finger. It was still aching. It would probably bruise.

Turning the volume up to full, she closed her eyes and watched the crimson clouds swirling, swirling.

Her parents were there, eyes open and motionless as they stared at her through hollow sockets. Their mouths were agape as blood bubbled and foamed upon their lips.

Crawling out from the darkness, stretching their tiny limbs from behind their yellowing teeth, the insects emerged. Their long antennae flicked this way and that as they pushed through the red and white bubbles spilling onto their chins.

Kirstin, she heard them call. Their faces were unchanging.

Neither one of them moved their mouths, formed the words, spoke a word. Yet, they called her name over and over.

Kirstin.

Kirstin.

No, you can't go to the movies, her father's voice told her. *How am I to know who you will meet up with there and what you will get up to?*

That boy only wants one thing, her mother said. *And you're nowhere near old enough to even be thinking things like that.*

Dirty minded, filthy boys who only want to have their way with you, her dad added.

Filthy girls, her mother hissed. *All of those girls wearing their short pants up their cracks. There is no way I'm letting you out with them. I won't have anyone calling my daughter a whore.*

Kirstin, do you hear what your mother just said? Her father's voice called.

Kirstin?

Kirstin?

Kirstin?

"Kirstin," a voice beside her beckoned.

She jumped in her skin as her eyes flickered open. Mister Redman, a young, attractive man, smiled down at her. He gestured for her to remove her earphones.

Kirstin turned her iPod off and stashed it in her bag.

"Thank you, Kirstin," the teacher said, as he moved to the middle of the room. Several other students had gathered in the library. Some others were hastily making their way in through the door. "Good morning, all."

"Good morning, Mister Redman," Kirstin replied, joining a droning chorus of greetings from those gathered in the library.

"Listen for your name," Redman instructed, "and call out *present* if you're here."

"And if we're not?" a young boy interjected.

"Hilarious, Mister Norritch," the teacher replied as he opened a folder while removing a pen from his shirt pocket. "Fiona Mabrey?"

"Present," a young girl replied from behind Kirstin.

"Greg Maddick?"

"Sir," a boy across the room called.

"Zain Maibling?"

"Here."

"Kirstin Matthews?"

"Present," she answered, tuning out thereafter as Mister Redman continued to call the morning roll.

His voice echoed away as she stared blankly at the desk. Her anger was still there, flooding the backs of her eyes with intense heat as the storm clouds built bit by bit.

Swirling, swirling.

The item she had carried in her bag seemed to reach out to her.

It wanted to be held by her.

It wanted to be set free.

But it wasn't time yet.

Soon, the calm voice told her. *It will be time soon.*

V

First period bell.

The swirling clouds dissipated, parting to make way for the reality around her, suppressing the reality within.

Like Pavlov's dog, the teenage animals rose from their seats and slung their backpacks over their shoulders before moving towards the door of the library as one organic mass. Squeezing against one another, pushing, shoving, the students forced their way through the relatively tiny passage way.

"One at a time," Redman shouted over the group.

Kirstin stayed at the back of the mob, letting them wrestle against each other as they shuffled through the narrow gap.

One student, two, then three, popped into the corridor beyond the door before they raced off toward their first class of the day.

"Why couldn't they all be sensible like you, Kirstin?" Redman commented with a smile.

Sensible, she thought. *Good old, sensible, reliable Kirstin. I'm sure you will change your mind about that before the end of the day, Mister Redman.*

She smiled back and moved behind the remaining students as the crowd thinned and made their way out of the room. Kirstin turned to her left and followed the passage to a set of steps that led up to the next level. There, she ascended the stairs, passing several students that raced down from their homerooms to their classes on the first floor.

As she neared the top of the steps, she reached into her jeans' pocket and retrieved a key. Turning to her right, she walked along the corridor, lined on either side with lockers. Some students were engaged in conversations about their weekends as they collected books and equipment for their morning classes.

The jocks, grouped together like pack hounds, taunted the nerds who carried laptops and tablet devices. Kirstin laughed inwardly at the stupidity of the muscle-bound sports freaks and their super cute cheerleading girlfriends wearing matching outfits. The boys had their green and black jackets with EHHS embroidered on the breast. The girls had their short green skirts and super tight tops with the same lettering across their boobs. One day, the football and baseball team members, if they weren't lucky enough to get a scholarship to some varsity college, would work for the tech-savvy Poindexters and Geekazoids. That's when the bullies would get a little taste of their own shit back.

She could see them cleaning muck and grime from cisterns, feeding pipe snakes into someone's sewers as thick, brown splash back soaked their overalls right through. Meanwhile, their cheerleading girlfriends waded waste deep in diapers as they bounced their fifth or sixth child on their over-ripe pregnant stomachs, chain smoking their full flavored Buffalos while watching their stories on the TV.

The nerds, however, bullied in the corridors of their high schools, would become CEOs and managerial material and would sit in high-backed chairs behind large mahogany desks, hiring and firing these assholes who once made their lives a living hell.

Thus completing the circle of life.

Kirstin used the key to open her locker. She placed her bag inside and retrieved a history textbook and writing pad that rested on their edges, pushed to one side of the locker's cavity.

"Slut," she heard a voice call behind her. Turning, she saw Steph and Nancy pass by as they made their way along the corridor.

Not yet, she thought as the two girls disappeared into a room farther along the passageway. Her hand was already in her bag. Her fingertips were touching the cold steel of the pistol.

Not yet.

Closing her locker, Kirstin returned along the corridor in the direction she had come from, making her way towards the stair-well. She crossed the passageway and entered a room directly opposite the stairs.

The room was filled with rows of desks and chairs, all facing a whiteboard at the front of the room, like soldiers on parade. Some of the more academic students had filled a few seats already and quietly prepared for the day's lesson, opening their text books to where they had left off and flipping through their notepads to their scribbling from the previous class.

Kirstin squeezed between two boys to sit in a vacant chair at the back of the room. She felt their eyes watching her, probably scrutinizing her ass in her jeans. If it had been a jock, she probably would have heard some snide comment to accompany the ogling.

Instead, the boys remained quiet and returned to their notes once she had passed them. She couldn't blame them for admiring her. It was in every boy's DNA to be attracted to women.

Well, she thought, *every straight boy.*

Not just that, but Kirstin had maintained her health and fitness with regular exercise and healthy eating, something her parents had enforced upon her through their rigid regime.

Sitting down, she placed her books on the desk and opened the textbook. As she did so, her eyes moved towards the front where they were met by those of one boy she had passed by. He was looking straight at her.

Probably the first time he noticed your face, she thought. *Probably only looks at your ass and boobs.*

He was cute. Even with the thick Coke-bottle glasses resting on his nose.

Red pigmentation appeared on his cheeks as he smiled sheepishly before turning away.

Kirstin felt the corners of her mouth rising. She found the experience quite flattering.

Her eyes moved to a poster that was positioned on the wall by the door. It was an old picture that had been hanging there since before she enrolled in the school.

It showed five native Americans adorned in face paint, feathers and *traditional* attire. Large letters stretched across the bottom, "Native American Heritage Month."

Heritage.

She laughed softly.

"What's so funny, Kirstin?" asked a young woman as she entered the room, placing her books on the large desk near the whiteboard.

"Nothing," she replied.

"You laugh at nothing?" the adult asked. "Even at your age, I would assume that would be a strange practice. No?"

Kirstin pursed her lips and pointed to the poster with her chin, "I'm laughing at that, Miss Posadas."

"The poster?" she asked. "Why do you find it so funny?"

Some of the other students turned in their seats to see Kirstin's reaction to the interrogation. Other students, jocks and cheerleaders, moved into the room, turning their jovial faces into serious expressions as they realized something was transpiring in the classroom. They quickly moved to their seats and joined the others in their gawking.

Kirstin didn't like this teacher. She was young, not much older than the students she taught. She was naïve, graduating from school to go to college, only to return to school again.

The young girl measured the teacher with her eyes. She was beautiful, exotic and voluptuous; the subject of adolescent male corridor discussions, and possibly the occupier of their dreams at night. Kirstin knew that the staff possessing penises had probably gone out of their way to please Miss Posadas in more ways than one in the hope of her to be the occupier of their beds.

More cream in your coffee, Miss Posadas? She imagined them asking her. *Let me get that for you.*

Are you cold, Miss Posadas? Here, have my jacket to keep you warm.

Walking home, Miss Posadas? Let me give you a ride.

"The poster isn't funny," Kirstin replied. "The concept of native Americans having the ability to maintain heritage is funny."

"I don't know whether to be offended or intrigued," Posadas said. "Explain yourself."

"I don't mean any disrespect to the native Americans, Miss Posadas," Kirstin began. "In fact, I find them to be the victims of a harsh race who attempted to conquer the world the only way they knew how. With technology.

"White man, my ancestors, came by sailing ship with muskets and gunpowder and wiped out quite a large number of the native Americans. And then, the ones they didn't hit with pellets or cannon balls were attacked by miniscule diseases.

"The ones who remained couldn't even be called lucky to have survived because then, they were thrown into fenced off zones that the conquerors called *reserves*."

"I think it was a little more complex than that," the teacher replied. "Don't you?"

"Not really," the student answered. The others around her stared, amazed that someone like Kirstin would bite back so readily.

"Please," Posadas gestured with her hand. "Go on."

"Okay." She nodded. "European explorers and settlers colonized many nations around the world, didn't they?"

"That's correct," Posadas admitted.

"In almost every one of those nations, they found an indigenous population that they needed to barter with or make treaties with. How many of them were successful in acquiring peace?"

"You don't believe that the settlers and the native Americans could establish peace?" the teacher questioned. "What about the traditional story of Thanksgiving?"

"Bullshit," Kirstin replied.

Several gasps resounded throughout the room.

Posadas looked surprised at the use of profanity, but didn't correct the girl for the foul language. Instead, she kept her eyes on the student, took a deep breath, and gestured for Kirstin to continue.

"Some historical texts would suggest that the transaction between the pilgrims and the natives ended in bloodshed. Others suggest that disease was passed over to the indigenous populations, such as smallpox being concealed in blankets that were given as gifts.

"And to say they established peace is a joke. There are innumerable accounts of settlers and travelers being mutilated as they moved across the plains to the west. At the same time, there are innumerable accounts of nations of native Americans being wiped out by white raiding parties in search of scalps.

"To deny any of that happening would be to deny the true heritage of the native Americans, but I think that poster does just that. It not only denies their heritage; it makes a joke of it."

"Your point is taken," Posadas relaxed. "But it is a very narrow one."

"This book..." Kirstin held up the textbook for all to see, "has a narrow point of view. My point of view spans the globe.

"Did you know that in Australia, when the ruling empire of the day claimed the continent, they declared it Terra Nullius, even though there was an indigenous people present?"

"What's a *terror nullerist*?" asked a beefy jock sitting by a window.

"Terra Nullius means that the land is unoccupied by a human civilization," returned the boy with Coke-bottle glasses.

"So?" said a girl in a cheerleader costume. "The Aborigines threw spears and lived in caves. They weren't civilized."

"Hold on," Posadas held her hands up.

"Yes, they were," another girl replied. "And they still are. They hold a rich culture, just like our own indigenous people. It was just stolen from them. Their land was taken and their babies were kidnapped."

"Did someone steal their babies from them, Miss Posadas?" a boy quizzed.

"Nobody stole anyone's babies," Posadas replied.

"They did too," said the boy with glasses. "They called it the Stolen Generation and the Australian President apologized to the Aborigines in two-thousand-and-eight."

"Prime Minister," another boy sitting beside him corrected.

"What?"

"The Australian political leader is called a Prime Minister."

"Oh." The boy with glasses nodded.

"I can't believe someone would steal babies from people." A girl shook her head.

"The same thing happened here," said another girl. "Babies were killed and soldiers raped women. The military called it *conquering,* but the natives called it *invasion.*

Kirstin sat back, admiring the look on Miss Posadas' face as the class erupted in discussion about anything but what the teacher had intended for them to be focusing upon.

The teacher threw her hands up in the air, calling out with her soft voice to regain the attention of the students, but it was too late. She had lost them.

Completely lost them.

Her eyes moved to Kirstin, who was silently scanning the room, listening to one conversation in part before turning her attention to another discussion. Eventually their eyes locked and the young girl knew she was going to pay for the disruption to the history class.

Well, Miss Posadas, Kirstin thought. *You're the one who asked me about why I was laughing at the poster. This is more your fault than mine. Besides, your students are talking about history in a history class. Why are you so upset with me?*

Kirstin held the stare, boring her own gaze deep into the burning glare of the teacher until Posadas turned her eyes back to the boisterous class. She shook her head, pulled the chair out from behind the desk at the front of the room, and plonked herself down.

There was nothing else she could do.

Can't get control of your students back, Miss Posadas? Kirstin thought. *Don't worry. It will all be over soon.*

VI

"She humiliated me in front of the class," Posadas barked as she stood before Richardson's desk, Kirstin seated at her side as the young teacher thrust a finger in her direction. "She caused the class to be disrupted and, as a result, they were uncontrollable."

"Please take a seat, Miss Posadas," Richardson requested as she peered over her glasses that were resting low upon the bridge of her nose. "I understand you are upset, but if you could please sit down, we both may be able to maintain our composure."

The young woman was breathing rapidly, remaining on her feet as her hands moved to her hips. Richardson couldn't stop her eyes from moving to Posadas' heaving chest. Every ounce of strength she had was holding back laughter as she observed the young teacher's breasts jiggle as they rose and fell with each inhale and exhale.

Richardson watched the teacher move her angry gaze from her to the young girl, where she kept her eyes as she lowered herself back to the seat beside the student. Kirstin wore the expression of a timid creature, fearful of the monster that sat within arm's length of her.

"Did you intend to disrupt the class like that, Kirstin?" Richardson questioned.

"She asked me about the poster," the student replied. "How could I intend to do anything? I was responding to her question."

"And what was the question?" the principal pressed.

"Why was I laughing at the poster?"

"And why were you laughing?"

Posadas huffed grumpily as she folded her arms and stared at a place on the wall.

"I found the concept of heritage and what the people in the picture were wearing to be contradictory," Kirstin replied. "I found it a little silly, that's all. Then she makes a big song and dance out of it."

"Excuse me," Posadas snapped. "I made the song and dance?"

Richardson held her hand up, "Miss Posadas, please. Let's try to remember who the adolescent person in the room is, thank you."

Kirstin almost laughed.

Focus.

She liked Missus Richardson. The principal had always been kind to her. She was kind to all the students, but seemed to have a soft spot for the quiet, the reserved, the academically gifted and those with interests in things that the majority overlooked.

It felt good to have an adult on her side, if only one.

"Kirstin..." The principal rested her elbows on the table. "I don't see a reason for keeping you from your next class. Where are you meant to be right now?"

"English with Missus Merrick," she replied.

Richardson looked at her watch.

"The period is almost over," the principal said. "If you want to wait in the office until the bell, you can."

"It's a double," Kirstin informed her.

"Well, you had better get there quick," Richardson instructed her. "Grab a hall pass from Miss Pearlman and give it to Missus Merrick when you arrive in class."

"Yes, Missus Richardson." Kirstin rose from her seat, hugging her books against her chest as Posadas glared confusedly at the two others in the room.

The young teacher shook her head and rose to her feet as the student opened the principal's office door and exited the room, closing the access behind her with a soft click.

She gestured to the door, staring at Richardson with wide eyes and mouth agape.

"Sit down, Miss Posadas," instructed Richardson, lowering her voice. "The girl may still be able to hear you and me."

"You're just letting her go?"

"I am," she replied.

"She ruined my well-planned lesson," the teacher told the other.

"From your perspective," Richardson reached for her coffee. She sipped on it. The contents had turned to room temperature from sitting for so long.

"From my perspective?"

"Sit down." The principal locked eyes with Posadas. The look was not one of comfort or sympathy. "Right now."

Posadas complied. Her countenance changed from fury to worry.

"I have reviewed your program and noted student feedback concerning your so-called *well-planned* lessons," Richardson began. "Teaching directly from a textbook is not, nor will it ever be, well planned.

"That girl did you a favor today. For the first time in the history of when you were employed by the state to teach at this school, your students were engaged in a discussion about history."

"It was off topic," Posadas interjected. "We were meant to be looking at the domestic and international impact of the US involvement in World War Two."

"Really?" Richardson sat back. "Well, I'm sorry if something sparked interest in some other historical debate that took you away from your well-planned lesson. But it seems to me that you started the discussion with a question."

"A question about her behavior," the teacher argued.

"A question about history," the principal replied. "A question about the heritage of native Americans to be exact."

Posadas shook her head.

"I know the poster Kirstin was referring to," Richardson continued. "It's old and far out of date. We should replace it. I had been thinking about doing it myself. But guess what? Today, I am so glad it is still there on that classroom's wall.

"Because of that poster, a young girl reflected upon what the meaning of *heritage* is to her. Today, you asked her a question, possibly hoping to ridicule her or admonish her in some way, but it backfired on you. Today, she answered your question. And, boy oh boy, what an answer. It was so good an answer that the rest of the class started talking about it.

"Today was the first day that your junior year class, the only class out of all of your classes, was truly engaged in learning. It didn't involve a text book. It didn't involve a YouTube video. It merely relied upon acquired information.

"You should be proud of her and your students for being able to discuss such deep and rich content. Instead, you come in here and point your finger at a young girl who is at a fragile, confused stage in her life.

"When it comes to your performance record," Richardson continued, "which I have not completed yet, what do you think I should jot down after today?"

"You've never liked me." Posadas scowled. "Not from the first day I arrived."

"I could say the very same thing regarding your attitude towards that young lady who was seated beside you only moments ago," the principal returned. "Why don't you like her? I don't understand.

"We have most of the cheerleaders with their constant texting during class, but that's okay with you. The other girls with their discussions about what the fashion of the day is and how to wear their hair, but you're fine with them too. We have an entire school of kids who are either geniuses in their fields or soon to be the dregs of society, but they don't even register on your radar.

"But Kirstin Matthews does, and I don't know why."

Posadas stared back to the principal, her chin lifting defiantly as she pursed her lips.

"Why her?" Richardson pressed. "I just want to know why you dislike that one student out of the hundreds we have walking our hallways every day. Why?"

"I don't know," Posadas replied, a tear streaking down her cheek. "Because she's smart. Because she's pretty. Because she doesn't fit in."

"Because she reminds you of yourself?"

"No," the young teacher replied adamantly.

Richardson peered at the teacher for what seemed an eternity. Suddenly, a light bulb flickered on and the principal believed she understood.

"You're in love with her," Richardson breathed.

Posadas remained silent, her wet eyes moving to the window.

"Why treat her so terribly if you like her in such a way?"

The principal's response surprised the young teacher. Richardson didn't appear offended by Posadas' silent admission of her fondness towards a student.

"Because it's wrong," Posadas explained. "Because it's criminal."

"You haven't committed a crime," Richardson told her. "The *act* is the crime. You haven't acted out your feelings. You're an adult who is in control of her faculties. For crying out loud, Rosina, get over it. You're reacting like one of those teenage, hormone infected, fruit loops we have out there.

"This kind of thing is going to happen from time to time. You'll see some attractive kid. Your heart will melt for them. Keep your composure. You're meant to be a professional."

Posadas nodded as Richardson extended a tissue box towards her.

The young teacher took two sheets of soft paper and wiped her eyes.

"I'm sorry," she said.

"For what?" the principal asked. "For being human or for being a lesbian who recognizes beauty when she sees it?"

Posadas smiled. "Please don't tell anyone."

"About this?" Richardson frowned. "Of course not. But you need to change your teaching habits before next semester. And you need to get your feelings in order. Here in this school, you are a teacher first. In this community, you are a teacher first. To these girls, both in and out of this building, you are a teacher first. Understand?"

Posadas nodded.

"Good," Richardson nodded. "Take the next period off. Relax in the lounge. I'll take your class."

VII

Kirstin stood at the receptionist's window, waiting for the hall pass from the young office assistant who was putting the date and time on the card. All could hear the conversation between the principal and the teacher.

The door was not as thick as one would hope, especially concerning such a private conversation that ensued from within Richardson's office.

When the discussion turned to why Posadas had taken a dislike to the student, Kirstin's ears perked up, focusing on the words. She didn't need to try too hard as the chat, though muffled a little by the barrier between the two spaces, was still clear as crystal.

The words spoken by Richardson, *you're in love with her,* made their way into the receptionist's office and through the little window where the student stood. The silent response from Posadas spoke volumes to the three females within eyesight of each other.

Kirstin's jaw dropped as she peered towards the principal's door. Both receptionists looked to the girl.

Tania Pearlman handed the hall pass to the student waiting by the reception window.

"Here, Kirstin," she said, observing the girl's reaction as the conversation continued.

Kirstin kept her eyes on the principal's door, dumbfounded and confused.

Miss Posadas loves me?

"Kirstin?" Pearlman called again. "Your hall pass."

The girl snapped back to reality and looked at the receptionist, taking the pass from her extended hand.

"Are you okay?" Pearlman asked.

"Huh?" Kirstin breathed, her mouth still wide open. "Yeah, thanks."

She pivoted and walked away, hoping anyone else who may have been passing the receptionist's office hadn't heard the conversation.

"That poor girl." Karly Childers sighed as she peered towards the little portal to the corridor.

Pearlman leant over the desk and peered down the passageway after her, concerned. A knot formed in her stomach as she felt like racing after the student, just to be an ear to talk to or a shoulder to lean on.

Her footfalls were brisk as her sneakers squeaked softly against the linoleum floor. Water welled up in her eyes and she looked around for a place to escape.

The girls' restroom was just ahead, to the left.

She ducked inside, finding the room empty.

Her feet directed her to the stall at the far end of the row, where she entered, locking the door behind her.

Sitting on the seat, she wept.

Why was she so mean to me?

She pulled a few sheets of paper from the dispenser beside her and wiped her eyes.

If she likes me, loves me, why would she be so mean?

I hate her.

Kirstin felt her mouth turn downward as tears streamed from her eyes. Her stomach tightened as she felt like screaming.

I hate her for making me feel like this.

Her shoulders shuddered, and her nose ran. She pressed more tissue against her face.

It doesn't change a thing.

She continued to weep profusely as her emotions rose, swirling like storm clouds.

I hate her and all the others.

Crimson wisps exploded into lightning, streaking across her mind, digging like sharp claws into her every thought.

I hate them all.

Lindsay Merrick, a dumpy woman in her mid-thirties, was in the middle of discussing correct and incorrect grammar use in a student's assignment.

"When you try to persuade me, Mister Fargus," she said wryly, reading from his paper, "please don't use text abbreviations such as... *O-M-G, this movie was the best...* or... *the character Charlie was so funny, LMFAO.* Not acceptable."

Kirstin stood at the door and knocked.

"Where have you been?" the teacher asked.

"I was with Missus Richardson," Kirstin replied, holding the hall pass out for Merrick to take. She felt the room bear down upon her. All gazes were crawling over her skin as she stood before the class, vulnerable.

The teacher glared at her, tilting her head up so she looked towards Kristin down the length of her nose. She made a clucking sound with her tongue as she reached over and took the card from Kirstin's hand.

"I've read your paper too," Merrick shifted her feet and tapped her toe against the linoleum floor. "A very dark interpretation of some of the more popular nursery rhymes. Well researched. You've used some good references, unlike many of your peers who decided the depths of Wikipedia were enough."

The teacher moved her gaze over the girl, pausing at her waist. She held her eyes there for a moment that seemed a little too long, making Kirstin feel even more discomfort than she had upon learning that Posadas had feelings for her.

She's envious, the girl supposed. *The woman has never had a waist like mine. She's always been tubby.*

"Still," Merrick finally said, moving her eyes to the class. "It was a narrow opinion and should have discussed more than one side instead of manipulating your research to endorse your point of view."

"I thought that was the point of writing an argument," Kirstin replied. "I thought we were meant to research and write a paper to persuade others to our point of view."

"Take a seat, Kirstin," the teacher replied, ignoring the student's answer.

The girl turned towards her peers, glancing over at the staring faces of the students seated before her. Some of them showed empathy towards her, having experienced the passive-aggressive antics of Lindsay Merrick themselves. Others, particularly some boys, stared at her boobs as she moved past the first row of desks towards a space near the middle of the room.

She saw three others near the back wall, glaring at her as she placed her books on the desk. Steph, Nancy and Angela huddled together, keeping their eyes on Kirstin as they whispered something to each other.

She sat down, the corners of her mouth drooping as she fought back more tears. A quick glance over to the desk next to her and she knew what page of the textbook she was meant to open to. As she flicked through the pages, Merrick turned towards the class, holding up another paper.

"Let's look at Miss Granger's work," the teacher announced.

Kirstin felt a chill move up her spine.

Belittling Stephanie Granger sounded like a good thing at the moment, but the aftereffect would be hell. Steph was the kind of person not to take criticism too well. She was likely to take rejection out on others, usually Kirstin.

"Total opinion," Merrick said as all heads turned towards the three girls sitting at the back of the room.

Kirstin kept her eyes on the pages of her book, not wanting to see what was happening around her.

"No research whatsoever," the teacher continued. "Absolute trash. I was tempted to put this on the bottom of my canary's cage, but it is not worthy of being covered with avian fecal matter, let alone any remarks that I could scribble upon it."

Merrick slammed the paper onto her desk at the front of the room so hard that it shook the floor.

Shit!

Kirstin closed her eyes. She knew the bitch and her two pets at the back of the room were going to find her during the day and humiliate her somehow. They always did when something didn't go their way.

She wiped her eyes. Her eyelids felt warm against the gelatinous orbs in their sockets as a sharp pain stabbed at them from deep inside.

The crimson clouds swirled and swirled as blood-red rain fell.

A storm was fast approaching, and she wasn't sure how much longer she could hold it in.

Focus, the calm voice whispered.

"I refuse to grade this," Merrick continued, her calm, gentle voice sweeping over the silent room as the rest of the class continued to peer towards Stephanie.

Kirstin could imagine the other girl staring coldly back at the teacher.

She couldn't see how the teacher's tactic of publicly humiliating her students could possibly assist in their learning and further academic improvement. While Kirstin held a secret spark of elation as Steph copped a mouthful from Merrick, she didn't believe the girl deserved such open treatment. A positive word once in a while would probably do much more than negative criticism.

But the teachers must know better than I do, she thought. *After all, they had the correct training on how to be effective educators. Perhaps ridiculing kids is one of the strategies they learn in college.*

"I wasted my time and energy looking this thing over." The teacher picked the paper back up from the desk and waved it violently in the air, scrunching it a little in her fingers' grasp. "And then there's the work of your two side-kicks."

Merrick put Steph's paper back on the desk and rifled through a small stack of students' work sitting nearby until she found the two papers for which she searched.

"Miss Cumberland and Miss Upton," the teacher said as she turned her face towards the girls at the back of the room once again. "This is absolute crud. It is clear to me that the three of you did this together. At least Miss Granger is intelligent enough to re-word her work, so it reads a little more independently than yours. But you two. Almost word for word is identical.

"And your topic." Merrick flipped a paper over to read the title. "Why we should listen to Kanye.

"Let's take a look at what you wrote, shall we?" Merrick put one paper on the desk as she moved herself to stand in front of it. "It doesn't matter which one I read from. They're both the same.

"Why we should listen to Kanye," she started. "He tells it how it is."

The teacher looked up from the paper to the three girls.

"It," she said. "What is *it* that he tells, ladies? Don't answer that. I sincerely don't care what *it* is. Let's continue.

"He *nows* how to move. I'm assuming this is a misspelt word, and you intended to write; He *knows* how to move. What is interesting about this is that both of you spelled *knows* incorrectly.

"Another important fact that you may have overlooked is that your title is *Why we should listen to Kanye*. Listen. Why would I want to know how he moves, sorry, why would I want to *now* how he moves when you are trying to convince me to *listen* to him?

"Let's skip down a little to where you wrote, *He is so bitchin hot*. I'm assuming you are referring to how he looks, not that he has a fever. Again, you are trying to convince me to *listen* to him, according to your title, not persuading me to agree that he is at-tractive, or perhaps has a higher internal temperature than most people."

You're not funny, Kirstin thought, watching the teacher as she waved the paper about.

"Also, the use of the word *bitchin* is inappropriate for inclusion into a class assignment. I will add a notification to your records and these papers will also be submitted as evidence."

Great, Kirstin supposed as she moved her eyes to the desk again. *Now I'll have all three of them on me. Thanks a lot.*

She closed her eyes, feeling the burning sensation again.

Overwhelming exhaustion pressed against her body as the inner tempest pulsated through her brain.

Membranous clouds burst open and grew, spinning in wide circles as lightning scraped against the sides of her mind. The rain fell, and the thunder roared.

She didn't know how much longer she could wait.

Soon, the voice told her.

Soon.

Missus Betty Walker pulled the white SUV to a stop in the same location from where she picked the children up in her yellow bus earlier in the morning. She was now undertaking her duties as one of the Edwards Hill Postal Delivery Officers.

She opened the door, which bore a blue banner with the outline of a white eagle stenciled on the exterior. At least, she thought it was an eagle and had never taken the time to ask. Under the banner were the words, *We Deliver for You.*

Moving to the rear of the vehicle, she placed her cell phone into her back pants pocket and opened the hatch-door before unloading a foldaway trolley. She quickly assembled the apparatus, placing two filled crates containing mailbags onto the upper and lower racks. She then placed a yellow satchel with a long strap over her shoulder and stepped away from the vehicle.

Closing the door, she held her remote key up to the SUV and pressed the locking mechanism. The vehicle honked back at her, signaling the vehicle was alarmed and locked.

Pushing the trolley back towards the crest of the hill far behind the SUV, she started along the side of the road, fishing through the mailbag for the first delivery. Betty Walker paused at the base of a driveway, locking the trolley's brakes with a simple push of a foot pedal.

Slowly walking towards the letterbox, she noticed the little orange flag sticking up at the side of the small container that rested on top of a post at the end of a long picket fence. She opened the flap at the front and retrieved a letter that was addressed for some law firm in Houston. This she placed in the satchel slung over her shoulder, resting on her waist. She put the letters in her hand into the letterbox and lowered the orange flag before she closed the flap.

She repeated this process along the stretch of road. Sometimes there was mail to take. Sometimes there was mail to be delivered. Mostly, there were bills that needed delivering. It was a rare occurrence, in the age of electronic interactions, to hand deliver an actual letter to someone.

Most long distance conversations existed only on e-mails or social media that she didn't care that much for. She didn't believe she had even seen a hand-written address on an envelope in nearly a decade. Instead, everything she delivered had been printed and was usually displayed through a little clear plastic window on the envelope.

Doesn't anyone know how to use a pen these days? she thought as she pushed the trolley towards the crest in the road.

She delivered a few more small articles to the last couple of houses before she crossed the road and moved down the sloping road towards where she had parked the SUV. It sat across the road from her now, far in the distance, appearing like a small white box.

Betty Walker took a moment to look at the world around her.

Sweeping grass and pasturelands extended in both directions from the houses along the road. Smooth, rounded hills capped with small thickets of trees rolled away in the distance. There were many shades of earthy colors showing through the green grass that carpeted the untended lands.

It's a pleasant spot out here. She smiled, pushing her cart down the hill towards the first house. As she pulled the trolley to a stop at the base of the driveway, she looked farther along her route and noticed a silver SUV parked in one yard.

Odd. She furrowed her brow.

She recognized the vehicle.

It belonged to Randal Matthews.

Betty Walker moved to the letterbox of the house she had reached. As she placed three envelopes with typed information in the box, she continued to peer towards the silver vehicle.

Randal was a senior banker at the National Mercantile in town. His wife, Jennifer, was a volunteer at the municipal library. When she wasn't helping to cover books and restocking shelves, they usually found her at the First Baptist Church on Main Street helping with canned food drives or packing bibles for the needy.

The silver Escape should not be there.

Continuing down the hill, sorting out the next delivery as she progressed towards the next driveway, she kept lifting her eyes to the yard with the vehicle.

A knot formed in her stomach.

She hoped everything was all right.

Betty remembered Kirstin had seemed a little distant over the past few weeks, but even more so today than usual.

Perhaps something terrible had happened at the Matthews' household. The old lady ran scenarios over in her head, considering the highly respected couple may be undergoing some changes in their relationship.

Not a divorce, she thought. *Oh, that poor little girl. No wonder she has been so withdrawn.*

She found this hard to believe. The Matthews were regular people, openly affectionate and compassionate towards others. Their status in the church wasn't just for show. It was who they were. They were the exemplary picture of good, bible thumping Christian do-gooders.

While Betty was not a frequenter of the First Baptist on Main, or a visitor of any other religious establishment, she regarded the Matthews family as friends.

Her concerns developed into heart-pounding stress as she drew nearer to the property with the silver Escape sitting in the yard. She was still trying to imagine why the vehicle was sitting in the driveway as the ground leveled out beneath her feet.

Even a divorce in motion wouldn't stop Randal from getting to work. The SUV should not be there.

Sick, she thought. *Maybe he's sick, and she's staying home to care for him today.*

But that didn't explain why Kirstin had been so quiet and introverted of late.

What can it be?

She paused at the end of their driveway, staring at the vehicle.

There was no mail for them and the little orange flag on the side of the letterbox was down. Nothing to pick up.

The Escape sat silently, facing towards the house under the shade of the large maple tree in the front yard.

Betty moved her gaze from the vehicle towards the neat house resting back in the yard. She noted the clean, white cladding over the exterior of the structure. Some white lattice along the façade beneath the windows housed red rose bushes.

Her eye followed the path to the tidy flower garden that bordered the patio before moving to the door.

The open door.

Betty Walker's heart almost stopped.

Why is the door open?

She pressed the foot brake and moved onto the driveway, precariously stepping closer to the parked Escape.

Did someone break in? she asked herself, keeping her eyes on the door as she placed one foot in front of the other, slowly, cautiously edging closer and closer.

It must have happened after Kirstin left for school, she surmised. *She would have said something if it happened before.*

She suddenly stopped moving when she reached the driver's door of the vehicle.

What if they're still here now?

Suddenly, her rapid heartbeat filled her ears and her soft breathing seemed to roar like a torrential wind.

"Hello," she called.

Stupid woman, she thought. *Now they know you are here. They'll come out and kill you now.*

"Hello," she called again.

Her feet started forwards again, slowly closing the ground between her and the house.

She shuffled along the path, tilting her head in an attempt to see inside.

It was dark, but she could hear the unmistakable sound of a television commercial playing.

Someone was inside.

"Hello," she called again. "Jennifer? Randal? Are you home?"

She lifted her foot onto the porch and stepped closer to the door.

"...and Access Hollywood is coming right up after the show," the television told her. "We'll be right back after this."

A commercial with a loud, steady electronic *doof-doof-doof* drum beat started as she stood in the open doorway.

Her eyes adjusted to the darkness slowly. Her surroundings became clearer.

Betty noticed a few pairs of shoes placed against the wall in the entry hall.

"Hello?" she called again.

"You know you want it," a young woman's voice said seductively. "You want it now."

"Randal?" Betty stepped inside, ignoring the commercial on the television.

Doof-doof-doof-doof.

"If you want it," the woman continued. "You got to move."

"Jennifer?" she called as she moved to an archway that led to the room where the noise from the television was coming from.

Doof-doof-doof.

"Re-Gen Fitness Wear and Apparel," the woman said as Betty stepped into the room. Her eyes fell onto Randal Matthews, slumped in an armchair facing the television.

Doof-doof-doof-doof.

"Randal?" The old lady peered towards him.

Her eyes fell upon the fallen coffee cup on the floor.

She couldn't breathe.

Her heart seemed to stop as her eyes followed his drooping arm that dangled above the mug.

The large red stain on his chest blared loudly in her vision.

Doof-doof-doof.

She found the hole under his eye where a thin trail of blood had trickled from onto the collar of his shirt.

"You know you want it," said the television.

Betty fell to her knees as she screamed.

PRIMUS INTERLUDIUM

9-1-1 TRANSCRIBED CALL
DATE: 04/24/2017   TIME: 10:48:27 – 10:52:43
LENGTH OF CALL: 00:07:16
CALL TAKER: Vanessa Parkes
POSITION: Dispatch Operator

CALL TAKER:

Houston 9-1-1 This is Vanessa. What's your emergency?

CALLER:

They're dead. They're dead.

CALL TAKER:

Calm down, please. Take a deep breath.

CALLER:

(Breathing)

CALL TAKER:

Can I take your name?

CALLER:

Betty. Betty Walker.

CALL TAKER:

Okay, Betty. Can I call you Betty?

CALLER:

Yeah.

CALL TAKER:

Betty, can I assume you require the police?

CALLER:

They've been shot.

CALL TAKER:

Is the shooter still nearby? Are you in danger?

CALLER:

Oh, God. I don't know. I'm in the kitchen and I...

CALL TAKER:

Where are you, Betty? What's the address?

CALLER:

Uh! Two Twenty-Seven Jackson Drive.

CALL TAKER:

And the suburb?

CALLER:

Edwards Hill. I'm at a house some ways from the town.

CALL TAKER:

Okay, Betty. I'm putting that into the computer now and notify-
ing the police in Edwards Hill.

CALLER:

Why would anyone do this?

CALL TAKER:

Can I ask why you're in the house, Betty?

CALLER:

I was making my deliveries and saw the door open. So I came inside to see if everything was okay. And I found them here... (A man's voice says something in the background.)

CALL TAKER:

Betty? Is somebody with you? Are you safe?

CALLER:

It's the TV. It was on when I came inside.

CALL TAKER:

There isn't anyone else with you?

CALLER:

No. Just me. Oh, that poor girl.

CALL TAKER:

Girl? Did you say, girl?

CALLER:

Yeah. I drive the school bus and dropped the young girl that lives here off at school this morning. She's going to fall apart when she hears about this.

CALL TAKER:

You dropped her at school and returned to the house?

CALLER:

I'm also a postal delivery officer.

CALL TAKER:

I see. I'm checking the communications, Betty. The police have been notified and are on their way. They're estimating a five-minute arrival. Paramedics are on their way too.

CALLER:

What do you need me to do?

CALL TAKER:

Are you able to move outside without disturbing anything?

CALLER:

Yes. Do I leave the TV on?

CALL TAKER:

Leave everything just as you found it. If you have moved any-thing, leave it where it is as well.

CALLER:

Okay. I'm moving to the door now.

CALL TAKER:

I can see that you're on a cell phone. Can you find a place to wait safely?

CALLER:

My truck is parked across the road and down the way a little. Can I wait there?

CALL TAKER:

That's good. Get in your vehicle and lock the doors.

CALLER:

Okay. I'm outside now. Oh, God. Oh, God.

CALL TAKER:

Try to remain calm, Betty. You're doing great. Tell me, what's the weather like over there in Edwards Hill?

CALLER:

It's a nice, clear day. Oh, my God. I think I'm going to be sick.

CALL TAKER:

That's okay, Betty. Take some deep breaths. If you need to throw up, go ahead. I'll be right here.

CALLER:

(Unclarified sound) Oh, God. I'm sorry. (Unclarified sound)

CALL TAKER:

Are you okay, Betty?

CALLER:

Dry reaching. Sorry.

CALL TAKER:

That's fine, Betty. Nothing to apologize for.

CALLER:

Oh, those poor people. Who could do such a thing?

CALL TAKER:

Police have a car nearby and are about one minute away. Are you in your vehicle yet?

CALLER:

Not yet. I'm still in the driveway.

CALL TAKER:

Try to move to your vehicle, please Betty.

CALLER:

Okay. (Shuffling sounds)

CALL TAKER:

What's that noise, Betty?

CALLER:

I'm trying to move my trolley.

CALL TAKER:

Your trolley?

CALLER:

It has all the mail in it.

CALL TAKER:

No. Leave it where it is, Betty.

CALLER:

Someone could take it.

CALL TAKER:

Your safety is more important than the mail, Betty. Please get to your vehicle and lock the doors.

CALLER:

Okay.

CALL TAKER:

Tell me when you get to your vehicle, Betty.

CALLER:

I'm getting my key out now. (A distinct beep in the background)

CALL TAKER:

What was that?

CALLER:

Me unlocking my truck.

CALL TAKER:

Good. Get inside, please Betty.

CALLER:

(Sound of the vehicle door opening. Some unclarified sounds. Sound of the vehicle door closing)

CALL TAKER:

Are you in your vehicle, Betty?

CALLER:

Yes. I'm locking the doors. (Sound of doors locking)

CALL TAKER:

I heard that. Okay. How are you feeling?

CALLER:

I don't know. My stomach feels strange. Oh, those poor people.

CALL TAKER:

Police are a couple of minutes out, Betty.

CALLER:

I can see them coming.

CALL TAKER:

You can see them?

CALLER:

I parked my truck facing towards town. I can see their lights.

CALL TAKER:

That's good, Betty. I'll stay with you until they arrive, okay?

CALLER:

Okay. Oh, God. (Sounds of crying)

CALL TAKER:

It's okay, Betty. You did well. You did well.

CALLER:

Oh, God. (Crying)

CALL TAKER:

You can relax now, Betty. They're almost there.

CALLER:

(Sound of sirens)

CALL TAKER:

You're safe, Betty. I'll stay with you until the police come to speak with you.

CALLER:

(Crying loudly. Sirens cut off)

CALL TAKER:

Can you see the police, Betty?

CALLER:

Mm-hmm!

(Officer Brandon Church: Ma'am, are you the caller to 9-1-1?)

Yes.

(Officer Brandon Church: My name is Officer Brandon Church from the Edwards Hill Police Department. Do you require medical assistance?)

No, I'm okay.

(Officer Brandon Church: Your name is Betty Walker, correct?)

That's right.

(Officer Brandon Church: Okay, Betty. Please wait in your vehicle while I check inside the premises with my partner, Officer Jolee Wulf. We'll be back in just a moment. Okay?)

Okay.

CALL TAKER:

Betty? Betty? It's Vanessa. Are you there?

CALLER:

I'm here.

CALL TAKER:

How are you holding up?

CALLER:

I'm okay. They've just gone into the house.

CALL TAKER:

I heard the officer ask if you need any medical assistance.

CALLER:

I'm fine.

CALL TAKER:

Betty, do me a favor.

CALLER:

Mm-hmm.

CALL TAKER:

Have the paramedics check you over when they arrive.

CALLER:

I feel absolutely fine.

CALL TAKER:

I know, but sometimes shock can set in late. Please, let them check you over. Promise?

CALLER:

I will. I promise.

CALL TAKER:

Good woman.

CALLER:

The police are coming back.

CALL TAKER:

Don't open the door until they come right up to the car, okay?

CALLER:

Okay. The lady cop is coming over.

CALL TAKER:

What's the other officer doing?

CALLER:

He's getting back into the car.

(Officer Jolee Wulf: Ma'am, could you step out of the vehicle, please?)

CALL TAKER:

This is where I leave you, Betty. You're in expert hands now. Don't forget to let the paramedics to check you over.

CALLER:

Thank you, Vanessa.

CALL TAKER:

You're welcome, Betty. Take care.

CALL ENDED: 10:52:43

VIGILUM : THE POLICE

Anger is a brief madness.

HORACE, *Epistles*

I

"Two dead. Gunshot wounds. Two Twenty-Seven Jackson," a man in his late forties said, pinching a piece of paper before him with a finger and thumb while holding his spectacles by the arm close to his eyes. He let the glasses fall. Attached to a cord, they swung down to his chest as he handed the paper to a young woman, dressed smartly and tapping away on a computer in a small cubicle.

"And how the fuck do you expect me to get out there, Jerry?" she asked.

"Take a van," he answered before waving his hand around to the others in the room that were chained to their keyboards behind the shoulder-high partitions separating the workspaces. "Or would you rather report on wheat pests, farmer revolts or the dreaded plight of Missus Montgomery when her cat got stuck up the tree again just like the rest of these deadbeats?"

"Hey," called a voice from across the room.

"You are the only one amongst us with any potential here," Jerry told her. "You're young. You look great on camera and people love you."

She stood up and grabbed her bag that was slung over her chair, "Okay, I'll go."

"Good." He stepped back for her to move past him. "Wayne is waiting downstairs for you. You've got thirty minutes to set up."

She started walking hastily through a thin passageway formed by the positioning of desks and workspaces. Jerry followed closely.

"Thirty minutes?"

"The networks in Houston will send choppers," he told her. "This is our chance to get the scoop."

"Would they have heard of this yet?" she asked, flipping the paper over in her hand as she read the details scribbled on it. "Surely they know."

"We just got this over the 9-1-1 feed," he told her. "This is happening right now. By the time they get their birds in the air, you'll be there. You might even beat the forensics if you're lucky."

"Shit." She pressed the button for the elevator. "Shot dead."

"First shooting in Edwards Hill since eighteen ninety-three," the man told her.

"You're joking?"

He shook his head. "Nope. And that one was self-induced. Poor bastard blew his brains out while cleaning his pistol. Do you wanna guess at what his last words were?"

"What?" she asked as the doors to the elevator opened.

"Don't worry," he replied with a wry smile. "It's not loaded."

"You sick prick." She laughed as she stepped into the lift.

"Thirty minutes, Samantha." He pointed to her as she pressed the button for the garage level. "You'll be reporting back to Phil Goldman in Dallas."

She nodded. "Thirty minutes."

The doors closed between them.

Strange music piped in over the speakers in the elevator. Something from the sixties or the seventies. She wasn't sure who it was. It was catchy and relaxing.

She used the time to read over the scribbles on the paper handed to her.

Man and woman shot.
Names unknown.
227 Jackson Drive
9-1-1 Call made by Missus Betty Walker.
School Bus Driver and Postal Delivery Officer.
First officers to arrive. Brendan Church and Jolee Wulf.

Placing the paper in her bag, she checked the illuminated number above the door of the lift. It blinked from 3 to 2. Two more floors to go.

Samantha straightened her tight navy blue skirt that ran from her knees to her waist, where a thick black belt rested on her hips. She tucked neatly a light sky blue shirt into the hem, buttoned up to the middle of her chest. She wore a dark, sleeveless vest with lace lining, ending in a V-shape near her cleavage.

She understood that the demographic of viewers that tuned in to watch her were males between the ages of twenty to forty, so she dressed to make sure they kept watching.

The doors opened to reveal a dark area with vehicles parked neatly into bays. Directly across from the elevator was a white van with **Edwards Hill News** printed on the side and a large, retractable antenna on the roof. A thirty-something man with a Cowboys cap on his head was sitting in the driver's seat waiting for her.

"That was fast," he called out to her as she opened the vehicle's door.

"Have you got everything?" she asked, sliding onto the seat and closing the door behind her.

"Double checked and loaded, sweetheart," he told her. "Your earpiece is on the dash."

"Let's go then," she said, grabbing a small receiver box that would clip onto the back hem of her skirt. Plugged into it was a long spiral cable with an earplug at one end.

"Seatbelt," he told her as she plugged the earpiece into her right ear.

She shook her head as she reached over her right shoulder to extend the strap over her chest.

"If this ruins my shirt…" She pursed her lips.

"I'd rather that than your pretty face all over my windshield," he replied, touching his foot to the gas.

"Do you know where we're going?" she asked him.

"Jackson Drive," he replied. "Shooting, right?"

He drove up a steep ramp and onto the street outside.

"Yeah," she nodded. "You ever covered one before?"

"Nope," he said as he steered the vehicle towards a set of traffic lights at the end of the block. He flicked the blinker to indicate a turn right before slowing down to take the corner. "You?"

"Not unless you count the duck hunt out at the National Park," she said, looking out of the window.

"Doesn't count," he said, bringing the van onto Main Street. "You look nice, by the way."

"Thanks." She smiled, flicking her blonde locks over her shoulder as she turned her head towards him.

"No flirting," he said with a straight face. "Trying to drive here."

She opened her mouth in mock outrage. He smiled, checking the mirrors as he moved the vehicle through the town.

"I'm kidding," he told her. "Flirt all you want."

"I forgot how dirty you are," she said, shaking her head.

"Forgot?" he questioned. "Why? How long has it been since we were on assignment?"

"Three months," she replied. "Or thereabouts."

"What was the report?" he asked. "Wait. Let me try to remember."

She watched him as he stared ahead, rummaging through the files in his head as he drove along Main Street.

"Sour milk," he said eventually.

"Sour milk?" She scrunched her nose. "What are you talking about?"

"You know," he answered. "That one where the farmer was feeding lemons to his cows out on the farming estate on thirty-six."

"Sour milk!" She laughed. "Yeah. That was the last time we did a story."

"This will be a little different," he told her. "This one will be live."

She took a deep breath as she considered his words.

"I'm a little nervous," she confessed.

"You'll be fine, Sam," he assured her. "Jerry wouldn't have given this to you if he didn't think you were up to it."

"Thanks, Wayne," she replied. "I think I'm going to be needing you a bit more before this is over."

"That's what I'm here for," he told her. "I got coffee and sandwiches in the back."

"Where did you find time to prepare all of that and get everything ready?" She turned to look over her shoulder at the equipment neatly packed in the back of the vehicle.

"I swiped the food from the cafeteria," he answered.

She stared at him, uncertain if he was telling the truth or having her on.

"I really did." He smiled.

"We could get into deep shit for that," she informed him jokingly.

"No fucking way," he chuckled. "This story is big. Nothing like this has ever happened out here before. We'll be the talk at the office for years to come. We'll be heroes."

II

McFarlan leaned back in her swivel chair, placing the heels of her boots on the edge of her desk as she moved the wireless mouse across the pad. On the screen in front of her was an electronic form that required her attention. It was a basic log for the time that she had applied towards the *Blue in the School* program, an initiative to integrate a police presence in the local educational facilities.

She had volunteered for the position of School Liaison Officer, hoping to avoid the grittier aspects of police duty. Tending to domestic disputes wasn't her idea of fun, and considering that in Texas everyone and their dog carried a firearm, she didn't want to be there when a bullet might go astray.

Luckily for her and the other officers of Edwards Hill Police Department, most local civilians were level-headed and well in control of their faculties. The worst crime that she needed to attend to during her post in Edwards Hill was a reported cow-tipping during the homecoming celebration over a year ago.

The log on the computer screen was for a visit to a local, one-teacher elementary school at least thirty miles out of town. She held a quick Q and A session with twelve students, the entire population of pupils.

Most of the children paid little attention to her talk about stranger awareness, focusing instead upon her sidearm and other objects she wore as part of her uniform. The students asked the usual questions when she opened the floor up to them, to which she had the over-rehearsed answers ready to go.

"What's that?" one would ask.

"Pepper spray," she'd reply.

"What's it for?

"To spray into people's eyes if they put me or someone else in danger."

"What's that?"

"That's a Taser," she'd say.

"What's it for?"

"To give a bad guy a little shock of electricity if they pose a threat."

"Can we see your gun?"

"No."

"Why not?"

"I'm only allowed to bring it out if there is a bad person with a gun," she'd answer.

"Do you got a boyfriend?"

"No."

"Why not?"

"Because I'm married to my job."

She clicked the drop-down menus placed throughout the form, showing place and time that she had dedicated towards the Blue in the School program. Once she had completed the relevant sections, she pressed save at the bottom of the form. This automatically kept a copy of the form in her account as well as sent one to her program supervisor.

McFarlan placed her hands behind her head, interlacing her fingers as she stretched in her chair, pushing her chest forward and pulling her shoulders back.

"Whoa," called a fifty-something man in a cheap tweed jacket, sitting at a desk near hers. "Could you do that again, but slower?"

"Dirty bastard," she said, smiling, sitting upright as she shook her head. "Your wife would have your balls if she caught you staring at my tits."

"She already has my balls," he chuckled. "She's had them since the wedding night."

"I need coffee," she said, standing up. She grabbed a mug from her desk and headed towards the kitchenette at the side of the office space. "You want some, Doug?"

"Nah," Doug Borden replied. "I need to cut back. The old bladder ain't what it used to be."

"More information than I need," she returned.

Two other plainclothes officers sat at their desks across the room from McFarlan's, closer to the sink and bench against the wall.

"How about you two?" she asked them.

"No thanks," a young male replied.

The other, a young woman roughly the same age as McFarlan, held her mug up and shook it in the air. The other took this as a sign that she wanted a refill and took the cup from her hand.

"Tell me something, Kimmie," Borden started. "Why didn't you take a job in Houston or Dallas? You know, somewhere exciting."

"I don't like noise," she replied as she poured hot black liquid into the other officer's mug. "It's quiet out here and not much happens."

"Yeah," the older man nodded, "but you got Roselia there who's yearning to work in the city and build a career."

"I just want to see some new meat," Roselia DeLong told him as she took the mug from McFarlan. "Thanks. This town doesn't offer much in the way of men."

"Hey!" the younger man snapped.

"She's right, son," Borden smiled. "You are butt ugly."

The younger man shook his head and returned to tapping the keys on his computer.

"But why here, Kimmie?" the older man pressed as he rolled a rubber band over his fingers. "This is where cops come to die. You know, set down roots, retire, grow some tomatoes and then push up daisies."

"I grew up in the city, Doug," she told him as she put the pot back onto the heating element and started across the room back to her desk. "I've seen it and I didn't like it then. I still don't like it now."

"But, Edwards Hill?"

"I didn't select it outright," she said as she sat back in her chair and sipped from her cup. "I put in for a bunch of places around the state. I was just lucky that I got put out here."

"All right," Borden conceded. "Something else I've wanted to know."

"What is it?" she asked him.

"Wait a second," DeLong called over. "You've been here two years, right?"

"Yeah," McFarlan replied. "Same as you."

"So how is it he's asking you all these questions and not me?"

"Everyone knows about you," the other male replied. "And I mean *everybody*."

"Shut up, Jaye." She scrunched her face up and shook her head at him.

"He's right," Borden told her. "You couldn't stop talking about yourself when you first arrived. You told us about how you were going to work your way up from the uniform to a plainclothes unit. Then how you would transfer to a location so that you could get promoted up the ladder to captain. And how you planned to do all of that before you turned thirty."

"I'm twenty-three now," she said, smiling. "I ain't doing too bad for myself."

"True." The older man smiled before turning his attention to the young woman sitting at the desk near him. "But back to my question for you. Why are you still wearing a uniform?"

"No, you can't see me naked, Doug," she replied.

DeLong almost spat her coffee.

"That's not what I mean," he said defensively.

"I know what you mean," she replied. "The uniform is why I got into the job. I love the uniform. I don't want to work plainclothes or climb the career ladder. I want to work with people and show that they can trust anyone who wears this. The uniform should be a symbol for people to know that we are keeping them safe. That's why I still wear a uniform."

"Good answer," said a voice from the doorway. All heads turned to see an older woman holding a sheet of paper in her hand.

"Captain." Borden saluted half-heartedly from his chair.

"Borden," she replied with a smile. She then turned her attention to the younger plainclothes officers. "I just got a call from Jolee. She and Brandon responded to a 9-1-1 call out to Jackson Drive. Two dead bodies. A woman and a man. Jennifer and Randall Matthews. Both shot twice. Presumably at close range. We need you two out there now to meet forensics when they arrive."

Roselia DeLong stood up and lifted the coat from the back of her chair. Jaye Hodder checked his sidearm, holstered beneath his jacket.

"Where do you want me, Captain?" Borden asked.

"You'll support Kimmie," she told him. "Turns out that the deceased have a daughter enrolled at the high school. I need you to head around there and bring her in for questioning."

McFarlan felt her heart sink. She dreaded informing individuals of a deceased loved one. It was her least favorite thing about the job.

Still, as the School Liaison Officer, it was her responsibility to perform such a duty involving students.

"Family?" she asked her captain as she stood up.

"We're still looking into it," she replied. "Looks like they weren't from here originally. You might want to check the school records before you inform the girl. Find out if there is an emergency contact."

"Name?"

"Kirstin Matthews." The captain glanced at the paper in her hand. "Sixteen."

"Shit on a shingle." Borden shook his head. "The poor girl."

"I know." The older woman looked at him. "Talk to the principal." She glanced at the paper again. "Frieda Richardson. Find out what you can about the girl before you ask to see her. Being sixteen can be strange and upsetting enough without this kind of thing lumped on top. See if she's one of those volatile types or not. I know you've not had to deal with this kind of thing before, Kimmie. But I need you to do this."

"It's my job, Captain," the young officer replied.

"Good luck, Kimmie." DeLong came to her side and placed a hand on her shoulder.

McFarlan pursed her lips and nodded a silent thank you.

She suddenly wished she was in plain clothes and given the task to oversee the operation at the place of the shooting.

"Come on, sweetheart," Borden said, grabbing the car keys from his desk and heading towards the door as the captain disappeared from sight, returning to her office at the end of the hallway.

III

The phone resounded, an annoying beeping noise that made the young receptionists want to answer it just to silence the device. Once or twice, they were tempted to just leave the receiver off the hook, but communications were essential in a school.

Callers could vary from some suit and tie sitting at a desk in the district office to a parent needing to speak to their child. From time to time, the girls let the answering machine intercept phone if they were engaged in other duties.

Karly Childers was speaking to a young female student at the reception window. Tania Pearlman wasn't paying much attention to the conversation, as she was too involved in crunching numbers as she moved digits from the school's budget into the many bills that needed to be paid.

She reached over and picked up the phone, clamping it between her ear and shoulder so she could free up her hands to continue tapping on the computer's keyboard.

"Edwards Hill State High School," she answered politely. "Tania Pearlman speaking. How may I help you?"

"Tania," the voice on the other end said. It belonged to a female that the young receptionist recognized. "Kimmie McFarlan from the police department."

"Hi Kimmie." Pearlman smiled. "How are you?"

"I'm well, thanks," the officer replied. "I'm calling on business. Is Missus Richardson available?"

"Sorry," the receptionist answered. "She's out on the floor doing the rounds. She's probably in the cafeteria right now. Should I get her to call you back?"

"I'm on my way over right now," McFarlan informed her. "I'm on my cell phone and moving along Main Street. I'll be there in a few minutes."

"Anything I should be worried about?" Pearlman's eyes widened and her mouth drooped.

"No," the other told her. "I need to speak to Missis Richardson when I arrive. It's important."

"I'll get her right now, Kimmie," Pearlman said, sensing the urgency in McFarlan's voice.

"Thanks, Tania. I'll see you when I get there."

The receptionist placed the phone back into the cradle and lifted herself from her chair.

"Miss Childers," Pearlman walked to the door, noticing the student still standing at the window. "Sorry to interrupt, but I need to find Missus Richardson. Could you manage without me for a moment?"

"Sure." Childers furrowed her brow as she watched her colleague exit the office and hurry along the corridor. Several male adolescents watched her like hungry wolves as she passed them.

Her heels tapped loudly against the linoleum floor as she stepped quickly along the passageway. She gave no mind to the ogling eyes that watched her ass in the tiny skirt she had squeezed herself into. Her ambition was to get her boss back into her office before the police arrived.

Turning a corner, more leering students who ignored their girlfriends as she moved by. The young girls rolled their eyes, and some grabbed their boyfriends' chins to forcefully turn their heads back.

Pearlman continued along the hallway, turning another corner that led to an open double-doorway to the cafeteria. A loud din of conversation and laughter reverberated from the large room. Thumping and clanking, scraping and screeching filled her ears as plates and cutlery rattled as chairs and tables moved about.

Several students sat about; several others were moving about to talk to friends at one location before moving to others across the room.

"Walk," yelled one male teacher, pointing to a boy in a jock jacket who was running through the aisle between the tables.

Pearlman caught the teacher's eye. He, like all the young males she had passed on her way to the cafeteria, leered at her for a moment too long.

She glared at him, causing him to look away sheepishly.

Pearlman moved her eyes around the room and found Richardson talking to one of the cafeteria staff near the service counter. She moved into the room and snaked her way around the obstacle course of children and furniture until she stood by the principal's side.

"Sorry Missus Richardson," she said before turning to the elderly lady chatting with the principal. "Missus Harrison. We just received a call from the police. You're needed immediately."

"All right," Richardson replied. "My apologies, Missus Harrison. We'll catch up soon."

"Quite all right," the older lady smiled.

Both Richardson and Pearlman hastily made their way out of the room.

Police.

Kirstin stared towards the cafeteria door, watching Richardson disappear.

She was sitting in a seat by the counter on her own. She had noticed Donny sitting with his friends a couple of rows away from her. He kept turning to look at her. She kept her head in a book, pretending not to notice.

It wasn't because she was afraid of what he might do if he saw her looking back at him. In fact, she was curious to know what he would do.

But Steph and her two cronies were also sitting nearby, another row over. They, too, were watching her.

By sitting by the counter, she was maintaining her safety. There were adults within talking distance to her, and adults were the enemy of people like Steph. It was as if some invisible force-field surrounded grown-ups.

On her own and with her friends, Steph was a bitch. When she was near adults, she changed her demeanor. Suddenly, she would be as sweet as pie and innocent.

Kirstin was convinced that all the male teachers would believe that butter wouldn't melt in Steph's mouth. How could they think otherwise when she flaunted herself in those high cut-off jeans that partially went up her crack, and that tight, low-cut singlet with her boobs almost popping out and over the top?

Maybe Richardson could see Steph for who she was. She seemed to have a good gauge of people's characters. Perhaps Missus Merrick understood her as well. But Merrick, it seemed, simply hated all students and exposed their true nature by ridiculing them before other students.

The police.

Kirstin looked over at Steph and the other two girls and considered whether she should risk her position of safety for the location of her locker.

Time was running out and that she would need to act sooner instead of later.

She was certain that the three girls would pursue her along the corridors and up the stairs to where she stored her belongings.

Perhaps that would work in her favor.

Perhaps leading them away would be what she needed to get this thing underway.

She moved her eyes to Donny.

The girl with braided hair he'd spoken to in the morning had moved to into the seat next to him. She leaned with her elbow onto the table, pushing her barely covered chest in his direction. It was an attempt to make him look at her.

Kirstin noticed Donny trying his best to ignore the gesture, but she knew boys couldn't help themselves. It was instinctive.

A natural reflex.

Still, he fought, keeping his gaze at eye level of those around the table.

It wasn't until the braided girl said his name that he turned his head in her direction. Then, and only then, did his eyes move to her cleavage.

It's not his fault, Kirstin told herself. *It's hers. She forced him to look.*

Donny quickly lifted his eyes and turned his face towards the younger girl sitting by herself. As the girl in braids talked in his ear, his eyes locked with Kirstin's.

Donny smiled at her.

The girl in braids noticed and glared sideways towards Kirstin as she continued her one-sided conversation with the young man.

Keeping her eyes on Donny, Kirstin could see Stephanie Granger and the girl with braided hair on either side of him. An opportunity presented itself that was too tempting to ignore.

As she lifted herself to her feet, she smiled and mouthed the words; *I love you.*

Donny's eyes widened, and a wide grin stretched across his face.

Behind him, Steph's face turned red with anger.

The braided girl's jaw dropped open.

Kirstin moved across the room towards the door. She knew Donny was watching her the whole way, but it was the burning eyes of Stephanie Granger and the girl seated by the young man's side that she felt boring into the back of her neck as she walked into the corridor.

IV

Richardson hurried along the corridor with Pearlman closely in tow. She turned the handle of the door to the small receptionist's office and, without slowing down, moved towards her office door.

"Officers Borden and McFarlan are waiting for you inside, Missus Richardson," Childers said, standing by the principal's door. "I was just going to get some coffee for them. Would you like some?"

"Thank you, Miss Childers." Richardson nodded. "That would be wonderful."

She entered the room and closed the door behind her, leaving the two receptionists behind. Sitting in the seats that faced her desk was a young uniformed officer and an older man in a cheap, well-worn suit.

"Good morning, officers," she said, moving around her desk to be seated. "How can I assist you?"

"Good morning, Missus Richardson," the young female officer responded. "I'm Kimmie McFarlan, the School Liaison Officer."

"I know who you are, Kimmie." Richardson smiled. "I also remember you, Mister Borden. The town's not that big that I could forget you both so quickly."

"Sorry, Missus Richardson," McFarlan said. "I simply reverted to protocol. I'm kind-a nervous and really don't know how to approach such a delicate situation."

"Delicate?" Richardson moved her eyes between the two seated across from her.

"A woman and man were shot in their home today," Borden blurted. "Their daughter is enrolled in your school. We need to ask her a few questions and take her back to the station as a precaution."

"Student?" the principal positioned herself upright. "Who?"

"Kirstin Matthews," McFarlan replied.

Kirstin, Richardson thought, picturing the girl in her head. She had been sitting in the very chair that McFarlan now occupied not even an hour before.

"We will need for someone to check her records for emergency contacts," Borden told her. "Family members. Close friends of the family. Anyone who can be of help to her during this time."

Richardson was staring at her desk. Her mind was swimming with her knowledge of the little girl she had spoken to not so long ago.

"Missus Richardson?" The man tilted his head, trying to gain her attention.

"Yes." she snapped back to reality. "Of course. I'll get one of my receptionists to get right on it. Do you want us to contact relatives or will...?"

"We'll take care of that from our end," McFarlan informed her. "It would be best if they heard such news from us rather than the school principal."

Richardson nodded. Her eyes were glistening with damp.

"Are you all right, ma'am?" Borden asked.

"Yes," she replied, reaching for a tissue from the dispenser on her desk. She wiped her eyes and shook her head as she rose to her feet. "That poor girl."

She moved around the desk and opened the door to speak to the girls in the receptionist's office. Tania Pearlman sat behind her desk, tapping away at the keys on her computer.

"Miss Pearlman," Richardson called softly. "Could you please retrieve the folder for Kirstin Matthews and bring it in to me? Thank you."

"Sure thing, Missus Richardson," came the reply as the principal closed the door before moving back around her desk to her seat.

"From recollection," Richardson began, "Kirstin has no family in Texas. I think her father has a brother in Wisconsin or somewhere like that. Her mother, I think, was from out east. Perhaps Boston."

"Does she have any living relatives out there?" Borden asked, pulling a notepad and pen from his pocket.

"I couldn't tell you without looking at the file. Sorry."

"That's all right, Missus Richardson. We should probably call the young lady in so that we can inform her."

"The students are at recess for the moment," Richardson explained. "Class resumes in a little under five minutes. It may be more discreet if we wait until the students are back in the classrooms. I'd prefer to gather her myself rather than call her over the speaker system, if that's okay?"

"Of course, Missus Richardson." McFarlan smiled. "We don't want to add any further complications to this situation. We can wait."

There was a gentle knock at the door before it opened. Pearlman entered, holding a manila folder stuffed with papers in her hand.

"The Kirstin Matthews file, Missus Richardson," Pearlman said as she reached between the two police officers to place the folder on the desk. "Coffee is here too."

"Thank you, Miss Pearlman." Richardson nodded.

McFarlan peered across to the older man as Pearlman moved out of the way to allow the other young receptionist through so that she could place a tray with three cups of coffee on the desk beside the manila folder. His eyes fixed on the woman's rump.

As she backed out of the tiny space between their chairs, Borden's eyes followed her a short way before catching McFarlan's eyes looking at him. She tilted her head slightly, silently scorning him. He grimaced defensively, moving his face towards the nearest coffee cup.

He leaned forward and took a mug before leaning back. He sipped slowly as he considered his bladder whilst making a mental note to not gawk at young females ever again. At least not while he was meant to be on the job.

"Who could have done such a thing?" Richardson asked. "From what I know of them, the Matthews were upstanding people."

"We have people at their house right now," McFarlan told her as she reached over for the closest mug to her. "I'm sure they'll turn something up that will help us find who is responsible."

"That poor girl," Richardson said again, reaching for another tissue.

"What kind of girl is she?" McFarlan asked, hoping to steer the principal's mind onto more positive reflections. "Is she smart, academically speaking?"

"Very bright for her age," Richardson replied, opening the manila folder. "Particularly talented in chemistry. I rarely get to say I have a straight-A student in my school. But this girl has always been one of those students who goes above and beyond expectations."

"How so?"

"Well..." The principal stopped to think. "Only today, I had a meeting with her history teacher about how she was able to stimulate a class discussion about social injustices towards indigenous populations around the world."

"She's an out-of-the-box kind of thinker, then?" McFarlan smiled.

"I guess so," Richardson agreed, reaching for the remaining cup on the table. "She reads a lot, knows a little Latin and hasn't been mingling with the other students too much lately."

"That didn't set any alarms off for you?"

"She's still friendly to everyone," the other informed her. "If we were to act upon every student who goes through a temporary moment of isolation, we wouldn't get any teaching done around here. They're teenagers who have constant emotional highs and lows."

"Wait," Borden interjected. "The kid knows Latin?"

"She knows a little bit," the principal replied.

"She's sixteen and knows Latin?"

"Yes," Richardson nodded.

"You don't find that strange?"

"Sure I do," she answered. "But some kids here have the strangest hobbies ever. We have a science fiction and fantasy club where the students come dressed as their favorite characters from books, movies and comics. We have students who can recite every Monty Python movie ever made. There are others who play ongoing board games like Dungeons and Dragons and World Conquest that last for months on end. When I consider all of that, I don't think a student knowing a little Latin is that peculiar."

Borden nodded. "When you look at it that way, I guess." He took a few notes before turning to McFarlan suddenly. "Hey! You know Latin, right?"

"I majored in the classics," she replied bashfully. "So, yeah. I know a little."

"Viri sunt viri," he said with a chuckle.

"Only those present in the room," McFarlan replied, shaking her head. "I apologize for him."

"No need." Richardson looked at the young woman. "And you shouldn't speak so negatively about your gender, Detective."

"What?" he looked up from his notepad wearing a confused expression. "Why? What did I...?"

"How would you describe her appearance?" McFarlan asked.

"Beautiful," the principal told her. "I don't just mean beautiful because she's a kid. She is stunningly attractive."

"And she's currently socially inept?" Borden questioned. "I don't get it."

"That's because you're old," McFarlan replied, before turning her attention to Richardson again. "What about boys? Do they avoid her also?"

"They're drawn to her," she said. "But I have never seen many talk to her outside of class."

"That is kind of strange, don't you think?" the young officer asked. "How old is she? Sixteen?"

"That's right." Richardson opened the manila folder and flipped through the papers as she perused the records within.

"You would think an attractive sixteen-year-old girl might have at least one boy trying to gain her affection," McFarlan suggested.

"I understand what you're saying," Richardson looked up to her. "But her parents are...were pretty strict religious types. As far as I know, she doesn't even have a computer at home. She'll stay back at school two days a week to use the tech in the library to complete her homework. Her father picks her up on his way home from work."

"Where was that?" Borden asked. "His place of work?"

"Ah..." She flipped a couple of leaves of paper over before running her finger down a page of information. "National Mercantile Financial."

"In Main Street," McFarlan said.

"What about the mother?" Borden pressed.

"She didn't work," the principal replied. "She volunteered at a couple of places around town. Whenever I've had to contact her, she was usually doing something at the First Baptist Church."

Borden scribbled the information onto his notepad as the bell signaled for class to resume.

"Should we send for her now?" he asked.

"There'll be a second bell," Richardson replied. "That one was to inform students to get to class. Some will stop to collect items from their lockers before moving to their next lesson. We should wait a little longer, Mister Borden. I apologize for the inconvenience."

"I fully understand." He held his hands up. "Last thing you really want is for kids to spread rumors."

"Precisely." She smiled, dabbing her wet eyes with the tissue she still held in her hand.

V

Kirstin deliberately took the stairs one step at a time, not too fast, not too slow, drawing her pursuers closer and closer as she neared the top.

"Where are you going, bitch?" Steph called after her. "Huh?"

Kirstin stepped onto the level where other students were hastily making their way to their lockers. The bell that signaled the beginning of fourth period had just sounded.

Most of the students of Edwards Hill State High had been trained well. They knew that the first of two bells was the alarm to move. Like Pavlov's dogs reacting to a chime with salivating mouths, the pupils ran to their lockers and fetched their required materials for their next classes.

Steph was in no rush.

Her next class was the same as Kirstin's.

Math with Mister Redman. The allotted room was at the far end of the corridor that the girls were now walking along. But she had no intention of attending.

She had no intention for any of them to attend any more classes today.

"I saw what you did," Steph hissed. The students filling the hallway looked at her, wondering if she was addressing them until they saw Kirstin walking ahead of them. Their questioning looks turned to disinterest, as they were used to the three adolescents ganging up on the one lone child.

This was the norm.

A few of the older students, jocks and cheerleaders mostly, pulled their phones from their pockets to video the exchange between the girls. They shared smiles as the thought of posting the event on the World Wide Web gave them a small amount of pleasure.

Others taunted the three pursuers, encouraging the bullying with calls emitting from the gathering crowd that could smell a fight about to happen like a shark can sense blood in the water from miles away.

"Go get her, bully bitches," an onlooker called. Laughter erupted in the corridor.

Kirstin paid no attention to those who surrounded her. She continued towards her locker.

Focus, the calm voice whispered. *It's almost time.*

The clouds swirled rapidly around and around as lightning flashed beneath the bulging, bursting surface.

"I saw you look at him," Steph said, ignoring the bustling crowd around her, feeling a sense of bravado as her two friends stayed by her side.

Kirstin kept her back to them, walking just far enough ahead to keep within earshot.

Just far enough ahead to do what she had to do.

Blood red rain teamed from the swirling vapors. Thunder exploded violently in her head.

"I saw what you said to him," the other spat.

Smiling, Kirstin continued along the corridor, drawing her pursuers onward. Leading them away from the stairwell and towards her locker.

"He doesn't love you." Steph frowned. "How could he? You're a disgusting whore."

Kirstin cackled softly.

The clouds stopped circling.

The thunder ceased its roaring.

The rain shut itself off as if someone had turned the faucet closed tight.

The students moving about stopped and peered towards her. Their countenances changed from placid to confused. Some stepped away, sensing something very different about the girl as she led the three others along the hallway.

"Are you laughing at me, bitch?"

Kirstin chuckled louder, turning to make eye contact with the three that continued to follow. She quickly turned her face back in the direction she was moving, eyeing her locker only a few paces away.

"Turn around and face me, slut," Steph called.

"Or what?" Kirstin asked.

"Or I'll smash your fucking face in," the other girl replied.

Kirstin reached for the key in her pocket.

"I'd like to see that," she said, placing the key in the lock and turning it.

The lock clicked, allowing Kirstin to open the locker door.

"I will," Steph barked. "I'll fucking do it."

Kirstin reached into the cavity of her storage compartment, deep into her bag where her fingers brushed against cold steel.

Her stomach tightened, filling with butterflies as her nerves engulfed her.

"How?" Kirstin asked her.

"What?" Steph stopped in her tracks as the other turned her face towards her pursuers.

The students watching in the corridor paused and observed the spectacle unfolding before them. Phones held steadily, continuing to record the scene. They had never seen Kirstin behave in such a manner towards the taunts of Stephanie Granger and her cronies.

Kirstin's face appeared calm. A tiny grin lifted the corners of her mouth, making her appear as if she was talking to a friend.

"How will you be able to smash my fucking face in when I do this to you?"

She pulled the handgun from her bag and leveled it at Nancy Upton.

Focus.

The bullet penetrated through the girl's eye.

She fell instantly to the floor, shaking with spasms in her arms and legs.

Thunder boomed as lightning flared, branching its fluorescent arms across her mind like twisted, gnarled branches.

The crimson clouds rushed around and around in widening circles.

Faster and faster.

The blood rain teamed down with ferocity.

She could feel it growing, pulsating from within.

Joy.

Such joy.

Kirstin moved her eyes to Steph and smiled. The two girls stared at their friend on the floor, mouths agape as time seemed to stand still.

"Tell me how, Steph?" Kirstin asked, her voice calm.

The bell rang, signaling commencement of lessons.

SECUNDO INTERLUDIUM

Extract from the Diary of Kirstin Matthews

Saturday, March 4 2017

My parents suck.
Kyle Fargus is having a party tonight and I'm not allowed to go.
The first night of Spring Break and I'm stuck at home again.
Why won't they ever let me enjoy myself?

Steph says she is going to wear her thong in Kyle's pool. She would too.
I don't know how she can be so free with herself. I could never do anything like that.
I would love to be there just to see the look on the other girls' faces. They will all be so jealous.
Steph has got a great ass.
A thong ass.
LOL.

I wonder if Donny will be there.
I wish I could go.
It just isn't fair.

I hate my mom and dad so much.
They won't even let me have a cell phone or a computer.

Steph said she would send some photos of what happens, but I can't even get them from her.

My iPod is the only piece of tech they let me have and it's useless without Wi-Fi.

Why don't they get the internet?
I can't even download new music unless I'm at school.

How can they be so closed off to the rest of the world?
We may as well have a horse and cart instead of the gas guzzler sitting in the front yard.

God, I hate them.

MORS : DEATH

In a mad world, only the mad are sane.

AKIRA KUROSAWA

I

She turned her head, hearing the distant crack of thunder.

"What was that?" McFarlan asked as she placed her mug delicately on the principal's desk.

Borden had already risen to his feet, sitting his coffee cup beside his partners as he reached for the walkie-talkie attached to his belt.

"Sounded like a gunshot," he replied. "I'll go check while you move Principal Richardson and her staff into the teacher's lounge."

"Stupid idea, Doug." McFarlan shook her head. "We should call it in and wait for backup."

"We don't even know what that was," he told her before turning his attention to Richardson. "You've got workshops and other things that make loud noises, right?"

The principal was staring silently towards the door. Her mind wiped blank after hearing the words *gunshot* come out of the male police officer's mouth.

"Missus Richardson?" he called softly.

"Huh?" she snapped out of her trance and turned to him, looking like they had shaken her awake after a deep sleep. "Yes. Yes. We have four workshops. Two metal and two timber construction rooms. There's the cafeteria and the art studios upstairs. They all emit some noise once in a while."

"See?" Borden smiled at the younger officer. "I should check it out first. It could be nothing."

"I hope you're right." McFarlan pulled her sidearm and released the clip, checking to see that it was loaded.

"You couldn't do that back at the station?" Borden asked.

"I don't like carrying a loaded weapon in schools," she told him.

"You all set?"

She pushed the magazine back into the P229, a compact pistol carried by all the officers of the Edwards Hill Police Department. "Ready," McFarlan answered, as she placed her sidearm back into the holster on her belt.

II

"What the hell was that?" called a thin man in jeans and a tie. He pushed through the gathered crowd of students, where his eyes immediately fell upon the fallen girl on the floor.

Dark blood expanded from beneath her body as a small thin stream ran from the hole in the middle of her chest to a small pool gathering in the tiny dip in the throat just above her sternum.

The man watched in silent horror as the blood overflowed, sending a tiny line of red down the girl's neck and onto the floor.

Kirstin swung her hand around and pointed the 92 Compact towards the teacher.

"Sorry, Mister Jamerson," she smiled, squeezing off another round.

He had no time to react. His eyes still fixed upon the dead body lying on the floor nearby.

The bullet entered his brow, just above his right eye, drilled a channel through his skull and brain tissue before exploding through the back of his head and burrowing itself into the doorframe of the nearest classroom.

The surrounding students screamed and yelled as a fine spray of blood-spattered their clothing and skin.

Jamerson dropped to the ground, landing awkwardly with his legs convulsing wildly, kicking the feet of onlookers.

Kirstin turned back towards her intended targets to see only Angela staring down at her friend.

Stephanie had disappeared.

"I'm coming for you, Steph," she shouted, peering past the crowd to see the other running away.

Kirstin leveled the pistol towards Angela.

"N- n- n- no," the girl stammered, holding her hands up defensively. "Please, Kirstin. Please don't."

BLAM!

The shot pierced Angela's hand and smacked through the skin near her jaw. The bullet lodged somewhere in her head, but it didn't kill her.

She fell, calling out with a gurgling noise as Kirstin returned her eyes to the corridor.

Steph was still running, but so were all the others that were watching or recording the event on their cell phones. The passageway was a mess with moving objects.

Using both hands to steady her aim, planting her feet solidly on the linoleum surface, Kirstin controlled her breathing and squeezed the trigger. Just as her father had taught her.

The bullet flew, heading directly for Stephanie Granger. If not for one young boy who bumped into another that fled from the scene, knocking him off balance and sending him slightly to his right just at the wrong moment in time, the projectile would have found her skull instead of his.

"Shit," Kirstin spat.

Steph bolted around the corner to the right and out of view.

Now, you'll need to go after her.

She looked down at Angela, who was pressing a hand against the wound. Blood flowed through the lines between her fingers as she stared fearfully up at her killer.

"What's that Angie?" Kirstin chided. "Nothing to say without your fearless leader to support you?"

Angie cried, shedding long lines of tears from the corners of her eyes as blood spilled from her mouth and over her cheeks.

Save your bullets, instructed the calm voice in Kirstin's head as she lowered the gun towards the girl. She thumbed the safety on and lifted her foot.

With two violent thrusts of her leg, she stomped her sneaker into Angela's face, smashing the fallen girl's nose and teeth into pulp with a loud, sickening, wet crunch.

Taking a deep breath and closing her eyes, she watched the clouds gather to swirl in tight formation. She hid the storm deep within, sending flashes of lightning to the surface in time with her heartbeat. It slowed, changing from the rapid adrenaline-fueled drumming to a steady thump.

Opening her eyes, she peered towards the far end of the corridor.

Now it was time to find Stephanie.

She stepped over the two bodies of the girls and made her way along the passage, towards the corner where she had seen the head bitch vanish. Some students cowered against the walls and inside the doors of the classrooms that she passed.

They meant nothing to her.

It was Steph she wanted.

Kirstin's shoes felt slippery on the floor as she moved. Looking down as she passed the body of the young boy who fell in the way of her shot, she saw the reason why. Her sneakers were leaving a neat trail of blood in her wake as she placed her feet onto the linoleum surface with each step.

So what?

She used her thumb to turn the Beretta's safety off as she rounded the corner.

More students pressed against the walls, cowering, crying.

Still, no Stephanie Granger to be seen.

Kirstin ducked her head into the nearest classroom to see more students hiding and sobbing.

Steph has to be here somewhere.

She continued along the hallway, stepping into each of the rooms in search of her prey.

There was no stopping until Stephanie Granger was dead.

Richardson stood on a green rug, adorned with floral decorations and patterns, in the center of the teachers' lounge. There was a coffee table beside her with several mismatched couches roughly placed in a U-shape around the edges of the floor covering. She was just about to sit down when she heard a second shot, the one that killed Mister Jamerson, echoing along the corridors.

"Dear God," she breathed, moving her eyes to the young receptionists standing nearby.

"Shit," McFarlan hissed before turning to her partner. "We need to call this in."

Another shot rang out.

"I should investigate," Borden told her. They were standing by the door, peering along the corridor towards the direction they believed the sound had resonated from.

"Not on your own," she replied.

Another shot.

"Stay here with them," he instructed her. "I'm senior officer here. Call it in and stay here."

"Doug," she objected, shaking her head as he moved into the corridor.

"Stay here," he ordered, placing his hand on the handle of his P229 reassuringly. "I'll be fine."

With that, he moved off.

McFarlan watched him walk away, intending to keep her eyes on him until he was out of view.

"What do we do?" Karly Childers asked, disturbing the female police officer from her observation.

McFarlan turned to see the three women standing, petrified in the middle of the room. She scanned the area quickly. The young officer saw a long table with chairs by a window. Against the far wall was a small kitchenette with a fridge, microwave oven, electric kettle and a coffee percolator that was a little more than half-filled. A line of desks with computers sat neatly against the adjacent wall, with a telephone sitting on the desk closest to her position. There were over-filled bookshelves and magazine stands placed throughout the room with material ranging from novels, textbooks, school photo-albums, and leaflets for Farraway's Lawn Cutting and Gardening Services.

"Make a fresh pot of coffee," McFarlan replied.

"Coffee?" she questioned. "You want coffee?"

"Sure," the officer answered. "White with two, please. You two could help her or take a seat. Up to you."

The three women stared towards McFarlan for what seemed a long time as she strode quickly across the room to the window. Pulling the curtains back, she noticed that a strong metal mesh covered the exterior of the portals.

"Are all the windows covered with this?" she asked, turning towards Richardson.

"Yes," the principal replied. "They've always been covered to prevent theft."

"Okay," the officer nodded, returning to the center of the room. The receptionists were still watching her. "Can we knock them out for emergency evacuation?"

"There's only two ways out of the school," Richardson pointed towards the street end of the structure. "The main entrance and a set of doors at the rear of the gymnasium that lead out to the sports fields."

"Can anyone open those doors or are they on an electronic release system?"

"Electronic release?"

"Some schools," McFarlan said, "particularly in the cities, have a central system controlled from the admin areas. No one can enter or leave without a button being pressed first. Does this school have a system like that?"

"No." Richardson shook her head. "We've never had cause to include such a thing."

"But there's mesh over the windows?"

"That was installed before my time here," the principal told her defensively. "Possibly before the invention of these electronic release systems you mentioned."

"My coffee?" McFarlan looked to Childers.

"Huh?" The receptionists seemed to snap out of a deep sleep. "Sorry. I was... I'll make a fresh pot."

Childers moved towards the kitchenette.

"I'll help," Pearlman offered, following her.

Richardson moved closer to the police officer and lowered her voice.

"They're scared," she said. "So am I. You're coming across a little hostile."

"I know." McFarlan locked eyes with the other. "I'm scared too. But sitting here doing nothing and just thinking about what might happen out there won't help. Idle hands are the Devil's playground, Missus Richardson. We should try to keep ourselves occupied. Making coffee was the first thing I could think about."

Richardson lowered her eyes.

"I'll get some fresh mugs and see what we have in the cupboards that is still safe to eat," she said.

McFarlan moved back towards the open door and reached for her walkie-talkie.

"Dispatch, come in," she said into the mouthpiece.

"Dispatch receiving," came a muffled reply.

"Dispatch, this is Officer Kimberley McFarlan of the Edwards Hill PD. We have multiple gunshots at the Edwards Hill State High School. Requesting backup."

"Multiple gunshots at Edwards Hill State High School. Requesting backup," the voice repeated. "Do you require medical assistance also, Officer McFarlan?"

"Unsure of the circumstances," McFarlan informed the other. "Officer Douglass Borden is investigating. I am in the teachers' lounge with the principal and two receptionist staff."

"Understood," the voice fizzed over the device. "I am relaying your message and request. Sit tight, Officer McFarlan."

"Will do," she said before turning her attention to the three others in the room with her. "Help is on the way."

Richardson turned quickly to face the police officer. Her hands were shaking as she fumbled with a mug she had just retrieved from the cupboard. It slipped out of her grasp and smashed onto the linoleum floor by her feet.

"Shit," she spat.

IV

"A shooting on the outskirts of the quiet community of Edwards Hill has resulted in two victims inside their own homes," announced a well-dressed, middle-aged man with a glowing blue orb with the rough outlines of the continents spinning on a screen behind him. The word, "SHOOTING" appeared behind him, just to the right of his head. "We cross live to our on-the-scene reporter, Samantha Patterson.

"Samantha, what can you tell us about the victims?"

Peterson flicked her hair over her shoulder. She peered directly into the lens of the camera that Wayne was holding upon her. The Matthews house was directly behind her, within frame. With a deep breath, she steadied her nerves and spoke.

"Phil," she said, "the two victims are well-known people to the town. Husband and wife Randal and Jennifer Matthews. Randal was a senior banker at the Edwards Hill National Mercantile Financial Institution and had his life taken from him at the young age of thirty-four. His wife, Jennifer, was only thirty-two and was a regular volunteer at the municipal library. Both were members of the First Baptist Church, here in town. I've been told that they have one daughter who is possibly with the police as we speak.

"What we know for certain is that the husband and wife were in their own house at the time and that both were shot at close range. They were discovered by a Missus Betty Walker, who delivers mail in this area and also works as the school bus driver. She has informed the police that she drove the daughter of Mister and Missus Matthews to school this morning. She is now assisting the detectives, who arrived only a few minutes ago, with their enquiries. Phil?"

"Thanks Samantha Patterson," the man replied, still staring down the lens of the studio camera. The word, "SHOOTING" vanished from behind him, replaced by, "HOLLYWOOD RED CARPET". "I'm sure we'll be crossing back to you as more information becomes available. On to other news, where the Hollywood press gallery gathered to recognize..."

"And we're out," Wayne Dwyers said as he lowered the camera.

Samantha lowered her microphone and shook her head, "The name's Peterson asshole."

"Don't worry." Dwyers smiled, patting her on the shoulder as she moved by him, heading back towards their van. "Everyone will know your name after today, sweetheart."

"...shots in Edwards Hill State High School," a muffled voice crackled over the speaker of the police scanner in the van.

"I mean, this story is the biggest thing we've ever encountered," Dwyers told her as he slid the side door open to place his camera inside. Samantha tried to focus on the police scanner attached to the console near the driver's seat.

"Repeat. Officer is requesting assistance. Reports of gunshots inside Edwards Hill State High School," the scanner warbled.

"This might even land you on network, baby," the cameraman continued.

"Shhh," she hissed at him. "Did you hear that?"

"What?" He put the camera into its well-padded bag and cocked an ear towards the scanner.

"Officer Cory Plasket responding," another voice crackled over the speaker. "I'm five minutes out and on my way back into town. Any chance someone will get there before me?"

"Sorry, Cory," the operator replied. "This is Naomi. We're mustering up who we can. The captain's busy doing that right now. Four officers are out at another crime scene as we speak. Borden and McFarlan are both at the school. That leaves you and Morris."

"Morris is out on the highway with the radar gun," Cory replied. "Radio reception is shit out there. You might want to try his cell phone."

"Will do," Naomi told him.

"Shit." Dwyers looked at the reporter. "We'll need to move fast. You up for it?"

"You bet your ass," she said, still holding the microphone as she opened the passenger door and slid inside the vehicle.

Dwyers slammed the sliding door and ran around the van to the driver's side.

Within moments, the van was speeding back along Jackson Drive towards the quiet community of Edwards Hill.

V

Climbing the stairs slowly, his gun trained ahead of him, his finger on the trigger guard, Borden moved forward cautiously. He placed his feet carefully on each step, trying to remain as silent as his aging body would allow him. His nerves were at their peak as his eyes grew level with the next floor.

His stomach tightened. His brow began to sweat. His bladder screamed.

Moving his eyes to the left as he hugged the wall on the right, keeping his back close to the brick surface as he moved up the final few stairs, he saw a boy's body lying on the ground. The arms and legs of the fallen students sprawled in an awkward position that would be uncomfortable to remain in for a conscious person.

Shit!

Some more students were cowering in the corridor, hugging the walls on either side of the long hallway.

He paused at the top of the stairs and moved his eyes around the corner of the wall to peer in the opposite direction of the passageway.

He saw more students crouching by the walls.

In the center of the passageway, about halfway along the length from his position to the far end, were three more bodies.

He lifted his walkie-talkie from his belt and turned the volume up just enough to hear.

"Dispatch, come in," he whispered.

"Dispatch," crackled a woman's voice.

"Officer Douglas Borden reporting four gunshot victims at Edwards Hill State High School," he whispered. "No sign of the shooter."

"Do you require medical assistance, Officer Borden?"

He looked towards the cluster of bodies to his right. The male adult had a great pool of blood around him. The two female victims were also lying in a puddle of red liquid. One of them had her entire face smashed in.

The sight made his stomach churn. His bladder burned as he tried to compose himself.

"They're all dead, dispatch," he replied.

"Understood," the woman said. "We have Officer Plasket on his way. Captain Reece has requested support from Houston."

"There are people here," Borden told the other. "I need to get them out."

"Can you do so without alerting the shooter?"

"If they stay here, they'll be targets for the shooter," he replied.

"Proceed with caution, Officer Borden," the woman advised.

"Doug, it's Kimmie," another voice warbled through the speaker. "I think we should evacuate as many as we can."

"My thoughts exactly," he replied as he stepped onto the floor, moving slowly towards the three bodies farther along the passageway. "I think the best way is back down the stairs I just came up and down the corridor to you."

There was a moment of silence.

Borden drew closer to the three victims. His eyes fell upon the girl with a caved in face. Deep red flesh and rippled broken skin gave way to protruding bone fragments.

His throat tightened as he forced himself to swallow.

"Doug," McFarlan's voice called through the walkie-talkie.

"Yeah," he replied, not able to move his eyes away from the mess of blood and bone.

"Principal Richardson has informed me that the mustering point for evacuation is on the front lawn," the other told him. "Under the trees to the side of the school. Near where we parked the car. Send all the people you can to us and we'll direct them there."

"Will do," he said, moving his eyes to the young boys and girls lining the corridor.

"And Doug?"

"Yeah," he called back.

"Don't be a hero," she told him. "Don't go after the shooter on your own. Come back here and wait for backup with me."

"Understood," he replied.

He turned his attention to the nearest group of people huddled by a classroom door. Placing a finger to his lips, he signaled for them to move down the stairs.

"Front door," he whispered. "Go."

Two boys and four girls, no more than fifteen-years-old, quietly moved towards the stairwell. Before they had disappeared from view, Borden had signaled for the next group to follow.

Eventually, he was able to clear the length of the passageway to the right of the stairwell, and the rooms on either side, of all students and teachers that were hiding and hoping to be saved.

He turned his attention to the other end of the corridor, noticing the bloody footprints leading away from the three bodies, back towards the stairs. Following them, he made his way back the way he had come, past the stairwell and towards the far end of the corridor.

As he moved forward, he signaled for the others cowering in classrooms and against the wall to move back along the passageway and down the stairs.

"Doug?" McFarlan called through the walkie-talkie.

"Yeah," he whispered.

"We just got the first group of people," she announced. "How many more?"

"I wasn't counting," he told her. "But there are a lot more. I've found footprints leading farther into the school. I think the shooter is still up here somewhere."

A young girl, hearing his conversation, pointed to the end of the corridor as she blubbered uncontrollably.

"They went that way?" he asked her.

She nodded.

"Okay," he replied. "Go down the stairs and head for the front door. Another officer is waiting there. Go quietly."

Her sneaker squeaked against the linoleum as she lifted herself to her feet.

Borden moved his eyes to her shoes, noticing the blood on the outer edges of the midsole.

Shit!

He lifted his gun, moving his finger inside the loop of the trigger guard of the P229.

She dropped to one knee, using both of her hands to level the Beretta towards his face.

BLAM!

The thunder roared and reverberated along the corridors of the school.

His ears rang loudly with a high-pitched screech as his vision blurred, growing darker and darker.

With a thud, he dropped to the ground in a heap.

Blood seeped from the socket where his left eye once was.

Kirstin heard several others around her scream as she lifted herself upright again. Peering around, she noticed the scared students cowering against the walls.

She moved to Borden's body and took the pistol from his hand, tucking it between the waist of her jeans and her back. Flipping his coat open, she searched his shoulder holster and pockets for spare magazines. She found two and put them in the right back pocket of her pants.

"Doug?" a woman's voice crackled over the walkie-talkie. "Doug? Come in? We heard a gunshot. Doug?"

Kirstin lifted the walkie-talkie out of the fallen police officer's hand before standing upright again. She looked around to the frightened faces of the boys and girls around her as she clipped the radio on her belt.

The clouds spun in a large circle. The thunder was distant; the lightning was dim. She felt composed. She felt serene.

Let them go, the calm voice told her.

"Make your way to the front door," she said to the students.

They peered at her questionably.

Fearfully.

Untrustingly.

"Go," she barked, waving the Beretta towards the stairwell. "Before I kill all of you."

With that, the girls and boys gathered near her, moved with haste, fleeing towards the stairs.

Three teachers, two women and an older man, emerged from the classrooms, following the released students.

"No," Kirstin snapped, pointing her pistol at them. "Not you."

She looked towards the stairs, waiting for all the students to vanish from view. With her gun, she gestured for the adults to move into a classroom at the end of the hallway.

"In there," she commanded.

"Kirstin," one of them, a middle-aged woman, pleaded. "Let us go. We have children and families. Please."

"Get in there, Missus Rostron," she barked at the woman.

The three adults moved into the room with the girl in tow.

"What are you going to do, Kirstin?" the older man asked. "Why are you doing this?"

The girl placed a finger to her lips.

"Shhhh," she hissed before lifting the walkie-talkie to her lips. "You have an officer down."

"Who is this?" a woman's voice called.

"There are more students coming your way." She looked to the door of the classroom, and added, "and there are three dead teachers in room one-one-nine."

She lowered the walkie-talkie, clipping it back to her belt as she aimed the Beretta towards the older male.

"Sorry, Mister Zelski," she said. "Missus Gaynor. Missus Rostron. But you're all to blame. It's all your fault too."

"What is, Kirstin?" Zelski asked. "Help us understand. Maybe we can fix it."

Kirstin squeezed the trigger.

VI

"Did you recognize the voice?" McFarlan asked the principal. They were standing on either side of the main doors to the building, ushering students out and directing them towards the receptionists, Childers and Pearlman. The two young women were standing on a large patch of grass under the shade of a Honey Mesquite.

The students gathered in small groups, some near the trunk, others on the grass near the two receptionists. Many of the girls were in tears, reaching for the comforting arms of their friends as they kept asking the same question to each other. *Why?*

"Missus Richardson?" the young police officer called gently.

The principal moved her eyes from the gathering children meeting under the tree to the uniformed woman across the doorway from her.

"Yes," she replied. "Sorry."

"Did you recognize the voice on the radio?"

"No." Richardson shook her head. "It sounded distorted. I don't..."

Tears welled in her eyes.

"It's okay," McFarlan told her. "I'm going to need to go inside."

"You can't leave me," the principal said, her eyes widening. "Please. There are still more students coming and she could be one of them."

Kimmie McFarlan looked into the building. A few students were still making their way towards them. It was true. The shooter could be amongst them, but gut instinct was telling the police officer the girl was still inside somewhere.

"When these kids come out," she said to the principal, "and are safe with the others over there, I'm going in."

"What do we do?"

"Stay with the kids," McFarlan replied. "Backup is on the way."

She peered past the approaching students towards the stairwell far in the distance.

"Is that the only way up to the next level?" she asked the principal.

"No," Richardson answered. "There are four more sets of stairs. One in each corner of the building."

"The hallways upstairs." McFarlan considered. "Any dead-ends?"

She suddenly wished she had chosen her words better. *Dead-ends.*

"No," the other replied. "All the hallways met up. It's a similar layout to this level. One hallway straight through the middle, like this, and a big rectangle to get to the outermost rooms."

McFarlan nodded. In her head, she pictured a square with a perpendicular line through the center.

The approaching students drew closer. One of the older boys looked towards the principal. His eyes were wet and blood had drained from his face. His breathing was shallow and rapid, wheezing with every exhale.

"It was Kirstin Matthews," he huffed. "It was Kirstin Matthews."

"The boy's in shock," McFarlan said, moving towards him to place his arm over her shoulder.

"Kirstin?" Richardson's chin quivered.

"Are there more people coming?" she asked a girl that had been walking with the wheezing boy.

"We were the last," the girl replied, her voice was shaking. "She told us to go or she would kill us. Missus Gaynor and Mister Zelski and Missus Rostron are still up there. I think she shot them. I heard the gun."

"It was Kirstin Matthews," the boy huffed again.

"It's okay," McFarlan told them. "You're okay now."

She helped the boy across the front yard of the school and lowered him onto the grass beneath the large mesquite.

"Lie down," the young police officer instructed the boy. He complied, placing his back on the soft, green blades of grass. McFarlan turned to the girl that had come with them. "Cross your legs and sit at his feet. I need you to put his feet in your lap."

"Elevate his legs to treat him for shock, you mean," the girl said.

"Yeah." McFarlan smiled. "You know what to do?"

"I took a course in First Aid during Spring Break." She looked to the boy as she placed herself on the ground, lifting his feet with her hands. "We both did."

"Sounds like fun." The police officer crouched beside her to help her elevate the boy's feet. "What's your name?"

"Jenny," she replied. "This is Mitchell."

"Your boyfriend?"

"Yes, Ma'am," the girl nodded.

"It was Kirstin Matthews," he said again.

"She knows, Mitchell," Jenny told him. The boy's eyes glazed over. His eyelids half closed.

"He's in shock," McFarlan said, looking around at the other students. "He'll probably say it again and again a few times more yet. What we need is something to cover him. You!"

Another boy, wearing a team jacket, looked back at the cop, surprised. He pointed to himself.

Who, me?

"Yeah, you," she called. "Come here."

The boy jogged over to her side, "Yes, Ma'am."

"I need your jacket," McFarlan told him. "Take it off and put it over Mitchell's chest."

The boy unzipped his coat and practically tore it off his body. He placed it over Mitchell's upper body like a blanket.

"Talk to him," the young officer instructed the girl. "Try to get him to respond."

"Mitchell," the girl started. "It's Jenny. Can you hear me?"

Mitchell moaned.

"Mitchell?"

"I can hear..."

"Stay with him," McFarlan told Richardson. "I need to get inside. I need to check if my partner needs my help."

"She said he was dead," the principal whispered.

"She said we have an officer down," the officer corrected. "That could mean he is injured."

McFarlan's gut told her that Doug Borden was lying dead upstairs in the building, but she couldn't live with herself knowing there was a chance he might still be alive.

Richardson nodded, understanding the police officer's plight.

"Go." The principal frowned. "Be safe."

"Backup's coming," McFarlan told her again before jogging back to the open doors of Edwards Hill State High School.

VII

Kirstin made her way along the corridor that stretched along the rear of the building and used one of the corner stairwells to reach the lower floor. Her backpack was slung over her left shoulder, now laden with the boxes of bullets, a spare magazine for her Beretta and the two for the P229 she still had stuffed down the back of her jeans.

She emerged near the doors to the gymnasium, which doubled as the school's basketball auditorium. There were still twenty or so students inside with one of the male coaching staff members. He was a robust young man, constantly blowing his whistle as he pointed to one student to move from running suicide laps to the next activity of jumping jacks. At the same time, he indicated to another pupil to move from doing push-ups to start the suicide run.

The students were all soaked in sweat, huffing and puffing as their sneakers squeaked and slapped against the polished timber floors. The noise reverberated loudly, possibly drowning any of the sounds of earlier gunshots.

Kirstin quickly looked about the room, up to the bleachers and around the students sitting on the court edge, catching their breath.

There was no sign of Stephanie Granger.

She moved past the open door to the gymnasium, by the entrances to the girls' and boys' change rooms, and to a little door with the word *MAINTENANCE* printed on it.

Kirstin tried the handle. The door swung inward quietly to reveal a small room lined with shelves loaded with various equipment that could be found in a hardware store. There were offcut pieces of pipes sticking out of containers, saws, and spades hanging from hooks on a wall. Some little trays sitting neatly in a rack contained different sized screws, bolts and nails. Above them was a wall panel with several tools hanging in a well-organized fashion. There were hammers, pliers, chisels, and screwdrivers.

It was a handyperson's wet dream.

The sour smell of paint, turpentine and fuel stung her nose as she peered around the room, looking for what she wanted.

"You kids should learn to knock before coming in here," a voice called from a high-backed swivel chair covered in worn faux leather with tattered edges, facing away from her. The occupier was watching the screen of a small television that sat beside a computer on top of an old teachers' desk pressed against the adjacent wall to the right of her.

Slowly, the chair spun around, revealing a scrawny, middle-aged man who was cleaning his thick spectacles with an old rag. His worker's shirt bore a nametag positioned just above the right pocket.

Lionel Jenkins.

He moved his eyes over the young girl slowly, absorbing her, pausing at her breasts before lifting his gaze to her face. She had noticed him do this many times, not just to her, but to all young, fit girls of Edwards Hill State High School.

"What can I do for you, pretty?" he asked with a crooked smile, placing his glasses on his nose.

The clouds spun in wide circles, gathering momentum as the lightning deep inside them increased their intervals.

"Spare padlocks and keys," she told him, hiding the Beretta behind her back, out of his view. "Where are they?"

"You could be a little nicer," he said, leaning back and placing his elbows on the armrests. "What do you need them for?"

"To lock the doors," she replied, looking across the shelves. "Where are they?"

He spread his knees apart and moved a hand to his crotch. She glanced briefly and wasn't able to determine whether he was trying to arouse himself or simply scratching an itch.

The clouds drew closer and closer, forming together as a pulsating mass as distant thunder echoed through her mind.

"What's the rush?" he said. "Is there an emergency? Why don't you relax and take a seat? Spend some time with old Lionel?"

Kirstin locked eyes with him.

"There are no other seats," she told him.

"Use your imagination, girl," he widened his grin to reveal a tobacco-stained yellow smile.

She smiled back, moving closer.

He giggled excitedly.

Before he could scarcely comprehend what was happening, she placed the muzzle of the Beretta against his crotch.

"Tell me where the padlocks and keys are," she said softly, "or I'll blow your balls off."

His chin quivered.

His hands shook.

His eyes grew wide with fear as they glared at the gun pressed against his crotch.

Nervously, he stretched his right hand out and pointed to a shelf with some old shoe boxes on it.

Kirstin kept the pistol leveled on the maintenance man as she moved to where he was gesturing. She lifted a box from the shelf with her left hand. It was heavy.

She placed it on a bench by the shelves and lifted the lid. Inside was a canvas library bag with the school's emblem printed on it.

Kirstin lifted the bag out and placed it on the bench, where she used one hand to open the top so that she could see inside. There were five large padlocks with the keys still plugged into them. There was also a thin chain with another padlock attached, but no key.

"Where's the key to the padlock?" she asked.

"They're in the locks," he muttered.

"There's one without a key." She pointed the gun towards his head. "Where is it?"

His shaking hand pointed to his pants pocket.

"Get it out," she ordered.

Jenkins reached into his right hip pocket and fished out his set of keys. Using his thumb and forefinger, he held them up for Kirstin to take.

"Toss them onto the bench," she instructed.

He did so, landing them precariously on the edge.

"Thank you," she said to Jenkins as she gripped the Beretta in both hands and aimed for his head.

The dull thumping of footfalls and the soft screech of the coach's whistle emitting from the gymnasium could still reach through the walls and into her ears. A gunshot would be louder and would cause alarm.

Her eyes darted across the many tools on the panel above the shelves, landing on a box cutter knife dangling next to a line of screwdrivers.

The clouds twisted ferociously, like a membranous creature forming, an unborn fetus growing organs, a darkness about to be unleashed.

"Turn around," she ordered the man as he backed up towards the tools.

"Don't hurt me," he blubbered, spinning in his seat to face the television again. "Please don't. I'm sorry for looking at you like that. I won't do it again."

She lifted the knife from the panel and extended the blade using her left thumb. The sharp razor emerged from the casing.

"I shouldn't have said those things to you," he continued, weeping profusely as she drew closer to him. "It was wrong. I know it was wrong."

She thumbed the safety of the Beretta with her right thumb and put the pistol's muzzle in her hip pocket.

"I'm sick," he told her. "I have a problem. I like young girls and it's wrong. I shouldn't be working here. I'll resign if you let me go. God help me."

Her right hand grabbed his forehead and pulled his head back as her left hand slid the blade across his throat.

Lightning exploded with a tremendous roar. The clouds burst to life, sending a shower of crimson rain.

A loud gurgling noise discharged from the wound as a gush of dark blood swept over his neck and over his shirt. His eyes moved towards her as she held him steady.

His arms and legs flailed wildly, knocking a few small things from the desk and onto the floor. He tried to breathe but sent a fine spray of red over the screen of the television.

Using both hands, she held his forehead in place, pressing the back of his head against the top of the high-backed swivel chair, keeping out of the reach of his flailing arms.

Jenkins' legs eventually stopped moving. His arms drooped to his sides.

Kirstin stood upright and dropped the blade on the floor. She turned her attention to the shoebox full of padlocks and lifted out five large, silver-colored items.

Twisting the keys, she checked the locks were operational before lifting her backpack off her shoulder and dropping the locks into a side pocket.

Taking the Beretta out of her pocket, she moved out of the maintenance room and started along the corridor towards the nearest door that led to the outside world.

She would have to move fast.

She would need to move quietly.

There was no doubt they would come for her.

But she still needed to find Stephanie Granger.

After that, it didn't matter.

The crimson clouds receded.

The blood rain slowed and died away.

The thunder grew quieter, and the lightning moved to the distance.

TERTIUS INTERLUDIUM

TRANSCRIPT OF KDY4 FM INTERVIEW WITH
SENATOR ELROY MITCHUM
WEDNESDAY APRIL 26 2017

The following is a transcript of an interview for KDY4 FM with Senator Elroy Mitchum and station announcer Morena Bollino.

BOLLINO:

Gun regulations reformation. A good idea? In the wake of the Edwards Hill tragedy, some would believe it's past time for changes to occur. Others would say that the mere concept of making such alterations to our constitution is outright sacrilege. I'm joined this morning by Senator Elroy Mitchum, a member of the Republican Party and an avid supporter of the NRA. Good morning Senator, thank you for joining us.

MITCHUM:

Thank you for having me on your program, Morena. I love the show.

BOLLINO:

Senator, the President has been somewhat quiet about the events that took place in Edwards Hill, and the incident at UT, surfacing only to express sorrow and offer condolences. Do you think this is because the previous administration was vocal about revisiting the second amendment to make alterations after an increase in gun crimes over the past decade?

MITCHUM:

I really can't speak for the president. What I can refer to in that question is how the previous leader of this nation wanted to change our constitution. It's our constitution. It can't be changed. It's black and white. We have the right to bear arms.

BOLLINO:

Sorry, Senator. You said that the constitution can't be changed?

MITCHUM:

That's right. It can't.

BOLLINO:

There are several people, including other senators, who would disagree with you.

MITCHUM:

Why? As I said. It's there in black and white.

BOLLINO:

It has been amended many times throughout history, and the portion that you are referring to is an amendment in itself. That means it was a change that was made to the original constitution.

MITCHUM:

But it's there now, and I don't think the American people want it changed or taken away. The second amendment was included to protect our sovereignty. It exists to guard the very principles for which the constitution stands for. Changing the second amendment, or any other portion of the constitution, will be like wiping our asses on Old Glory herself.

BOLLINO:

Colorful.

MITCHUM:

I'm sorry. But that's how I see it.

BOLLINO:

You said the second amendment exists to protect our sovereignty. But in this day and age, isn't that what we have our military forces for?

MITCHUM:

The military protects us, and the free world. We can't expect them to look after our own backyards. If someone breaks into your house and threatens your family, wouldn't you feel safer knowing that you have a gun at hand?

BOLLINO:

I'm afraid I don't see the link. You were talking about sovereignty before. Now you're talking about home protection. The two are not really related.

MITCHUM:

Of course, they are, Morena. Of course, they are. I'm protecting the sovereignty of my house.

BOLLINO:

I still don't see the link. From a historical point of view, the second amendment was an addition that allowed citizens to carry firearms to protect themselves against a genuine threat of the time. Given that the British are now an ally of the United States, and that we don't have any potential, great threats similar to the day the amendment was added, don't you think it's time that we revisit the need for such an amendment?

MITCHUM:

Al-Qaeda, ISIS, the Taliban. The list goes on and on. How can you say there are no threats against our sovereignty? Sure, the British are no threat to us. But Mohammad, who moves in next door to you, may not be as innocent as he appears. We've seen trained doctors and lawyers strap bombs to themselves and blow-up schools filled with children all over the Middle East. Those bastards who crashed into the towers in New York and the Pentagon on nine-eleven were all university students or graduates. There's your threat against our sovereignty.

BOLLINO:

But how will a gun in your house stop that from occurring?

MITCHUM:

Well, if you... That's not the point. You were questioning the reason why we have the second amendment. I was giving you an answer. A gun in the home would be a protection against a burglar or an invader.

BOLLINO:

According to Texan regulations, firearms need to be secured in a place which cannot be accessed by a child under the age of 17, or secured with a trigger lock if there is reason to know that a child under 17 may gain access to the firearm. This being the case, and that some who experience a break in might have children, by the time a person is able to navigate all of that security, surely the intruder would have completed their deed. I mean, you're not going to ask the burglar to wait while you retrieve your gun from the safe and remove the trigger lock mechanism. Are you?

MITCHUM:

The regulations don't mention the need for a safe and only require a trigger lock for any child that may gain access to the firearm. It doesn't say, you gotta have a safe for your gun. It just says, make sure your kids can't get to it.

BOLLINO:

Which would mean that it's not hanging on your bed post or on the nightstand within arm's reach, just in case your house is broken into. Right?

MITCHUM:

Of course not. But you still would feel safer knowing that you had a gun in your house.

BOLLINO:

But you couldn't get to it in time.

MITCHUM:

But you'd feel safer.

BOLLINO:

But you couldn't get to it in time.

MITCHUM:

Listen. You wanted me to come on here and talk about gun reform laws.

BOLLINO:

I'm questioning the need for the second amendment.

MITCHUM:

And I'm thinking that you sit more to the left-wing than I originally thought you did.

BOLLINO:

You said you loved the show. I assumed that meant you had tuned
in and listened once or twice. Let's move on to gun categorization.
Under current laws in several states throughout the US, ownership extends past handguns and single-shot, bolt-action, lever-
action rifles to semi-automatic assault weaponry. Is there a need
for such high caliber firearms to be available to the average Joe?

MITCHUM:

Some use such firearms for hunting.

BOLLINO:

What exactly are they hunting that requires an AR-15? The weapon of choice used by the shooter at UT.

MITCHUM:

Look. We could get into specifics, Morena, but the fact remains that the American people are entitled to purchase such a weapon under the current legislation.

BOLLINO:

But why? Shouldn't access to such weaponry be questioned? Isn't a bolt-action or lever-action rifle good enough to kill a duck or a deer these days? Are the animals wearing Kevlar, Senator?

MITCHUM:

This kind of questioning is ridiculous. Consider this. The latest mass shooting in Edwards Hill didn't involve an assault rifle. It didn't involve a bolt-action or lever-action rifle. It was a young girl with a hand-gun. A hand-gun that obviously wasn't kept out of her reach. I really hate to speak ill of the dead, but if there is any- one to blame besides the girl... Kerry? Karren?

BOLLINO:

Kirstin Matthews.

MITCHUM:

Kirstin. Yeah. Well, if there was anyone else who could be blamed, besides Kirstin for the tragedy that unfolded on Monday, it would be her parents for not adhering to the laws and regulations.

BOLLINO:

Some might say Kirstin Matthews was a victim herself.

MITCHUM:

She pulled the trigger. She's no victim. I just wish the teachers were allowed to carry guns in schools. One of them could have dropped her before she went on that rampage.

BOLLINO:

Isn't that a risk to the teachers? What if a student, say a large male in his senior years, decides to attack his teacher and takes the gun from him or her?

MITCHUM:

Well, teachers would need to undergo some training, of course. But think of this. If one of the staff members of that school was able to end that before it began, we could have ended with maybe only two or three victims instead of seventy-three.

BOLLINO:

Seventy-four.

MITCHUM:

I stand by what I said. The girl is not a victim in this.

BOLLINO:

Senator Elroy Mitchum, we've run out of time. Thank you for coming in today.

MITCHUM:

A pleasure.

BOLLINO:

And we'll be right back with comedian, Randy Sanders, after the news and the traffic report.

VENATURA : HUNTING

Madness borrowed its face from the mask of the beast.

MICHEL FOUCAULT

I

Holding her P229 in front of her as she cautiously climbed the stairwell, McFarlan peered up to the top of the steps looking for movement. Her finger was resting on the trigger guard, hoping the only other person she might see would be another fleeing student or some teachers.

She stepped upon the upper floor and into the hallway, moving her eyes to her right first. She immediately saw the two bodies of young girls and one male adult roughly halfway along the passage.

Her head snapped to the left, where she saw the body of one young boy not too far from her. Much farther along, nearer to the western end of the corridor, lay the unmistakable form of Doug Borden.

Her stomach tightened as a lump formed in her throat. Even from this distance, she could see the wound where his left eye used to be.

She steadied her breathing as she turned towards the three slain individuals to her right. She moved towards them, keeping both of her hands around the pistol's grip.

The ghastly sight of the concave face of one of the female victims filled her vision.

"Dear God," she exhaled as she drew alongside the fallen. Her eyes fell upon an open locker that was all but empty, save for a pencil case and one large exercise book.

McFarlan lifted the book out of the cavity and read the name on the front.

Kirstin Matthews.

She placed the notebook back into the locker and moved past the stairs she had just climbed and towards her fallen partner.

She stopped momentarily to look at the boy. The damp hole in the back of his head was the only wound she could see.

Continuing on, she reached Borden and crouched beside him. His good eye was closed shut.

She placed her hand on his cheek.

"Oh, Doug." She frowned, fighting back tears, noticing the wet patch on his trousers and remembering his complaining of a weak bladder.

She studied him, focusing particularly on his shoulder holster. His weapon was missing. No doubt taken by Kirstin Matthews.

A quick summary of what she had seen so far told her that the young girl knew how to handle a weapon. All of her victims that McFarlan inspected had been taken down with one shot. Just one shot.

She's good, the cop reflected. *She knows how to control her emotions.*

Another thought crossed her mind.

Perhaps she is just conserving ammunition? Perhaps she has a limited number of clips for her gun. That would explain why one victim had her head caved in.

Doesn't matter now, she argued with herself. *Now she has two guns and more ammunition.*

"Why?" McFarlan hissed, shaking her head slowly as she stared at the body of her friend.

She's hunting.

Lifting the walkie-talkie from her belt, she called in a brief situation report.

"Dispatch, come in," she called softly into the radio.

"Dispatch, go ahead," replied a woman's voice.

"Officer McFarlan reporting an officer down." She almost choked on the words as they came out of her mouth. "One Officer Doug Borden, shot through the left eye. Deceased. His sidearm is missing. I repeat, his sidearm is missing.

"I have counted four other victims so far. Two adolescent females. One adolescent male and one adult male.

"Suspect is a Kirstin Matthews. A student of Edwards Hill State High School. I believe the suspect is still on site. I repeat, I believe the suspect is still on site.

"Several students, some teachers, the receptionist staff and the principal have been evacuated from the building. There are still many students and staff members inside.

"I desperately need backup, dispatch. How long before the cavalry gets here?"

"We're fully aware of the situation there, officer," the woman replied. "All available officers are being relocated to your location. We have made a request for tactical response to Houston. They're sending a task force by chopper."

"How long?"

"Thirty, maybe forty minutes," the woman answered. "That's what they told me. I really can't be certain. You just keep your head down. Help is on the way."

McFarlan stood to her feet and moved farther along the passage, peering into the open doors of the classroom as she passed by.

"Understood," she said disappointedly into the walkie-talkie, moving closer to the T-intersection at the end of the passage.

Something gripped her attention in the corner of her eye. She turned to see another three bodies inside the last classroom on the left. Three adults. Two females, one male.

"Dispatch, I've just found three more bodies in a classroom not too far from Officer Borden's position."

"Noted, Officer McFarlan," the voice warbled back. "Keep us updated. You're doing great."

II

Crouching by an emergency exit door on the southern wall of the lower level, Kirstin listened to the conversation between the dispatch lady and the police officer inside the school with her.

She kept her breathing steady as the clouds swirled around her head violently again.

Not yet, the voice said. *Calm down.*

She closed her eyes and felt the intense heat of a fire that laced the insides of her eyelids.

The clouds receded a little. Her anxiety subsided.

She opened her eyes and reached into the library bag slung over her shoulder. Retrieving a padlock, she twisted the key to open it before threading it through the hole just below the locking mechanism on the door.

With a click, she locked it shut and tossed the key into the bag.

That's two, she considered. *Four more to go.*

She moved out of the thin passage that ran down the side of the library and onto the passageway that ran from south to north near the front of the school.

Her ears were straining to hear noises from upstairs. There were still students and classes in progress along the outer corridors. The students and teachers here had not heard the gunshots, or if they had, they hadn't recognized them as such.

She could walk casually by the classes in clear sight of everyone without arousing suspicion. It wasn't unusual to see a student or two moving along the hallways during class time.

People continued to work in the library, none of which was Steph. If she had made it here, she would have raised the alarm. It was Kirstin's best guess that the girl was still upstairs, hiding in a classroom with others who were aware of what was happening.

The big problem was, there was a cop up there too, and she knew who Kirstin was.

She moved towards the front door, passing the reception office and staff lounge, reaching the double doors that led to the outside world. Peering through the glass panels, she could see the students and teachers who had made it out, gathered under the trees on the edge of the grass.

Reaching into her pocket, she retrieved Jenkins' keys and found two possible matches to the lock on the door.

She tried one, but it didn't fit. It was then that she noticed a sliding bolt at the base of the door. Bending, she moved the bolt into place, locking one door.

Kirstin tried the other key in the lock. It slid in with ease.

With a hard counterclockwise turn, the lock clicked shut. She then reached into the bag and pulled the chain loop out. Using the same key, she unlocked the padlock and threaded the chain through the door's handles twice, making a tight loop. She reattached the padlock and hurried away from the doors, back into the corridor.

Three down. Three more to go.

The need to move fast was overbearing. The next period bell would ring soon. She intended to have all the doors locked before the change of class.

She hurried along the passageway towards the northern end of the school.

Briskly, she moved partway along the northern corridor, heading towards the cafeteria. She disappeared down the passageway between the girls' and boys' bathrooms, leading to the emergency door at the end.

As she approached, she took a padlock from the library bag and unlocked it.

Stay focused, the calm voice told her.

Placing the lock through the hole beneath the door's locking mechanism, she clamped the padlock shut and spun around to return to the northern hallway.

Next stop, the cafeteria.

She smiled, drawing closer to the main passageway. The task was almost complete. Just two more doors to go.

She was almost there.

Suddenly, a large figure blocked her view.

It was Mister Thompson, the Deputy Principal.

"Kirstin?" He looked surprised. "Why aren't you in class? Why are you here of all places?"

She stopped dead in her tracks, moving her right hand behind her back, touching the grip of the Beretta.

"Ah," she let out nervously.

"This isn't an area permissible to students." He lowered his brow, giving her an angry look. "Now I know some students go down there to make out, and truth be told, I do sometimes look the other way. But that's usually during break times, and you're on your own."

"I wasn't feeling well, Mister Thompson," she told him, taking a step backwards. "I was heading for the bathroom but I took the wrong turn."

"Bathroom's just there." He pointed. "I don't see how you could mistake a hallway for a bathroom. Maybe you need to go to sick-bay?"

"I just need some water," she answered, trying to think of something to make him move on. She took another step backwards.

He furrowed his brow, looking to her feet before moving his gaze to her eyes.

"What's the matter, Kirstin?" he asked. "Why are you moving away from me?"

"I..." She shut her eyes. They burned hot. The clouds spun around and around, faster and faster.

Not now, she pleaded with herself. *Please not now.*

Focus, the calm voice instructed her.

"Kirstin?" He stepped towards the girl.

"I don't know," she replied. It was true. She was moving backwards slowly, so very slowly, and she didn't know why.

Thunder grumbled from inside the swirling vapors as they intensified.

"I think you need to come with me," he told her, stepping towards her. "We can chat in my office. Okay?"

Her fingers wrapped themselves around the Beretta's grip.

Please. Not this man. He's a good man.

It doesn't matter, the calm voice argued. *They're all at fault.*

The blood rain fell as lightning erupted from the pulsating tempest deep within her.

"I don't think that would be a good idea," she told him.

His eyes moved to her right arm, disappearing behind her back.

"What have you got there?" Thompson asked her.

She shook her head, pursing her lips tightly as she took another step backwards.

He moved towards her, reaching his hands towards her arm.

"Show me what you have hidden there," he commanded.

Focus.

Her countenance changed.

Let me have this one.

Something dark passed over her eyes.

Give him to me.

She locked her gaze with his and grimaced sinisterly.

"Okay, Mister Thompson," she replied.

As quick as a flash, she swung the pistol around from behind her, took two steps forward, and pressed the muzzle hard against his soft belly.

Thunder and lightning exploded.

The crimson clouds erupted with light as the blood rain poured down.

The muffled gunshot, absorbed by the man's body mass, sounded more like a large, deep drum being struck hard.

Thompson fell to the ground.

Kirstin placed the pistol in between the lining of her jeans and her back before reaching down to grab the deputy principal's feet.

He was still alive, gasping for air and looking at her with shocked, wide eyes.

With all of her might, she dragged him into the side passageway, out of the immediate view of anyone in the northern hallway.

She repositioned herself beside his head and peered down at him.

Tears streamed from his eyes. His stare kept asking her over and over, *Why?*

"I am so sorry, Mister Thompson," she said apologetically.

Kirstin placed the sole of her right sneaker against his neck and applied all of her weight.

Thompson made loud gasping noises for a brief moment before she heard the unmistakable sound of a wet snap as the vertebra in the man's neck separated.

Stepping over the body, she moved back into the main passageway and made her way towards the cafeteria, leaving Thompson to stare lifelessly towards the florescent light in the ceiling above.

III

Moving towards eastward along the southern corridor on the upper level, McFarlan gathered students and staff from the classrooms, informing them of danger and the need to evacuate. A long line of timid people crept as quietly as they could along the passageway as they drew towards the stairwell in the south-east corner of the building.

The police officer's intent was to descend to the lower level and move to the front doors of the building, collecting as many people as they could along the way. So far, she had collected seven teachers and at least one-hundred-and-fifty students.

It was a hard journey as she found either herself or another adult needing to hush the students with a raised finger to the lips and a loud hiss emitting from between her teeth. Silence would ensue, but only for a short moment before some young boy or girl would start up a conversation with a whisper, which would escalate into murmuring before the volume increased.

"Shhh." An older female student turned and stared at a group of young boys. They nodded politely, apologetically before continuing forward.

The pattern repeated again and again as they entered more classrooms, interrupting lessons and more people joined the gathering crowd. Confused by what was happening, unaware that a student was on a killing rampage, students asked questions while teachers demanded answers.

As McFarlan reached two-thirds of the hallway's length, she heard another gunshot.

Many of those following her jumped in fright, gasping noisily.

The wide eyes of both adults and children stared at her, hoping she could help them and bring them to safety.

Another loud explosion from a firearm followed shortly after.

Tears and nervous whimpers resounded along the length of the corridor. Others hissed a chorus of sounds to silence the upset students and teachers.

The gunshots came from downstairs, but the reverberations and echoes traveling along the hallways made it hard to tell from which direction.

McFarlan risked moving on.

She needed to get these people out of the building.

Another shot thundered through the building.

The young officer's stomach tightened, and her mouth seemed to turn dry in an instant. She tried to swallow with little luck.

Edging towards the end of the upper level's passageway, she turned and signaled a short, tubby female teacher over to her.

"What's your name?" McFarlan asked her.

"Missus Merrick," she replied, shaking her head as she realized her situation and that she was talking to another adult. "Lindsay."

"Lindsay," McFarlan confirmed. "My name is Kimmie. I need a favor from you. You won't like it, but I need you to do it.

"I'm going to lead us down these stairs. I want you to stay behind and be the last person to follow. I need someone to make sure everyone gets downstairs. Can you do this for me?"

Merrick nodded. "I think so, yes."

There was another shot fired downstairs.

Merrick closed her eyes and shuddered at the sound.

"It's all right," McFarlan lied. "It came from far on the other side of the building. We're safe here for the moment. But we really need to get outside."

Merrick nodded.

Another shot rang out, followed by another and another and another.

McFarlan held her firearm in front of her with both hands as she moved towards the stairs. She signaled the students near to her to follow her as she descended towards the lower level.

Hugging the wall, trying to keep the lower corridor in view as she turned on the landing halfway down. The path ahead appeared clear.

She signaled for the students to remain on the landing as she continued to the bottom of the stairwell, keeping as tight to the wall as she could.

The stairs spilled onto the lower level from the eastern wall, allowing McFarlan to see only the southern hallway that stretched from her location to another stairwell set into the western wall at the far end. To her right, and just out of her view, was the lengthy western corridor that led in the gymnasium's direction and the cafeteria.

Moving her eyes around the edge of the corner, she peered along the brickwork of the eastern wall to look into the passageway.

Empty.

Her heart almost stopped beating.

There was no sign of the shooter.

A deep panic set in.

Kirstin could be anywhere in the building.

McFarlan was about to pull her head back and signal for the students to follow her down, but movement caught her eye at the far end of the eastern hallway.

It was her.

Kirstin was backing out of a doorway on the right at the very far end of the passage. She had a backpack slung over her left shoulder and a pistol in both hands, leveled at something or someone inside the room.

She was saying something, but the girl was too far for the police officer to hear.

McFarlan considered lifting her walkie-talkie and calling in what she could see, but her eyes fell upon a little black box that was attached to Kirstin's belt.

Borden's radio.

She's been listening in.

McFarlan turned quickly to the students on the stairwell and placed a finger to her lips.

Keep quiet.

The children gathered nearby nodded and repeated the gesture, passing the message up the stairs to the others waiting behind them.

The police officer moved her left eye around the corner to find Kirstin moving towards her.

Shit.

The girl was still a long way from her, but she was moving briskly towards the southern end of the building.

McFarlan moved her sidearm in front of her and thumbed the safety off. Her chest seemed to shake as her jaw quivered.

She didn't want to shoot the girl if she could avoid it.

McFarlan saw a young, beautiful child with a face of innocence.

How could this little creature do what she was doing?

The police officer pulled the hammer all the way back, feeling it click into place.

Kirstin veered to the left of the passageway, on the opposite side of McFarlan's position.

What are you doing?

With knees of jelly, McFarlan fought to compose herself, feeling an icy trickle of sweat dribble down her spine.

Kirstin suddenly vanished from view, turning into the corridor that split the building in two. She was now heading along the passageway that took her directly towards the front doors.

McFarlan breathed a sigh of relief, replacing the hammer to a neutral position before thumbing the safety back on. She waited for thirty seconds to make sure the girl wouldn't double back.

Her gut instinct told her that Kirstin was gone for now and that it was safe to move on. She signaled for the students to follow before stepping quietly into the corridor.

IV

Emerging on the upper level after taking the center stairwell, Kirstin glanced quickly back at the bodies of Nancy and Angela. She saw the figure of the dead teacher, Mister Jameson, but felt indifferent about his demise. It was the two girls that had her attention. They were two-thirds of the problem that needed to be remedied before moving on to the next phase.

Placing her backpack on the floor, she crouched to retrieve a box of bullets so she could top up the clip in her Beretta. As she did so, she kept her ear tuned to her surroundings.

The walkie-talkie fizzled momentarily, but she had heard no voices for some time. Not since the female cop inside the building had last spoken to the dispatch lady.

The murmurs and whimpers inside the middle corridor had silenced. Kirstin guessed the police officer had got quite a few people out of this section of the building by now.

No matter.

The students and teachers weren't her chief priority. Neither was the cop.

Her prey was one Stephanie Granger.

The bitch has to die.

Returning the box of bullets to the bag, raising herself to her feet and slinging the backpack over her left shoulder, Kirstin peered back down the stairs, listening intently.

When she was certain she was alone, she moved past the body of the fallen boy, towards the dead cop at the end of the passageway. Her intention was to revisit her path and turn right at the far intersection.

She was going to search the northern side of the upper level before moving back along the eastern corridor to the southern hallway.

If she couldn't find Stephanie upstairs, her next move would be to go down again.

If she's not here, the calm voice told her, *you'll just have to kill whoever is left. Time will run out before you know it.*

She stepped past the body of the dead cop. He stared up at her with a bloodied, eyeless socket. His other eye had been closed. Kirstin surmised the female cop had probably done that out of respect.

Respect for who? she questioned. *For the body? He's dead. He wouldn't care if his eye is open or not.*

She crouched beside the dead man and stared into his face.

The soulless, lifeless mass didn't twitch or smile. It didn't react when she approached. It felt neither fear nor shame.

It was a lump of meat.

Using her finger and thumb of her left hand, she pried the eyelid open.

There was no weeping or retraction of the iris.

Nothing.

Kirstin stood and peered down at the corpse.

"Now you see me," she said before spitting on the dead man's face.

Foamy saliva dribbled down the bridge of his nose and into the open socket where his left eye used to be.

She watched with a mixture of feelings, awestruck and disgusted at the same time.

The calm voice, the essence behind it, seemed pleased.

Taking a deep breath, she turned on her heels and continued along the passageway, resuming her hunt.

V

"Dammit!" McFarlan huffed as she glared at the padlock and chain threaded through the main doors.

The girl has been busy.

The young police officer turned back to the few faces that she could see at the head of the quiet mob. Wide-eyed students and teachers looked back at her in hope.

She shook her head and watched as their expressions dropped.

Carefully, she walked back to them, making sure her shoes neither squeaked nor scuffed upon the hard floor. Keeping her voice low, she whispered to those nearby.

"We need to move around to the cafeteria," she told them. "The doors are locked here. I think it would be best for us if we were to get to a place where we could all gather and lock the doors behind us."

The group's disappointment was obvious as soft murmurs and disgruntled groans moved down the line of students and teachers like an audible wave. They had moved past the wood and metal shop classrooms, the library and two science labs and now slunk around the corner by a couple of art rooms before ending up near the center corridor. They had gathered more people along the way, adding to the growing number of wannabe survivors.

"What about the people upstairs?" asked an older female student. "There are still people up there."

"Who cares?" said a younger boy with a slightly oversized belly grumpily. Sweat was beading on his brow and his hands were shaking.

"They're our friends," the girl hissed back.

"Are you okay?" McFarlan asked the boy.

"I think my sugars are low," he replied.

"Shit," she spat. "Have you got anything on you to take?"

"No." He shook his head. "I left my backpack upstairs."

"For fuck's sake," another girl grunted, pulling her bag off her shoulder and reaching inside as tears streamed from her eyes. She pulled out a roll of lifesavers and offered them to the sweaty student. "Here. It's all I've got."

"Thanks," the boy replied, taking the candy.

Reaching her hand over, McFarlan squeezed the girl's shoulder and nodded.

"Can we just keep moving before that psycho bitch finds us?"

"What's your name?" McFarlan asked the Good Samaritan.

"Stephanie," the girl replied.

"Thank you, Stephanie," the cop said before turning her attention to the others gathered nearby. "We need to move quickly and quietly."

Continuing northward, McFarlan led the mass away from the front doors. Gradually, they passed more classrooms before edging around the corner into the northern hallway.

The young police officer kept her eye on the stairwell where the two passageways met. She could hear footfalls that seemed to come from within the alcove that led to the level above. They seemed to move away from the group. Still, she held a finger to her lips to signal those around her to keep silent. She then pointed up, telling them she believed the shooter was above them.

Stephanie turned white as blood drained from her face. Her mascara, applied rather thickly, was running down her cheeks as she panicked.

"She's coming for me," she gasped softly. "She's coming for me. She's coming for me."

McFarlan put her arm around the blubbering girl and guided her along the corridor towards the cafeteria towards the far end.

"Come on, Stephanie," the police officer whispered. "You're doing great. How old are you?"

"Sixteen," the girl replied.

"Sixteen?" McFarlan raised her eyebrows. She had seen the girl's attire and felt a knot tighten in her stomach.

What kind of parents let their sixteen-year-old daughter wear slutty clothing like that?

"You're very brave for sixteen," the police officer said. "And very quick to help that boy out with his problem. If it wasn't for you, he could have passed out. Did you know that?"

"My cousin is a diabetic," Stephanie sniffled.

"Well, I'm glad you knew what to do."

"I'm scared," the girl told the cop.

"When we get into the cafeteria," McFarlan said, "we'll close and bolt the doors behind us. They're big wooden doors, right?"

"I don't know." The girl frowned. "She killed my friends."

McFarlan looked at the girl sideways.

"Where?"

"Upstairs." Stephanie wiped her snotty nose on the back of her hand.

"Two girls?"

The girl nodded, bursting into tears. "And I ran away. I left them there."

"You did the right thing, Stephanie. Okay? You didn't have a choice."

Stephanie was crying profusely. Her legs almost buckled underneath her as the weight of reality hit her hard.

They moved past the thin passageway that cut between the boys' and girls' bathrooms against the northern wall of the corridor. The wide-open doors to the cafeteria were just a short distance ahead of them on the left.

"Almost there," McFarlan said, more to herself than to those around her. She could see the groups of tables and chairs around the large room.

With her arm still around Stephanie's shoulders, she guided the long line of people into the cafeteria.

"Holy fuck!" she heard a male call from farther along the corridor. She quickly glanced over her shoulder, but couldn't see the cause of such a remark.

"Shhh!" several people hissed to the noisemaker.

"Go inside and find a seat," she told Stephanie.

"Don't leave me." The girl's eyes widened.

"I need to see what the problem is back there," the cop explained. "Go inside. I'll be right back."

She ushered the girl into the room, directing her towards a table and chair not too far from the doors. It was then that the young police officer noticed four large wooden panels that sat on rollers positioned on either side of two entries into the cafeteria. There were sliding bolts at both the top and bottom of each panel that would lock the doors into the floor and ceiling.

"Close those doors," she instructed two older boys, pointing to the entryway a little farther towards the eastern side of the room. "And bolt them shut."

The boys nodded and moved immediately through the cafeteria towards the other doorway.

McFarlan moved back along the corridor, shuffling past the students and teachers, making their way towards the closest entry to the large room.

"Keep moving," the police officer instructed them quietly. She could see a few students and two teachers peering into the small passageway between the two bathroom blocks.

Following their gaze, she noticed the body of a dead man lying on his back.

The bloodstain on his shirt told McFarlan he had been shot in the gut. The odd angle of his head showed his neck had been broken.

This girl has an acquired taste for this, the cop thought.

"Keep moving," she instructed the gawkers. "You're not safe here."

She used her hands and pushed the gathering onlookers towards the cafeteria. Standing by the passageway's entrance, she guided the rest of the students and teachers on, waiting for the last in line to get to her.

Lindsay Merrick approached her, shaking slightly as she attempted to maintain her composure.

"I'm the last," she said as she drew near to the officer. Her eyes instinctively fell upon the mass on the floor inside the passageway. "Ohmygod."

"Don't look." McFarlan placed her hands on the teacher's shoulders, steering her away from the scene.

"Was that Harry Thompson?" Merrick asked. "I think that was Harry Thompson."

"Who's Harry Thompson?" McFarlan asked, knowing it was a stupid question considering the timing.

"He's our Deputy Principal," the teacher replied. "Is he dead?"

"I'm afraid so," the cop said, directing the teacher into the cafeteria.

"Oh God, no." Merrick breathed rapidly, hyperventilating. "Oh, God. Oh, God. Oh, God."

"Here." McFarlan steered the teacher to a seat beside Stephanie. "try to control your breathing."

Merrick continued to take shorter and shorter breaths.

"In through your nose," McFarlan instructed. "Out through your mouth. Slower. Slower." The police officer demonstrated the process.

Merrick tried to imitate the cop. Her exhaling was shaky at best, an intermittent sigh escaping her lungs with each attempt.

"Keep trying," McFarlan told her, worried that the teacher was about to pass out. "Stay here. I'll be back."

The officer turned back to the doors behind her and slid the one on the right closed with a loud rattle and thud. She bent and dropped the sliding bolt into the floor.

She moved across the open gap to take hold of the left door. With a heave, she pulled the large wooden panel towards the other.

Something caught her eye.

Something in the hallway.

Her gaze moved from the wooden panel to a space just to the right.

Standing at the far end of the corridor, just at the base of the north-east stairwell, was Kirstin.

She held the Beretta down at her side in her right hand. Her head tilted slightly to one side to see past the young female police officer to something just behind her.

To someone just behind her.

A sudden shrill scream drilled into McFarlan's ears painfully.

It was Stephanie.

Her eyes were wide in horror as she spied the other girl sneering back at her.

"Found you, bitch," Kirstin called, raising her pistol towards the open doorway.

At that moment, the school bell sounded, marking the transition into the fifth period.

QUARTUS INTERLUDIUM

Extract from the Diary of Kirstin Matthews

Wednesday March 8 2017

Spring Break and I'm either stuck at home with Mom or helping her out at the library or church.

God, I hate the church.

It's a place overflowing with of hypocrisy and lies.

On the surface, they all dress modestly and act all clean and "godly." The women in their so-called casual wear still dress as if they are attending the Sunday service. They talk politely to one another when they meet together, sorting through second-hand clothing and canned food that has been donated to charity. But the moment one of them leaves the room to piss, the others come out with the knives and start stabbing their "friend" in the back.

I've learned that Mrs. Shoal has been screwing Mr. Lawson. Apparently, everyone knew about it except for Mrs. Lawson and Mr. Shoal.

Who knows?

Maybe they're banging each other too.

There are rumors that the deacon, Mr. Orvell, is skimming from the tithes. I don't know how much he's taking. My guess that it wouldn't even be enough to buy a burger considering that nobody ever puts the full tenth into the plate as it goes around.

I've only ever seen a fiver at most as far as paper money goes. The rest is usually nickels and dimes. Maybe a bottle cap or two.

But, oh, how we love Jesus.

I caught Pastor Shane looking down the ladies' tops today as he paid us a visit this morning. I'm so glad I was wearing a T-shirt under my blouse.

Dirty, gross old man.

The building itself is a reflection of what they all are. The main room is all neat and clean and tidy. The chairs are all in straight rows and columns. The carpet's vacuumed and wooden panels along the base of the walls polished.

But the back rooms are all seriously fucked up.

Holes in the walls. Stains on the doors where hands have been touching them. Torn rugs and the smell of mold reeks from the very back rooms where they have the crèche during the services.

It makes me want to puke.

Working in the library wasn't too bad. At least I got to read a few books. They even let me take some home, even though Mom and Dad won't let me get my own library card. I've almost finished reading *Emma* by Jane Austen. I've never seen any of the movies, and I don't intend to. I don't think Austen is my kind of author.

I'll finish the book tonight and return it when I visit the library tomorrow. I guess that I'll get the task of sorting the returns again and maybe I'll even get to stack shelves.

Most of the library staff and the volunteers got in my face with their cheesy grins the last time I was there. They all said things like, ...It's so good to see someone so young interested in reading... or ...Books are better than the inter-webby...

I felt like putting my heel into their teeth.

I would rather be with my friends swimming or watching TV or sitting in a giant pile of shit than hang out with old people.

One good thing that happened during yesterday was Dad took me out to the gun range after dinner. He said he felt the need to let off a few rounds after a day of angry phone calls. Mom didn't really want me to go, but he insisted. He later told me he felt bad that I wasn't spending most of the break with any of my friends, but he and Mom both agreed that some of my friends were not people they wanted me to associate with.

I could see his point. Steph and Nancy have behaved and flaunted themselves around in ways that are not to my taste. But that's their choice.

I would never do anything like that.

I tried to tell Dad this, but he just shook his head and started talking about boys and how all they wanted to do was have S-E-X with girls like me.

Yes, he actually spelled it out.

A full grown man that can't even say "sex."

I mean, for fuck's sake, how did he and Mom come to make me if he can't even say the word?

For the second time in my life, he let me fire his gun.

I loved it.

The smell of the gunpowder and the sound of the blast were exciting. The kick from the gun as I squeezed off each round send vibrations up my arms and into my chest.

The target sheet looks kind of like a man. There are four zones on the body that start at 7 points on the outer zone to 9 on the inner one before the red zone in the middle. I don't know what amount of points the red zone is worth.

My score was higher than Dad's. From seven rounds, he landed four shots in the 8 zone and three in the 9.

I put four in the 9 zone, two in the middle of the target and one on the head.

He smiled and said he was proud of me, but I could see that he was a little jealous.

I would have written about it in my diary last night when we got home, but Mom made me bush my teeth and go to bed. Lights out. It was after 10 pm.

Fucking bitch!

I really did like firing that gun.

SANGUIS : BLOOD

Sanity brings pain
but madness is a vile thing.

EURIPIDES, *Hippolytus*

"Push the door shut," McFarlan bellowed to the two senior boys who had closed and locked the other entrance into the cafeteria.

As Kirstin raised her Beretta, the cop reached for her P229 that still sat in her hip holster. The two boys raced along the wall that separated them from the corridor outside, reaching the thick, wooden panel just as the young police officer brought her weapon out of her holster. Just as Kirstin opened fire towards the opening into the room.

Students and teachers instinctively screamed and ducked in fear for their lives as three rounds exploded in rapid succession. Each smacked hard against the large panel that was moving as the boys pushed with all of their might.

McFarlan fired one round back, aiming for the wall across the way, near to Kirstin's position.

A tiny cloud of dust and brick fiber burst into the air around the girl's head.

She dropped to the floor without a second thought, squatting as she slowly moved backwards in an attempt to find cover.

Squeezing off two more rounds, she reached the corner of the passageway and slid into the eastern hallway. There she dropped to her belly and positioned herself so her hands could keep her weapon pointed towards the cafeteria door and one eye on her objective.

McFarlan fired back several times. Her target was small. Each of her slugs smacked into the walls either in front or behind the girl, producing small puffs of debris.

The door slammed shut with a loud thud.

McFarlan lowered her pistol to her side as the boys busied themselves with the sliding bolts.

Sharp knocks against the door from outside caused them to retreat a little as Kirstin continued to fire at the panel in frustration.

"Are you okay?" the cop asked the two boys.

"Fuck, that was scary," one of them blurted nervously.

The other simply shook his head in disbelief.

"You did good," McFarlan told them as they heard two more bullets slamming against the door. "You did real good."

The bell sounded again, signaling the scheduled time for class to resume.

"Why?" the second boy suddenly asked. "Why is she doing this? I thought she was nice."

"It doesn't matter why," the cop answered, glancing over to Stephanie, who was sobbing in her chair. Her heels were resting on the edge of her seat, forcing her knees up to her chin. Her arms were hugging her legs as she rocked back and forth slightly.

McFarlan turned back to the boys. "What are your names?"

"Donny Shepherd," the second boy replied.

"Freddie Morris," said the other.

"Morris?" the young officer quizzed. "Any relation to Randy Morris?"

"He's my dad, Ma'am," Freddie told her.

"I'm sure he's on his way," she said. "Bet you wish he was in here instead of me, right?"

"No Ma'am," the boy replied. "You're a badass. He knows how to drive a car real good. But you shooting that gun and all. That was awesome."

McFarlan smiled politely and shook her head, lifting her walkie-talkie from her belt.

"Dispatch, come in," she said into the radio.

"Dispatch." The response was fuzzy. The static was thick. McFarlan put the interference down to the structure of the room.

Perhaps the radio signals were having difficulty penetrating the building here.

"More shots fired at Edwards Hill High," the cop said. "Confirmation and sighting of the shooter, Kirstin Matthews. I have engaged in a firefight with the individual. No new casualties. The shooter is still at large. I have a number of people in the school cafeteria. We have barricaded ourselves in and are awaiting backup."

"Understood, Officer McFarlan," the crackled voice replied. "Backup is on the way."

"Officer McFarlan?" a fresh voice called. It was crisp and clear, almost as if it was someone in the room, only it emitted from the speaker on the walkie-talkie.

The voice was that of a young girl. Calm. Emotionless. Almost surreal.

"Can you hear me, Officer McFarlan?"

"It's her!" Stephanie gasped. "It's her! It's her! It's her! It's her!"

"Stephanie..." Donnie moved towards the girl. He crouched beside her and placed his arms around her shoulders. "She's not in here. She can't get in. You're okay."

The cop glanced around at the other adults in the room. They were clearly shaken up by the ordeal, but she would have expected one of them to comfort a stressed student. Not one of them moved. They huddled together like a frightened flock of sheep near the serving counter on the far side of the room, staring back towards the door and the children with confusion engraved on their faces.

Out of twelve adults who could have responded, it was a boy who reacted.

A student.

"This frequency is for emergency service communications only," the crackled voice of the dispatch office warbled. "Please leave the line clear."

"I'm sorry," Kirstin replied. "But I thought you might want to talk to me. Considering I'm the one you have been discussing."

McFarlan lifted the walkie-talkie to her lips.

"McFarlan here," she said. "Is this Kirstin that I'm speaking to?"

"Yes, Ma'am," replied the girl.

"Don't speak to her," Stephanie pleaded.

"Shhh." Donny pulled her into him.

"What do you want, Kirstin?" the cop asked. "Why are you doing this to your friends?"

"Friends?" the voice quipped. "I have no friends, Officer McFarlan. My parents saw to that. But I fixed them this morning."

"I heard about that." The young officer moved along the wall towards the other doorway of the cafeteria. "What did they do to you to make you so mad at them?"

"We're not going to discuss what they did or didn't do, Officer McFarlan," Kirstin replied. "We're going to discuss what I want right now."

"Okay." McFarlan stopped by the door, checking that the bolts were secure. "What do you want?"

There was a moment of silence.

There was a soft hiss of static just before the girl replied.

"I want Stephanie Granger."

II

The crimson storm clouds circled slowly. A gentle rumble emitted from deep within as soft flashes of light burst alive far beneath the surface.

She was in control.

She was focused.

But she knew it wouldn't be long before the need to feed the storm gripped her once again.

The emotional high of pure elation that swept over her as the blood rain-soaked into her soul was intoxicating.

She wanted more.

Kirstin was rifling through the drawers and boxes in the maintenance office with one hand as she held the walkie-talkie she had taken from Doug Borden's body.

Lionel Jenkins continued to stare blankly towards his television, the sound turned down so the girl could hold a decent conversation with the police officer in the cafeteria.

Blood dripped slowly from the large gash in his neck and had spilled over the floor into a thick puddle at the base of the tattered, high back swivel chair.

"I can't do that," the officer told her, rejecting Kirstin's demand.

"I know you can't," the girl replied. "Not without some persuasion. So I'm going to force your hand, Officer McFarlan."

She lifted a small container from a shelf and saw something that would meet her immediate needs.

Long cable ties.

They were thin strips of plastic that had grooves, or teeth, along the length and something that resembled a belt buckle at one end. The other end of the strip could be threaded through the buckle freely in one direction. The grooves prevented the strip from moving back, locking it in place.

Exactly what she was looking for.

"What do you mean, Kirstin?" McFarlan asked.

The girl took her backpack off her shoulder and placed it on the bench before her. Unzipping the front pocket, she placed the walkie-talkie beside the bag before shoving all the cable ties into the open compartment.

"Kirstin?"

She lifted the walkie-talkie to her lips again.

"There are still people out here," she informed the police officer. "You don't have everyone in the cafeteria with you. I have my dad's gun and the dead police officer's gun. I also have a lot of ammunition."

Her eyes fell onto two red jerry cans. She reached over with her free hand and lifted one, checking its weight before placing it back on the floor before repeating the process with the other.

"I have enough bullets for all of them, Officer McFarlan," she smiled. "But there are other ways to die, too. Fun ways. Give me Stephanie Granger."

"I can't do that, Kirstin," the cop told her. "Please. Put the guns down and turn yourself over to me. I can get you some help."

Kirstin checked behind the open door of the maintenance office, partially closing the door, to find a bright yellow slicker hanging on a hook.

"I don't need help, Officer McFarlan," she replied as she lifted the raincoat off the hook. "They tried to help me before we moved here. But, truthfully, I've never felt more at peace. This is right. This is the way it must be."

"It doesn't have to be like this," McFarlan said.

The girl draped the slicker over the jerry cans before searching through the drawers of the old teacher's desk that Lionel Jenkins sat facing towards. She found what she was looking for in the bottom compartment.

A book of matches.

The casing was a bright yellow with a logo covering the face of the small, square envelope.

PACER MOTEL, MIAMI.

"Please, Kirstin," the cop continued, trying to reach what remained of the girl's empathy. "People are scared and hurt."

Kirstin flipped the cover of the matchbook open and noticed three matches missing. She searched farther into the drawer from where she found the matchbook. Nestled in the back corner was a pack of cigarettes.

She lifted the packet from the drawer and gave it a quick shake. A few thin cylinders of paper and tobacco rattled inside.

"Naughty boy, Mister Jenkins," she said to the corpse. "These things will kill you."

She tossed the cigarettes onto the desk and shoved the matchbook into the hip pocket of her jeans.

"They just want to go home, Kirstin," McFarlan persisted.

"Then give me Stephanie Granger," the girl replied. "And I'll let them all go free."

She knew what the answer would be.

She knew the police officer wouldn't simply give someone up to be shot.

Kirstin was betting on this.

Only one would not appease the storm.

Stephanie would not be enough.

"I can't give Stephanie to you," replied McFarlan.

"Then, what is about to happen," the girl articulated, "will be on your head."

III

With sirens blaring and lights flashing, the police vehicle slid around the corner from Main Street, into the road that led to Edwards Hill State High School. The tires screeched loudly, piercing the near quiet air as the sedan straightened up before lunging forward at a great pace.

Within moments, the vehicle pulled to a stop in the school's driveway. It parked at an awkward angle with its headlights pointing towards the corner of the building, its trunk still sticking out over the road.

"Dispatch, come in," the driver said into his radio.

"Dispatch," the voice replied.

"Officer Randy Morris," the cop started. "I've arrived at the high school. I can see some students and teachers gathered on the grass outside. There's at least one lying down, possibly in need of medical assistance."

"Officer McFarlan has requested the paramedics," Dispatch told him. "An ambulance is on the way."

"Any news from Officer McFarlan?"

"She is still using the alternative frequency," the woman's voice answered. "We don't know how to inform her that we are working on the new one without alerting the shooter."

"Understood," Morris nodded nervously. "Anything from the captain?"

"Captain is a little preoccupied at the mo—"

"I'm here," another female voice interrupted. "I'm here, Randy. I'm here."

"Captain Reece," the cop in the car responded. "What do you want me to do? Do you want me to find a way in there? Where do you want me?"

"I want you to stay outside and wait for backup," Reece instructed.

"My son's in there, Captain. I need to get in there. I can't see him out here."

"Remember your job, Randy. Look after those people outside. Keep them together and keep calm."

Morris felt the corners of his mouth pull downwards as his eyes welled with tears. He nodded silently, accepting his orders. Accepting his duty.

"Randy?" Captain Reece called.

"I'm here," he replied. "How long until backup arrives?"

"We're low on staff," the captain informed him. "We still have a crime scene out on Jackson Drive. I just got off the phone with Houston and they're sending a tactical team to take charge once they arrive."

"SWAT?"

"They said, tactical team," Reece stated. "I don't know what that means exactly. But I'm sure they know what they're doing."

"It's one girl," Morris put in. "We could just go in ourselves and take her down. Better yet, we could overrun her and take her in."

"She's already killed one cop." The captain's voice seemed extremely loud in his head. "I don't want anyone else risking their lives if we can avoid it."

As she was speaking, a white van crossed the street and pulled up across the road, in front of the elementary school. The stenciled logo for Edwards Hill News reflecting in the rear vision mirror caught his eye immediately.

"Aw shit," he slurred, lifting the radio receiver to his mouth. "Television's here."

There was a pause at the other end. Morris pictured the captain saying a vilification or two of her own.

"Keep them back," the captain ordered. "I don't want them interviewing kids or staff. Tell them they are to stay on the grass outside the elementary school. They can film and report from there."

"Okay," Morris replied, placing the mouthpiece back into the cradle before exiting the car.

The passenger door opened and a long-legged young woman stepped out, holding a wireless microphone in her hand. She saw the police officer approaching and tried to intercept him as Wayne Dwyers, her camera operator, rushed to the side of the vehicle to retrieve his equipment.

"Officer," she called to him. "Officer. Samantha Peterson from Edwards Hill News. Can you tell us what is happening inside the high school at the moment? We understand that there have been distinct sounds of gunshots from inside. Are there any wounded? Has anyone been killed?"

"Listen." Morris held his hand up to her as he approached. He pointed over to the elementary school and kept heading towards her. "You and your colleague there will need to stay on that side of the road. For your safety, I'm going to have to order you back off the road. You can set up over there."

"Do you know who the shooter is?" she pressed, ignoring his instructions. "Is this at all related to the double homicide on Jackson Drive? Is it the same shooter?"

Quite possibly, he thought.

"Miss Peterson," he continued, speaking over her. "If you don't get back, I'm going to have to cuff you and place you in the back of my vehicle for your safety. Please get yourself off the road and over there."

"What about those people?" She pointed to the students and staff members on the lawn outside the high school.

"Those people have rallied there after evacuating the school," he told her. "They will remain there until emergency services have assessed the situation and determine that it is or isn't safe to move them."

"So everybody's out of the building then?" Peterson asked as her cameraman joined her at her side, lens pointing directly to the unprepared police officer. "What about the elementary school? Have they been evacuated yet?

"No comments will be made about the current situation until all authorities have been notified and full assessments can be made," he answered, continuing to point towards the elementary school.

"So you admit that there is a situation?"

"No further comment," he replied. "Now get back off the road before I arrest you for obstruction."

"Okay," she said. "Okay. "I get it. You're just doing your job. So are we."

"I'm not disputing that, Miss Peterson," Morris told her. "I'm concerned for your safety, and I have orders to keep you away from those kids for now. So, if you don't mind, remove yourself from the road and set up over there somewhere. Please."

The two looked at each other for what seemed a long time. Eventually, the young reporter caved, lowering the microphone with a nod.

"We'll set up over there," she agreed.

"Thanks," he said, turning back towards the high school as Dwyers switched his camera off.

"What was that?" he asked as the police officer retreated across the street.

"A small favor," she told him. "Maybe he'll return one later."

"Maybe he won't." Dwyers shook his head.

She shrugged. "Doesn't matter. We're the first crew here. Let's get set up."

IV

With the bright yellow rain slicker draped over her, the hood pulled over her head; she tightened the cable ties on the last student's hands. There were fifteen of them, eight girls and seven boys, kneeling in a line along the middle of the gymnasium floor.

Each of them had bound the other at gunpoint. All except the last boy to whom she applied the plastic ties herself, securing their hands were behind their backs and strapping their ankles together.

"Why are you doing this?" one girl blubbered. "We didn't do anything to you."

She was younger than Kirstin. *Maybe fourteen*, she thought.

Get the gas, the calm one inside of her said.

Kirstin obeyed, watching the storm clouds in her mind gathering closer and closer. The lightning inside flashed with the words of the relaxed voice.

She carried the first jerry can past the students kneeling on the polished timber floor. Each of the youngsters was a weeping mess.

"I want to go home," one girl blurted.

"Soon," Kirstin said reassuringly. "You'll all be there soon."

She took the canister to five bodies that lay on the floor in a neat line. Kirstin had made the students drag each of the fallen to the location before forcing them to bind themselves. The slain comprised of the coach and four male students she had shot earlier.

After stuffing her Beretta down the back of her jeans, she took the cap off the jerry can and hoisted it with a grunt. Carefully, she poured the gas over the five bodies, moving towards the kneeling students.

The aroma was strong and biting.

The students wept or screamed as she edged towards them, continuing to pour the liquid over the dead.

She moved to the first student and tipped gas over his head. He screamed as the fuel burned into his eyes. He called for the help of a deity she once prayed to.

But no longer.

It was the calm voice she listened to now.

Pour it all out, the voice told her.

Kirstin moved to the next in line, a young girl. She screamed as well.

By the time she reached the fifth student, the fuel had run dry. She tossed the jerry can across the floor where it slid and thudded noisily against the bleachers that nestled the northern wall of the gymnasium.

She moved to retrieve the second jerry can from the corridor just outside the door. The students continued to blubber, cry, scream and plead with her.

Ignoring them, she returned with the can, popped its cap and continued dousing the children with fuel.

"I want to go home," the girl continued to cry. "I want to go home."

Kirstin threw the now empty jerry can towards the bleachers where the other had landed. She then reached under the yellow rain slicker and took the book of matches from her pocket.

She read the logo on the packet one last time.

PACER MOTEL, MIAMI.

Carefully, she scrutinized the faces of her intended victims. Tears were streaming down their youthful faces.

"I want to go home," the girl continued to say with each outgoing breath.

Kirstin lifted the walkie-talkie from her belt.

"McFarlan?" she called. "Are you there?"

"I'm here, Kirstin," a voice replied over the speaker.

"Help us," a boy next to the blubbering girl shouted.

She continued to mutter the same thing over and over, "I want to go home. I want to go home."

"Help us. Please, help us."

Kirstin held the walkie-talkie out towards them, capturing every cry, call and sniffle that she could.

"You hear that?" she asked.

There was silence emitting from the speaker. Too much silence for Kirstin to take.

"McFarlan?" she barked.

"I heard it," the cop replied.

"I told you that there are other ways to die," Kirstin said. "These little boys and girls are about to be burned. Or you could give me Stephanie Granger."

"I- I can't," the police officer answered. Kirstin recognized some reluctance in the voice. "Please, Kirstin. Don't hurt them."

"Have you ever been to Miami, Officer McFarlan?"

"Miami?" the cop said. "What has Miami got to do with this? Will you let them go if I talk to you about Miami? Is that where you want to go? Is that why you're doing this?"

"No," Kirstin replied, turning the matchbook over in her hand. "I don't think I'll be going anywhere after today. It just says Miami on the matches I have. I took them from the maintenance guy after I cut his throat with a box cutter."

"Kirstin, please."

The girl in the yellow slicker peered towards the ceiling.

"You might want to find a table to shelter under, Officer McFarlan," Kirstin told her before returning the walkie-talkie to her belt.

"Kirstin," McFarlan called. "You don't have to do this. Kirstin, please."

"I want to go home. I want to go home," the little girl continued.

"Help us, somebody," the boy screamed.

The others cried and called.

Kirstin flipped the book of matches open and tore one stick free. She took a deep breath as she slid the match along the striker strip. The head burst into flame.

Holding the stick at an angle, she made sure that the match had a solid light to it before igniting the other matches, still attached to the book.

The line of students screamed and called for someone to help. Some tried to move away on their knees in desperation. The girl continued crying, "I want to go home. I want to go home."

Kirstin threw the flaming matchbook towards the middle of lined students.

Flames spread over them like an orange wave, expanding to the left and right. The fire consumed the fuel that had soaked deep into their clothing, beaded upon their skin and dripped from their hair.

She stepped back from the heat as the glare of the flames intensified.

The screaming reverberated around the gymnasium, drilling into her ears as she watched in awe.

No longer was the boy shouting for help.

No longer was the girl wanting to go home.

There were no more tears.

There was no more sadness.

There was just pain.

Excruciating pain.

Kirstin moved her eyes along the line of writhing, screaming children.

Her heart pounded excitedly as she gazed, transfixed by the sight before her.

It's glorious, she thought as a smile built on her face.

It's magnificent.

It's wonderful.

It's pure.

She giggled with delight as the first of the burning girls fell upon her side. Her hands went to her mouth as tears of joy streamed down her face.

"It's magic!"

V

McFarlan stood motionless in the center of the cafeteria. She held the walkie-talkie inches from her face. Her mouth was open, unable to speak.

All eyes fixed upon her. Some filled with tears, others with shock, and a few with anger.

The cop lowered the walkie-talkie to her side, relaxing her arm as she moved her eyes over the faces of the crowd surrounding her. She suddenly felt as if she was on display in a storefront window. She was about to turn and make her way to the adults clustered by the serving counter.

"Why didn't you just hand her over?" one student cried. "She's just one person."

A few other students joined in, supporting the boy's point of view.

"She's a bitch." One of the younger girls pointed to Stephanie, who was still curled in the chair, crying. Donny continued to hold her, trying to keep her calm. "She picks on everybody. That's why Kirstin wants her. We should give her up."

"What if it was you she was asking for?" another girl retorted. "What if it was your name she was asking for? Should we just give you up?"

"She's not asking for me," the girl replied. "She's asking for that bitch."

The crowd roughly divided in two.

One half was to support throwing Stephanie out the door. The other was in favor of protecting her.

"You let them die," the first girl shouted to McFarlan. "You let all of them die because you won't give that skank over."

The young officer looked at the teachers for support.

None came.

Their eyes flickered across the students, full of fear, drained of hope.

"Shut up!"

The words seemed to echo around the room.

All voices fell silent and stared at the police officer. It was then that she realized the words had come from her. She swallowed hard and took a deep breath.

"I can't give anyone over to that girl," McFarlan began. "No matter how much someone has been a bitch to you, or how much you think they deserve it. It's against the law and my job is to uphold the law.

"There was no guarantee that Kirstin would have let them go even if I *did* give her Stephanie. There is no guarantee that she will let us go, either.

"As far as I know," the cop continued, directing her speech to the first girl, "we are all marked. Every single one of us. Even you.

"So, I would appreciate it if you kept that shit to yourselves."

With all young eyes wide and staring at her, McFarlan turned back to the clustered adults and approached them.

"And you can start acting more like grown-ups instead of cowering like frightened sheep in the corner," she told them. "How about you get out amongst your students and talk to them? Try to keep them calm."

"We *are* scared," one of the male teachers told her.

"And I'm not?" She gave him a questioning glance before moving her gaze over the rest of them, pausing when she found Lindsay Merrick.

The English teacher met her stare for a moment before her eyes welled up. She turned her head away shamefully.

McFarlan moved past them, around the counter and towards the kitchen.

"Where are you going?" asked one teacher.

"To see if I can find a way out," she replied. "Or to get something to eat."

"You're thinking of food at a time like this?" he pressed.

"Look around you, shit for brains," she said, her anger at its peak. "We're trapped in here. We've got over one hundred kids who are scared and confused. Soon, they're going to get hungry.

"Later, they're going to want to go to the bathroom. Last I checked, the bathrooms were back out in the hallway. We need to organize ourselves just in case we are here for a long time.

"We need food, water and places to piss. Got it."

The man lowered his eyes sheepishly.

"I'm sorry," he murmured.

At that moment, the sprinklers burst open and a heavy spray of cold water fell from the ceiling.

Shrieks and screams filled the room as the florescent lights dangling from the rafters flickered out. Students and staff bustled about, clambering for the cover of tables.

Emergency lighting positioned at wide intervals high upon the walls flashed alive. The room still appeared dark, with strong shadows being emitted by the angle of the new lighting.

Donny pulled Stephanie under a cluster of benches nearby. There, with several other students, they huddled as the water fell like rain.

McFarlan stood in the kitchen, her uniform soaking through. She watched as everyone slipped under some cover.

Taking a deep breath, she turned towards the counters and cooktops in the center of the room. Stainless steel vats filled with hot oil hissed and bubbled as the water fell into their wells. Skillets and grills fizzled loudly, filling the area with a tremendous sizzle.

"Shit," the cop spat as she realized everything had been on the entire time. She moved to the cookers and started turning the knobs, closing the lines, extinguishing the flames in the ovens and switching off the electrical circuits to the deep fryers and grills.

Some oil spluttered over the edge of the vat as she twisted the dial, hitting on her right hand. She recoiled. "Motherfucker."

It burned into the skin on the back of her hand, just below the index and middle fingers. Looking around, she saw no one had heard her brief outburst. The murmurs from frightened people cowering under tables, the constant hiss of spraying water falling from the ceiling was too loud for them to hear anything she was doing.

McFarlan spotted a large sink on the far side of the room, past the cookers and near a wide alcove that expanded behind the wall to the left.

It seemed odd that she would run cold water over the affected area, considering that it was raining inside. But she remembered her first-aid training and didn't want to take any risks.

Standing by the sink, allowing the water to flow over her hand, she peered around her and into the alcove to her left. It was a wide corridor.

There were two cool rooms on the left and an open pantry to the right.

At the end was a closed-door with emergency lights above it, blaring into her eyes.

She squinted, bringing her left hand up to shield against the glare.

Instantly, her eyes fell towards the dark floor where odd-shaped shadows gathered.

McFarlan twisted the faucet off and stepped towards the hall-way, moving slowly towards the door. Her vision was slowly adjusting to the strange lighting as she drew closer to the shadows.

She saw the clear outline of people prostrate on the floor. Three women.

On closer inspection, the police officer noticed blood-soaked wounds in the back of each of their heads.

The three women were lying with their heads closest to the door. The first was not too far from the kitchen. The last was not too far from the door.

They had been trying to get away.

They had been trying to escape.

They had been trying for this door.

McFarlan stepped over the fallen bodies and made her way to the access to the outside world at the far end of the hallway.

With a hefty shove, she pushed the door. It rattled loudly, but did not open.

She tried again, but with no success.

Carefully, McFarlan checked for sliding bolts at the top and bottom of the door. Finding none, she searched along the rod that was attached to the locking mechanism.

Someone had fitted a padlock in place.

"Shit!"

They were trapped.

VI

The water built from puddles to streams before flooding an inch thick on the floor throughout the school. The sprinklers continued to shower down into every room throughout the building.

Kirstin could hear faint screams coming from inside the cafeteria and from upstairs as she moved along the eastern hallway, back to the maintenance office once again. She ignored the noise, focusing on the sound of water striking her slicker as she stepped carefully on the wet linoleum.

Her sneakers and socks soaked through. The lower parts of her jeans' legs felt heavy. The raincoat only covered her to her knees.

She didn't mind.

It didn't make her feel any less comfortable than she already felt.

Right now, as the sprinklers rained down on her, she felt her best.

The crimson clouds swirled like a magnificent merry-go-round. Lights burst and exploded from deep within excitedly as blood rain streamed from the sky.

She was happy.

Content.

Pushing the door open, creating a small wave that expanded through the room, Kirstin stepped into the small office where Lionel Jenkins continued to watch his television through dead eyes. She saw what she had returned for, lying on the floor beneath the water.

Bending down, she reached for the item, wrapping her fingers around it tightly before standing upright again. She looked at it, turning it over in her hand and expanding and retracting the blade by sliding the release mechanism with her thumb.

As she moved out of the little room and back into the corridor, the sprinklers slowed their flow of water, as if someone was turning the tap off somewhere. Kirstin knew it was merely because the tanks were running dry.

No matter.

They had served their purpose and doused the flames.

She had no intent of setting anything else on fire and probably couldn't, now that everything in the building was drenched.

She returned to the gymnasium to find the line of bodies still smoking.

The stench was horrendous.

Stinging fumes of melted clothing, burned flesh, and wet ash wafted into her nostrils. She scrunched her nose up in disgust as she moved towards the body that lay closest to her, fully extending the blade of the utility knife in her hand.

Her feet sloshed loudly in the inch-thick water that covered the polished floorboards of the basketball court. Large drops of water fell periodically, sporadically from the tiny outlets high above her as the pipes to the sprinkler system emptied themselves of their contents.

The water moved slowly, unnoticeably towards the east, where four double doors, evenly positioned apart, rested along the far wall. They were locked; only ever opened for a game on the field, or when the football team and cheerleading squad were engaged in training.

Never opened on Mondays.

She crouched next to the body at her end of the line and moved it so it was lying on its back. It made a loud crunching sound as the charred skin cracked and peeled slightly from the disturbance.

Although, with all distinguishable features gone, Kirstin could tell from the shape that it was a boy.

His blackened face stared blankly at the ceiling with empty sockets. The flesh of his mouth had burned away, revealing a white smile surrounded by dark, flaky crust where his lips once were.

Portions of singed hair still stuck from his scalp, but she wasn't able to determine what color it once was. It was all black.

With a solid thrust, she plunged the blade as deep as she could into the boy's abdomen. She felt the muscles separate with a sudden pop.

Attempting to slide the blade down towards the groin, Kirstin felt intense resistance. This would not be as easy as she had hoped it to be.

She tried sawing with the knife, forcing the blade through the skin that was charred and hardened by the flames.

Thick, dark blood oozed from the wound, spilling across her fingers and into the water covering the floor.

It built around the body like a cloud.

Thunder filled her head.

She smiled, feeling delight as she watched the cloud spread.

Focus, the calm voice told her.

She continued to cut through the boy's torso, creating a long gash that reached from the sternum to where she believed that the belly-button once was.

Retracting the blade, she placed the utility knife in her back pocket before reaching into the opening with both hands.

The smell of human meat and wet, carbonized flesh bit into her senses as she lifted the boy's intestines from his body.

He was still raw and warm inside.

She dragged the innards to the floor beside the body, where they slapped into the water. The sight of them reminded her of a mix between wet rubber, raw sausages still strung together and slime-covered eels.

Using the box-cutter blade, she reached back into the cavity and released the organs from the body. She then hoisted the heavy innards onto her shoulder, where they drained some dark fluid and some solid matter over her slicker before dripping into the water about her feet. They slipped and stretched, dangling over her back and dragging behind her as she crossed the floor.

The stench was far worse than that of the burned flesh.

Everything that the boy had eaten, drank and digested trailed behind her, dripped over her and wafted into the air surrounding her.

The thought of what she was doing made her snort a quick laugh as she carried the organs towards the southern edge of the basketball court. Releasing the intestines, she heard them smack onto the floor with a loud splash.

With her hands and the utility knife, she started organizing the mess, cutting here and there, stretching the transverse colon this way and turning the small intestine that way. It wasn't too long before she stood upright again to admire her work in progress.

It's the right thing to do, the calm voice acknowledged. *It's the only way they could fully understand.*

"I know," she replied out loud.

She turned and made her way towards the next body, extending the blade as she drew nearer.

This one used to be a girl, she thought as she crouched by the charred remains.

QUINTUS INTERLUDIUM

Extract from the Diary of Kirstin Matthews

Tuesday, March 14 2017

Back to school yesterday. I said 'Hi' to Steph and the girls. For some reason, they ignored me and kept talking like I wasn't even there.

Donny spoke to me.

He always does.

I think I really like him, but I don't know if he likes me. I should ask, but some might not agree with that approach.

It's not proper for a girl to ask a boy out.

Why is it I can hear my mother's voice saying that?

I tried to sit with the girls on the bus, but they put their bags on the seat.

I got the message.

I sat behind Mrs. Walker in the dreaded 'no one sits here' seat. It wasn't long before I found out why no one sits there.

Mrs. Walker knows how to talk the ears off a rabbit.

All the way to school, she jabbered about her garden and her grandchildren. Apparently, her son (Rusty or Randall) has a four-year-old son that suffers from epileptic fits. He ended up in hospital because he went into convulsions while jumping on his trampoline. She said that he went straight down the gap between the canvas and the metal bar, banging his head on the ground below.

She shook her head, quite saddened by the story, while I tried not to laugh.

The idea of a little kid falling down and hitting his head seemed funny at that moment.

I don't know why.

I heard the sound effects of cartoon springs as I pictured the boy jumping.

BOING, BOING, BOING...

Then a slide whistle as he tumbled down with a deep bass drum being struck as his skull hit the dirt.

It was wrong of me.

I know it.

But I don't feel bad.

Mrs. Walker didn't pick up on my reaction.

The girls avoided me for the entire day. I sat near the serving counter during recess and lunch. Donny waved to me. I thought I was going to die.

By the time I mustered the courage to wave back, he was talking with his friends and not looking at me anymore.

Stephanie was, though.

I think she saw me looking at Donny. I don't think she likes me watching him.

Maybe if I could go to parties with them, instead of being kept at home by my parents, she wouldn't be this way.

It's not my fault. What else can I do?

My parents made me stay home. They made me volunteer at the library and the church.

I hate them so much.

I hate being dragged along to service every Sunday. The church smells like old people waiting for death to come and take them away.

Their prayers and token pocket change offerings given in some hope that the Lord will prolong their lives and keep them in this godforsaken world a little longer.

It's all bullshit!

I've read the book they claim to follow.

'Claim' to.

I don't think there are too many in that place that follow anything much in their holy book.

Their self-centered prayers remain unanswered merely because they are self-centered. Their silver change clinking noisily in the basket wouldn't even buy them a small bag of fries from the local burger joint.

Hypocrites.

Pretenders.

Liars, all of them.

God isn't in that church.

God isn't in this town.

He's abandoned us all to our own devices.

If Stephanie is no longer my friend, because she has some fickle idea that my absence is a sign of animosity, then perhaps I need to look for friends elsewhere. Her two cronies, Nancy and Angela, are too shallow to see past Stephanie's hold that she has over them, so they won't need my affection either.

The truth is, I never truly liked them. They were friends out of mere convenience. All three live only a short walk away. That was a useful reason to keep them as friends when I was younger.

Not any longer.

If they can move outwards and expand their social circles, why can't I?

Oh yes.

That's right.

My fucking parents.

It appears that I won't be able to make new friends because they keep me locked away from people my own age, like I'm some disfigured retard who might fall over and cut myself on a blade of grass.

Mom is too worried that I will fall in with the wrong crowd.

Dad believes I'll accidentally trip and find some boy's cock inside me as I walk down the street.

I can't, and will never, get a chance to prove to them I can be trusted.

I hate them both so much.

I hate their god too.

I hate everyone.

IUGUOLO : BUTCHER

Though this be madness, yet there is method in it

WILLIAM SHAKESPEARE

I

"Don't order takeout," she said into the receiver. She held the phone against her ear as a watchful eye remained trained on the door to her office. "I've got a feeling you won't be able to get anything."

A young female officer in full uniform appeared in the glass viewing panel, holding some papers in her hand. She wore a white bandage on her right hand that was wrapped over her wrist. She tapped her knuckles gently against the glass where the words CAPTAIN JULIA REECE were inscribed in gold lettering before opening the door.

"I don't think I'll be home early, baby." The captain held a finger up, silently instructing the officer to wait. "I think this one is gonna keep me here a while."

There were words spoken on the other end.

"Okay," Reece replied.

More words were said before a slight smile crossed the captain's face.

"I love you too," she told the other before resting the receiver back into the cradle. Her attention moved directly to the young woman standing in the doorway. "What do you have for me, Summer?"

"Ah..." The girl flipped the papers over in her hand until she found what she was looking for. "We just had word from the inbound chopper. They're about fifteen minutes out. They want to know if they should come here or go directly to the school."

"Send them to the school." Reece stood up and straightened her attire before reaching for the jacket draped over the back of her chair. "Tell them they can land on the football field to the east of the building."

"Okay." The young cop scribbled a note on the paper with a pencil.

"Anything else?" the captain asked, moving around her desk and making for the door.

"Yeah." She appeared withdrawn. "Some of us stuck in the office were wondering if we could go out to the scene. I know I'm meant to stick to admin duties until my wrist heals, but it's not too bad now."

The captain brushed by her and started down the hallway with the young officer in tow.

"I've been sleeping with the bandage off most nights," Summer continued. "And besides, we are limited on people here. I can help out there."

Reece stopped and faced the girl, smirking slightly as they looked at one another.

"The clerical staff can do what I've been doing, Captain," the young officer said. "Answering phones sucks. Please, Captain."

"Remind me," Reece said. "How did you injure yourself?"

"I tried to fire a five-hundred one-handed," she said and lowered her eyes sheepishly.

"You tried to fire a Smith & Wesson five-hundred Magnum with one hand?"

"I know." The girl furrowed her brow. "It was really stupid. The doctor said I was lucky that only a tendon snapped and not a bone or two. But I don't need to fire my gun out there. I can't shoot left-handed, anyway. I tried."

"You tried?" the captain quizzed, turning to continue along the hallway.

"I went to the range with my service revolver." She stepped in line to follow the other.

"Did you now?"

"I followed protocol," she said defensively. "I signed it out and everything."

"So, how did you do?" Reece asked, still smirking.

"I missed every time," Summer replied. "But I don't need it. I just want to help."

"Answering phones isn't helping?"

"Please Captain," the girl begged. "I'm going stir crazy here."

Reece stopped at the end of the passageway and turned back to the young officer.

"The gun is part of the uniform," she said. "You will wear it at all times."

"Yes, Ma'am." The young officer nodded excitedly.

"You will stand on the line to keep people from entering the zone. Especially reporters and family members of people inside."

"Yes, Ma'am."

"Before you go, I'll need you to contact the chopper and tell them where to land and that I'll meet them there. Got it?"

"Yes, Ma'am." Summer couldn't contain her smile any longer.

"And I'll need the forms to release you from light duties and place you back in the field."

"Already filled out and waiting for your signature, Ma'am," the girl replied, holding the papers out in front of her.

II

"To some breaking news." Phil Gouldman swiveled in his chair to look down the barrel of camera two. It zoomed in a little closer, framing his shoulders and head tightly, allowing a space to his right for a graphic, with the words *BREAKING NEWS* flaring across it, to be slotted in place by the editors in another room.

"Gunshots have been heard coming from Edwards Hill State High School. We cross live to our on-the-scene reporter, Samantha Peterson. Samantha, this is the same town as the double homicide that you reported to us about earlier. Is there any connection?"

Got my name right that time, didn't you, you bastard?

"Phil," she began. Dwyers had placed her to the side of frame, allowing for a wide view of the school building in the background. "At this stage, we can't confirm that there is any direct correlation between the crime scene at Jackson Drive and the incident that is still unfolding in the Edwards Hill State High School behind me.

"We have heard some loud explosions that were like fireworks. We are presuming the sound to be gunshots.

"There are several students and staff members assembled on the lawn of the school just across the road. At this stage, we have been unable to interview any of the people gathered across the way."

Dwyers moved the camera and zoomed into the section of lawn where a male student was prone on his back. Two ambulance officers were crouching beside the boy, obstructing any clear vision that the cameraman hoped to get.

"Paramedics have arrived and seem to be assessing one student who is lying down under a tree. It's unclear if the student has obtained an injury or is suffering from some condition brought on by stress."

The camera zoomed back out to its original angle. Peterson turned, holding her microphone in front of her, and pointed to the roof of the high school.

"I can report that smoke was seen coming from the back of the building a short time ago. It's uncertain what caused the fire, but it appears that it was extinguished by the internal sprinkler system."

She turned back to face the camera.

"In the meantime, the elementary school directly across the road from the high school has been placed into lock-down and the one police officer on site is waiting for more law enforcers to arrive. Phil."

"Did I hear correctly, Samantha?" the anchorman asked. "There is only one police officer on site?"

"That we can see," she replied. She thought of the announcement over the police scanner that both she and Dwyers had heard earlier. Knowing that using such devices might land them in trouble with the authorities, she chose her words carefully. "We have it on great source that there are two officers inside, but we are still waiting for confirmation. Phil."

"Thanks Samantha," he said into the camera. "We'll cross back to you as news becomes available in this still unfolding situation.

"In other news, reports of an outbreak in the northern regions of Idaho and Washington have alerted the attention of the CDC. The origin of the outbreak is still uncertain but reports of extremely high fever, migraines and excessive sweating are among some symptoms associated with the illness. Some patients have expressed erratic behavior and violent tendencies..."

"And we're out," Dwyers said, switching off the lamp positioned above the lens before lowering the camera to his side. "You did good."

"I was a nervous as hell." Peterson moved her hand to the back of her neck and rubbed a tiny space between two vertebrae. She then lowered her arms and rolled her shoulders.

"You okay?"

"I feel a little stiff." She tilted her head from side to side.

"I could give you back rub," Dwyers suggested as he approached the open side door of the van.

"Ha, ha," she retorted. "I don't think so."

She opened the passenger door and retrieved a bottle of water.

"I wasn't kidding," he said.

She almost choked and spat some water back out. "What?"

"About you doing good. You looked good, and you kept to the facts. It was impressive."

"Really?"

"Yeah," he answered. "I mean, they'll cross back to us later and who knows. Maybe someone at network will see you. This could be a step up for you, Sam."

A broad smile grew on her face as she screwed the top back onto the bottle.

III

"This door's locked, too," Lindsay Merrick called from the back of the cafeteria. She started towards the young police officer, who was standing near the sink in the kitchen area. "Can we try to pry the padlock loose with something from the kitchen?"

"Not yet," McFarlan replied quickly, stopping the teacher from approaching. The three bodies of the cafeteria staff members were still on the floor in the small hallway that led to the other door to the outside world. "I need two men to help me with something back here first."

Donny stood to his feet and raised his hand. "I can help."

Stephanie, sitting on the chair again, reached up and grabbed his other hand frantically, frightened.

"Don't go," she begged. Her voice trembled.

"No," McFarlan told him, not wanting to expose the students to any more unnecessary death than they had already seen. "I need two male teachers, please. You stay with her. I think she needs you more."

Stephanie gripped his hand with both hands. She was sopping wet. They all were.

Her eye make-up had run down her cheeks, making her look like a sad panda.

"Please don't go," she pleaded again.

He crouched beside her again, gripping her hands in both of his.

"I'm not going anywhere," he assured her. "It's okay."

"You and you." McFarlan pointed to two teachers. "I need your help."

Two men moved through the tiny access between the wall and the serving counter before routing around the stainless steel cookers towards the waiting police officer.

"Wait," she whispered, holding her hand up. The two men stopped in their tracks and looked at her quizzically. "There are three dead bodies here. I need you to prepare yourself for what you are about to see. What I need from you is your help to move them into the freezer. I've found some blankets and towels in the pantry. We'll wrap them up first."

"Shouldn't you leave them for the crime investigation people?" one man asked. He was a broad chested man with thick arms. If she had to guess, she would have placed him in his mid-forties.

McFarlan thought about his question for a moment. She reached into her pocket for her cell phone.

"I'll take some photographs first," she told them.

It wasn't there.

"Shit!"

You probably left it on your desk again, she thought.

"We need to access this area and we can't simply step over the deceased to get food and supplies," she told the others. "I'm making the call. We need to move the bodies."

She stepped into the hallway with the two men close behind her.

"Oh dear god." The other man placed his hand over his mouth. He was shorter than the first man, slightly softer in the middle but of a similar age.

"Are you all right?" she asked him. He looked as if he was about to vomit. "Do you need to leave? I can get someone else if you're not up to this."

"I'll be fine." He moved his hand to his chest and took a deep breath. "I'll be fine."

"Are you sure?" the other man questioned him.

"I can do this."

McFarlan stepped into the pantry area recessed into the wall on the right. She crouched and retrieved three folded blankets from the lowest shelf. Moving along the hallway, she dropped one by the side of the body nearest to the door before moving back towards the men. She dropped another by the fallen woman near the middle of the passageway before unfurling the last blanket and wafting it out so that it landed open on the wet linoleum near the first body.

"We need to lift her into the blanket," the cop told the men. "We will place her arms across her body like an Egyptian mummy and wrap her in the blanket as tightly as we can."

"Will all three of them fit in there?" The first man nodded towards the freezer door.

"It's a walk-in freezer. I'm hoping it will be big enough," she replied. "We'll just have to do the best we can. If one of you can take the feet and the other takes the arms, I'll get you to lift her onto the blanket while I straighten it out a little better. Okay?"

Both men nodded. The first man moved to the woman's arms.

"Should we turn her over first or wait until she's on the blanket?" the second man asked, pointing out that the dead woman was lying on her stomach. He didn't like the idea of lifting her by the arms and legs while she was still in this position. It would cause her spine to arch unnaturally, causing her abdomen to bow towards the floor.

The picture in his head almost made him sick.

"Turn her first," McFarlan instructed them both. She kneeled on the blanket and reached across the body of the woman, gripping the body by the waist. Both men straightened the legs and arms and helped to guide to body as the young police officer rolled the woman towards her.

The body lifted onto its side slowly before slumping quickly onto its back.

"Okay, lift her up," McFarlan instructed them.

The two men complied, lifting the woman by her wrists and ankles, allowing the young officer to straighten and stretch the blanket out more.

"Okay," she said again, signaling the men to lower the woman onto the spread.

They placed her gently in the center of the blanket as best as they could. McFarlan straightened the woman's clothing to give her some dignity. She lifted the arms and placed them across the body, making the fingertips touch the shoulders.

"This was Nelly," the second man said. There were tears in his eyes. "I don't know her last name. She usually wears a name tag, but she doesn't have it on today. I just thought you might want to know her name.

"She was a real nice lady. I don't think there were any kids that had a mean thing to say about her, and I don't remember her saying anything nasty about the kids. She could have, though. The way some of these kids behave towards the staff here.

"Working here could be enough to make you lose your smile forever. Not Nelly. She always smiled and spoke nicely to everyone. I don't know why anyone would want to do this to her. She didn't deserve this."

McFarlan wrapped Nelly tightly, covering her body and face carefully before tucking one half of the blanket under the body. She then pulled the other half of the spread back over the body.

She rose to her feet, crossed the passageway, and opened the freezer door. A fluorescent light flickered inside, illuminating wisps of frosty air that circled the roof and seemed to spill from the shelving like a vaporous waterfall.

The floor was cold concrete and just long and wide enough to fit the three bodies if not for a stack of boxed frozen fries. She looked to the shelving for space to move the items to, but found none.

"We need to move these boxes," she told the men. "We can put them in the passage to make way for..."

She paused for a moment. The first woman had a name now. Referring to them simply as *the deceased* or *the bodies* didn't seem right anymore.

"...for Nelly and the other two ladies," she finished.

The first man stepped into the freezer and lifted two boxes from the stack and shifted them outside, placing them against the wall to the side of the freezer door. Before long, they moved the eight boxes and wrapped the three bodies of the fallen cafeteria workers before placing them on the cold, hard floor of the freezer.

As McFarlan closed the door with a loud thud, the locking mechanism click-clacking noisily, the second man burst into tears. The cop wasn't sure if it was because he was mourning the three women lying in the freezer, or because of the fear that gripped all of them getting the better of him.

Perhaps it was both.

She returned to the pantry area and lifted more blankets and towels from the lower shelves. The second man followed her and held out his arms to take them from her.

"Are they dry?" he asked her.

"The sprinklers didn't reach in here," she answered. "The water on the floor is runoff from the kitchen." She crouched and made a quick calculation regarding the linen and the population of the cafeteria.

"There's not enough to go around," she told him. "They're going to have to share the towels and huddle together under the blankets. I think the girls wearing next to nothing out there should take precedence."

"Agreed," he nodded. "I think most of the boys will play the chivalrous role and offer these to the girls and female teachers, anyway. Which is why I'm going to suggest using one to dry yourself off with first before Martin and I take care of ourselves."

"Absolutely," Martin acknowledged.

"I'm an officer of the law," she told them, "and my priority is *your* safety."

"What sort of gentlemen would we be if we let you go about sopping wet?" Martin stepped towards them. "If I could muster up some dry clothing for you, I would see you changed as well."

"You want to watch me get changed, Martin?"

"Don't flatter yourself, honey," he replied. "I'm gay."

"What about you?" she asked the other man.

"No, I'm not gay," he replied. "But I'm too much a student of the old school to admit that I would like to watch you get dressed."

She smiled.

"I meant your name." She shook her head. "He's Martin, and you are?"

"Aiden," he answered. "Aiden Fisk."

"Kimmie McFarlan," she told him, placing the stack of linen into his arms before reaching for a towel to dry herself. She watched him walk away as she started toweling her hair.

Martin stepped towards her and waited for the other man to disappear from view before speaking.

"Yes, he is," he whispered to her.

"Yes he is, what?"

"Very single," he replied. "Very available and ready for someone new to enter his life."

"I don't think that would be very appropriate for me." She draped the towel over her shoulder and reached down for another stack of linen for Martin to take out to the others.

"If we all waited for appropriate moments," he said as she dropped the towels into his arms, "we'd all be waiting forever, honey."

IV

Tiny cascading waterfalls filled the stairwell in the north-east corner of the building. Kirstin slowly made her way up, carefully placing her feet on each step.

The area above her was dark.

The lights were out and the emergency globes had failed to turn on in the stairwell and the corridor on the next level.

She knew there were still people hiding in the northern passageway of the top floor. The sound of girls screaming when the sprinklers had kicked in had made its way to her as she moved along the floor below.

She took the last step, then stood upon the floor and peered along the passageway before her. She was at an intersection, the corner where the hallway turned to move along to the south, or to the west towards the front of the building.

Kirstin had already been through the area to the south, passing through the center corridor and the southern passageway. There was a chance that some people might have moved to the rooms down there, but she hadn't checked these yet.

A fluorescent globe at the far end of the hallway flickered sporadically, intermittently, reminding her of lightning.

She closed her eyes and felt the heat emitting from her skin. She could see the flashes discharging from the real world and the vision that lived in her head.

The crimson clouds swirled again.

Focus, the calm voice, the distant lightning, told her.

She took a deep breath in through her nose and filled her lungs to their capacity. Slowly, she exhaled the air, feeling her heart throbbing in her chest.

Her eyes opened, adjusting to see the dark walls lined with lockers and doors.

There were no windows here.

Only the lightning showed her the way.

The sound of falling water filled her ears as it constantly hissed and trickled behind her, tumbling down the stairs to the floor below.

She moved past the first set of lockers set into the wall to her right as she pulled the yellow slicker off her body. Her hands were still smeared with blood after the act she had performed in the gymnasium.

Dropping the raincoat to the floor, letting it slap loudly onto the wet linoleum, she moved to the first door on the right. She adjusted her backpack by sliding her thumbs under both straps over her shoulders. Some of the blood smeared onto her tee-shirt as she pulled the straps tighter.

She reached around her back and took the Beretta from the hem of her jeans. Easing the slide back, she checked to see if a round was in the chamber.

It was.

She tried the handle of the door.

Locked from the inside.

She backed up a little and kicked out towards the door with her right leg, landing her foot beside the handle.

The door frame cracked a little, but not quite enough.

A few sudden and quick yelps and screams resounded from inside the room.

She kicked again.

The door burst open violently, sending a few small splinters of wood into the room. It smacked into the wall to the side of the room and bounced back towards Kirstin.

She held her hand out and stopped the door from hitting her, holding the pistol steadily in the other hand.

Scanning the room, Kirstin saw twelve soaked students cowering against the wall at the back of the room. They were all younger than her and extremely scared out of their minds.

It surprised her to see both female and male students huddling together, crouching on the floor with their arms around one another. In her mind, she imagined the girls huddling while the boys put on some false bravado.

But this wasn't to be.

They were all cowering.

They were all cowards.

A male teacher stood between her and the children.

His back bowed, and one of his hands raised up towards her defensively.

"P- p- please," he stammered fearfully. His wet white shirt clung to him so she could see his nipples. "D- d- d- don't hurt th- th- them."

She moved her head to look past him to the frightened faces of the students under his care.

It's his fault too, the calm voice told her. *You should let him know that.*

Kirstin moved to aim the Beretta at the students directly behind the teacher.

Without hesitation, she opened fire. With careful deliberation, she aimed and squeezed the trigger.

Twelve students.

Twelve shots.

The teacher turned slowly.

The shooting had stopped, and there seemed to be a deafening silence hanging heavily in the room.

His eyes moved over the students. They were still cowering with their arms around each other, pressed against the wall with their eyes wide open in everlasting fear.

All of them had wounds to their heads.

All of them were silent and still.

He dropped to his knees uncontrollably, a loud guttural sound bursting from his open mouth.

"You have failed them," she told him.

Her voice sounded distant, as if it came from somewhere deep within a cavern.

"This is your fault," she continued.

His body sucked in a deep, noisy breath.

A loud cry exploded from his chest as he reached his hands out to the children.

"It's all your fault," she said, placing the barrel of the pistol against his head.

V

The gunshot rang out through the building.

It echoed like thunder and rattled the door a little as the reverberation rushed along the corridor.

Rosina Posadas and Samuel Redman had locked themselves with seven students into a classroom halfway along the northern passageway.

Four sixteen-year-old girls pressed themselves against the female teacher as they huddled on the floor in the corner farthest away from the door.

The three boys and Redman started to quietly move furniture in front of the door, creating a barricade with the teacher's and students' desks. It was a flimsy construction at best, and with the linoleum floor being wet, it most likely wouldn't hold in place.

Redman knew this, but wanted to try. It also gave him and the boys a chance to get their minds onto something productive, rather than thinking about what was coming for them down the hallway.

He needed an excuse to get his and their eyes off the young women with wet, clinging clothing in the corner. The last thing he wanted was for them to feel uncomfortable with these young men and himself in such a moment of horror.

"It's all right, girls," he heard Posadas tell the sniveling teenagers.

There was another loud crack from down the corridor as another door busted open.

The sound made his heart leap and a lump to form in his throat.

"Can we put something else there?" asked a boy in Coke-bottle glasses, glancing over to the barricade. "I don't think that will stay in place."

"We might have to hold it ourselves," another boy replied.

"I think you're right," Redman told him. "We might have to push back against the desks if they try to break in."

"Who's doing this?" asked one girl.

"It doesn't matter," Posadas replied, pulling the girl's head towards her chest.

"I don't want to die," the girl blurted.

The others started crying louder.

"Shhh." Posadas tried to give some comfort, reaching her arms around them.

None of us does, Redman thought as he locked eyes with the other teacher.

She looked at him with little hope in her eyes. He wanted to put his arms around her and comfort her in this moment.

But he couldn't.

A sudden barrage of explosive popping noises filled the air, reminding him of fireworks. His stomach tightened and his heart dropped as he knew the sounds announced another group of people meeting their ends.

How many colleagues? he thought. *How many kids?*

Who is doing this?

Why?

The girls gripped onto their teacher tighter. They weren't coping with the situation at all. Neither was Posadas.

Neither am I.

The boys had frozen in place, staring at the door as the sound of gunfire erupted from outside their room somewhere.

"We should have chosen a room across the hall," said the boy wearing Coke-bottle glasses. "We came to the wrong room. We're going to die here."

"I don't think location would change our situation." Redman placed his hand on the other's shoulder. It was a meager attempt at bringing any reassurance. His hands were shaking, and he knew the lad felt his nervousness emitting from his fingers.

"There are windows over there," the boy continued. "We could have opened them and called for help."

"My phone," the other boy blurted suddenly. "We can call out with my phone."

"They won't work," the third boy informed them as the other reached into his back pocket. "I tried mine. It's got water all through it."

The girls moved their eyes to the boys, listening to their conversation.

"Mine too," said the boy with spectacles. "The screen is blank."

Two of the girls reached into their pockets, pulling out their phones, checking to see if they were operational.

"Anything?" one boy asked.

A girl shook her head.

"Nothing," the other replied, pressing the home-screen button over and over, hoping, by some miracle, it would turn on.

"It's the water," the third boy shook his head. "They're all fucked."

"Try the phone on the wall, Mister Redman," one girl suggested.

"They only phone through to the office or to other rooms," he replied to her before turning his attention back to the boy in glasses. "And the rooms on the other side of the hallway have bars on all the windows. We'd be just as much trapped over there as we are here."

He turned his face towards the door.

It had been silent out there for some time.

"Maybe they're gone," Posadas said wishfully.

THUMP!

The girls resumed their positions, gripping onto the female teacher, sobbing profusely.

The boys jumped back from the door.

THUMP! CRUNCH!

Another door somewhere along the corridor smashed open.

Whoever it was out there was making their way along the passageway, entering every room.

It would only be a matter of time before they were smashing through the door in front of Samuel Redman.

Gunshots rang out again.

A girl screamed hysterically.

"Shhh." Posadas stroked the teen's wet hair.

Redman felt helpless.

He had done everything he could physically do to keep them safe. But the torment was unbearable.

He couldn't bring these children any comfort or sensation of safety with the sound outside invading their senses.

Closer and closer, it approached.

Louder and louder, with each door breaking.

The fear and horror intensified on the faces of those around him as the sound of impending doom resounded with each thunderous blast of the gun.

They were trapped; he knew it.

They were in trouble.

There was no way out, and someone was coming for them.

He had already come to the finite conclusion that there was only going to be one way out of this mess.

They were going to die.

VI

"Oh dear god." Frieda Richardson covered the lower half of her face with her hands as she peered towards the upper level of the building. The unmistakable sound of gunshots rang across the air. "Oh dear god."

"Missus Richardson," a voice called to her. "You need to come back over here."

She turned to see the uniformed police officer standing by the students gathered under the trees. Not realizing she had ventured so far away from them, she turned and retreated towards the cop, turning her head towards the upper windows of the building as more gunshots resounded.

"Jesus," he hissed as he took the principal by the arm, his eyes fixed on an area of the building from where he thought the noise was coming. He directed the woman back towards her two staff members, who were watching her with concern.

When she was closer to them, they took her arms and held onto her. Karly Childers wrapped her arms around her boss and rested her head on the older woman's shoulder.

"Don't do that again," she ordered Richardson.

"I'm okay," she assured the two young women. Richardson looked over at the uniformed man standing near to her. "Why aren't you doing something?"

"Backup is on the way, Missus Richardson," he replied. "I have my orders to stay out here and make sure you and these people here remain safe until we can get you all out of here."

"Then what?" She pulled herself away from her receptionists, facing the police officer with anger in her eyes. "You'll just stay out here and let more of my students and teachers get shot?"

"I am sorry, Missus Richardson," he answered. His eyes were wet and red. "I truly am. But I have my orders to stay out here regardless of what I want to do. My son is in there. Freddie Morris."

Richardson's heart almost stopped. She glanced over to Tania Pearlman, who stood with an open jaw, staring towards the man. Her eyes moved to meet with those of her principal.

Both women shared a moment, a memory of the boy that was flirting with the young receptionist early in the morning.

"I'm sorry, Mister Morris." She lowered her head and tried to swallow. "Have you had any word from the officers inside?"

"Not much," he told her, peering back to the building as silence filled the air once again. "We had confirmation that one is dead. Doug Borden. He was a friend of mine."

She didn't have any words to say.

Sorry could be said only so many times before it sounded insincere.

Instead, she nodded solemnly and frowned.

"Officer McFarlan has barricaded numerous people in the cafeteria," he informed her. "I don't know who. She told dispatch that there are about a hundred or so, including a few staff members."

"Is she trying to find Kirstin?"

"She can't," Morris answered. "Her priority is for those in the room with her. Her hands are tied as much as mine are at the moment. I'm sure if Officer McFarlan is anything like me, she would want to be in there trying to stop this girl. But I really don't know her situation and I would only guess if I was to say anything more."

Richardson nodded. She understood where the police officer was coming from.

"I'm sorry to have taken your time, Mister Morris," she breathed. "And I really do hope your son is okay in there."

"Thank you, Ma'am." He frowned, lowering his head as he turned away. "I should return to my post on the line."

She watched him walk away towards the road. A long strip of police tape had stretched from the door of his car and across the extent of the front lawn of the school, wrapped around a couple of lamp posts at intervals to keep it up off the ground before being tied to a telegraph pole on the far side of the grounds.

The familiar popping sound of gunfire resumed.

Richardson turned to face the school building again. Her hands instinctively went to her face as tears welled in her eyes.

Weakness overcame her, and her knees buckled. She fell to the lawn, where she cried uncontrollably.

Each shot rang out loudly, filling her heart with increasing dread.

Each shot was a life.

A student.

A staff member.

Someone she knew.

VII

Dwyers rested the camera steadily on his shoulder, focusing on the upper windows to the northern side of the school's façade. He wasn't able to see anything, but the sound was loud and he hoped the multi-directional microphone fitted into the camera could pick it up.

He moved, pointing the lens towards the lone police officer standing by his vehicle. The cop was facing back towards the building, listening to the sharp bursts emanating from somewhere inside the structure across the road.

The cameraman panned up and across the lawn to the people gathered under the trees. He found a well-dressed woman that he presumed to be a teacher, on her knees and bawling hysterically.

That's the money shot, he thought, zooming in slowly on the woman and holding her in frame as the gunfire continued to ring out.

When silence ensued, the sound of the last shot ripping through the air. He held the lens on the woman. Two others, much younger ladies, joined her. They lowered themselves beside her, where they wrapped their arms around her shoulders.

The shot was perfect.

"Christ almighty," he gasped. "How many was that?"

"I counted eighteen," Peterson replied, standing by the open passenger door of the van, scribbling onto a notepad. "She must have two guns."

"She?" He panned over the crowd of students, holding the frame, when he saw someone in emotional distress.

"It's got to be the girl from Jackson Drive," the reporter said. "She killed her parents and then came here to do this."

"That's speculation," he pointed out. "Did you hear anything like that over the scanner?"

"The scanner is all but dead," she replied, peering up towards the building. "All I'm hearing is traffic cops from highway patrol."

"You would think with this shit going on, we'd be hearing constant chatter." He moved the camera to record a small group of girls sobbing near the edge of the lawn where the driveway moved past.

"Maybe they changed frequency," she suggested, placing her notepad on the passenger seat before retrieving her water bottle.

"Frequency?" he blurted. "We need a way to change the frequency."

"Hmm?" She had the bottle pressed to her lips, gulping down a mouthful of water.

"We've been listening to dispatch conversations that relay to vehicles," he told her. "We haven't been listening to cop chatter on their mobile systems. They could be talking to each other on walkie-talkie."

"So," she said, screwing the lid back onto the bottle, "let's change the station on the scanner."

"Can't," he replied disappointedly. "Someone at the station rigged it to stay on that frequency."

"Can't you fix it?"

"I'm just a camera operator, baby," he said. "I'm not a techie."

"Shit," she spat. "So we can only listen in to traffic chatter?"

"And the occasional call out from dispatch."

"Fuck me sideways!"

He lowered the camera and raised an eyebrow. "Was that a request?"

"You wish." She shook her head.

Gunfire suddenly started up again.

"Crap!" Dwyers frantically lifted the camera back onto his shoulder and started recording again. "Whoever it is, is one harsh motherfucker."

"Maybe you should use the tripod." Peterson ducked behind the door. It was more of a reflexive action that one of necessity.

"You know how to set it up?" he asked. "I kind-a got my hands full at the moment."

"Sure," she said, moving to the sliding door on the side of the vehicle.

VIII

Tires squealing farther down the road caused Morris to turn abruptly. Flashing lights informed him that another police vehicle was on its way.

Gunshots continued to ring out behind him as he crouched under the police tape and waved to the approaching car. He signaled the driver to slow down and pointed to a place next to his own car for the other to pull into.

The driver complied, screeching to a halt before jumping out of his vehicle with his hand resting on his holstered pistol.

"Sorry." The other held up his free hand apologetically.

"Where the fuck have you been, Cory?"

"A tire blew on the other side of town." He pointed over his shoulder. "I just managed to change it and then I tore ass over here. Sorry."

"Why didn't you radio it in?" Morris held the tape up so that the other officer could duck beneath it.

"Damn thing just died when I pulled up to change the tire," he replied. "There's no way I could have picked it if I tried. It took, I don't know how many tries, to kick the car back over. I thought the battery might have blown or something. I thought I might have had to walk back to the station."

Another shot rang out.

Cory Plasket pulled his sidearm out instinctively.

"Put that away," Morris barked. "She's inside and out of range."

"She?" Plasket raised his eyebrows as he placed his pistol back into his hip holster. "So it *is* the girl?"

"Yeah," the other replied. "Listen. Don't tell anyone. Especially not the media parked across the road there."

Turning his head, Plasket could see the camera operator moving the lens towards him. Beside the man was a well-dressed, very attractive woman setting up a tripod.

"How long have they been there?"

"Since I arrived," Morris answered.

"So where do we get inside?" Plasket asked eagerly.

"We don't," the other told him, moving his eyes back to the building.

Plasket furrowed his brow and quickly glanced over to the other officer.

"Orders are to stay here until backup arrives," he explained.

"And then what?"

"Who the fuck knows?"

Plasket sensed some unease in the other.

"Are you all right?"

"My son's still in there," he replied.

Plasket nodded as he panned his eyes across the windows of the upper level.

"Shooting's stopped," he said eventually, realizing it had been silent for some time.

"It'll start up again soon," Morris informed him. "I think she's making her way from room to room up there."

"What about them?" Plasket nodded towards the people gathered in the shade of the trees on the lawn.

"I think we should move them across the road," the other suggested. "I was waiting for the paramedics to finish up."

"Paramedics?"

"They had a kid go into shock," Morris explained. "They took him to the hospital a while ago. I just hadn't got around to finding a suitable location to move the rest of them to."

Looking around, Plasket locked his eyes on the school across the road.

"What about over there?" he asked. "Surely they'll be safe inside there."

"The elementary school?"

"Yeah."

"They're in lockdown," answered Morris, peering across the road, past the reporters to the large brick building behind them.

"Maybe we can put them on the ground behind the school then," Plasket suggested. "At least they'll have some cover if this girl starts shooting through the windows."

Nodding, Morris kept his eyes on the building across the road.

Gunshots started erupting from inside the building again.

Both officers snapped their heads back to the upper level of the high school. Morris didn't need any more convincing.

"Let's get them over there now," he said to the other officer.

IX

"They're coming," one girl blurted. She clung tightly onto Rosina Posadas, causing a button in the middle of the teacher's blouse to pop. "They're coming."

The other girls blubbered noisily. All the while, the young female teacher tried to console them as best she could.

"Shhh." She wrapped her arms around all of them before telling a lie. "It'll be fine."

Redman gazed over at her and saw fresh tears rolling over her cheeks. She knew as well as he did that this might be the end for all of them.

"Boys," he called softly as he pushed against the barricade, planting his feet as securely as he could on the slippery linoleum floor. The three lads joined him on his left, the boy wearing glasses standing by the teacher's side as they leaned their combined weight against the desks and chairs they had stacked in place.

The gunshots had stopped some time ago, and the silence seemed drawn out.

As they prepared themselves, Redman hoped and silently prayed the shooter had moved on. That they had simply left the area to allow the survivors to live another day.

Still, he maintained his position, pushing against the furniture, ready for an attack.

"They're coming," the girl said again.

Redman glanced over and saw all five females shivering in the far corner. They were cold, thanks to the drenching they had received from the sprinklers in the ceiling. But the fear they all felt wasn't helping them through the situation.

His jaw quivered because of his nerves, not from feeling cold.

Side by side, the boys pushed the barricade.

Waiting.

Waiting.

Waiting for the inevitable.

"Maybe they gave up," the boy with Coke-bottle glasses suggested.

THUD!

The door shuddered, but didn't budge.

"Shit," one of the other lads hissed.

A girl screamed. Another groaned fearfully.

The boys repositioned their feet and readied themselves for another blow.

THUD!

There was a sound of something cracking. Redman couldn't tell if it was a piece if the barricade breaking or whether the sound came from the door itself.

"Come on, boys," he grunted, pushing with all of his might.

THUD!

The cracking was louder this time.

Definitely the door, Redman thought.

His eyes scanned through the piled furniture in search of the origin of the sound. He couldn't see anything significant.

"They can't get through," one boy said, a smirk growing on his face.

BLAM!

BLAM!

BLAM!

Three loud shots thundered into the room.

Three bullet holes appeared in the door.

Redman was still standing. He was still holding the barricade in place.

"Oh fuck," another boy shouted. "Fuck!"

Redman turned to see the three boys in place on his left, still pushing against the piled up furniture.

"Jesus," the other boy whispered, slackening his grip on the barricade.

"Keep pushing," Redman told him.

The boy wearing glasses turned his head towards the teacher.

"I don't feel too good, Mister Redman," he slurred.

The left lens of the boy's glasses was missing.

A small amount of blood was dribbling from the socket where his eye once existed. Another hole oozed thick, red liquid from his cheek bone from where the second bullet had penetrated. The last slug had smashed through the top lip, just below the left nostril, knocking his central left incisor and lateral incisor to somewhere in the back of his throat.

The boy's right eye rolled upwards as he collapsed lifelessly to the floor.

A girl let out a shrill scream that rang loudly and painfully in Redman's ears.

His heart leaped into his throat as he stared at the young boy lying on the ground beside him.

THUD!

The furniture scraped loudly over the floor an inch. The door opened slightly.

Redman quickly snapped back to reality and pushed against the barricade.

"Boys," he called desperately. "Help me."

The two lads quickly put their attention back onto the door, joining their teacher in a last ditch effort to keep the intruder out.

"Fuck off," one boy hollered as he pushed with all of his might.

The barricade slid back against the door with a thump, forcing the door shut again.

THUD!

The intruder was strong.

The jarring impact sent a jarring ache along the teacher's arms.

"Leave us alone," the boy cried.

THUD!

THUD!

THUD!

SEXTUS INTERLUDIUM

Extract from the Diary of Kirstin Matthews

Friday, March 31 2017

I heard it again last night.

It seemed like it was right there, in my room with me.

Talking to me.

It didn't say much, but I know what it wants. I think I know.

I think it wants to help me. Maybe it wants to be my guide.

It called to me, just as it did before. I was almost asleep, but not quite. Just like the other times.

I wasn't scared this time.

The first time was freaky. It felt like someone was there with me.

I prayed for it to leave me alone.

It did. But it returned the next night, and the next.

I couldn't see anyone when I finally got the courage to look.

Last night was different from the other nights.

I wasn't half-asleep in my bed. I was wide-awake and sitting at my desk reading.

All I could think about was how Stephanie and her bitches have been teasing me lately. They've been calling me a slut and whore every chance they get.

When I pass them in the hallway or when they stand near me in the cafeteria, they whisper so that the teachers don't hear them.

I want to hurt them so much.

I want to cut them to pieces.

That's when I usually hear the voice.

Whenever I think about those girls or how my parents keep me as their prisoner, the voice comes.

It tells me it will all be all right.

It tells me I am right to feel the way I feel.

It said that one day I will be free to do whatever I want.

I'm not afraid of it anymore. I don't know if it comes from inside me or from somewhere else.

I told Mum, but she just said it was my inner voice trying to make heads and tails of confusing moments in life. She said that everyone has an inner voice to help them decide.

I don't think she's right.

It definitely sounds like someone else, like someone that is in the room with me.

Someone that is not me.

The voice is always calm, quiet and gentle. It never gets loud or irritating. It doesn't sound bossy or spiteful.

It seems like someone who cares for me.

Someone who loves me.

I can't tell if the voice is that of a boy or a girl. I guess if it was my inner voice, it should probably sound like me, but it doesn't. That kind of puts a spur in Mum's theory.

It's almost a whisper.

Like a cloud.

Like a soft breeze.

Like distant thunder or gentle rain falling on a tin roof.

I think it wants to guide me.

I think it wants to help me.

I think it loves me.

I think I love it too.

I know I do.

LEGIONES : SOLDIERS

To think that the spectre you see is an illusion does not rob him of his terrors: it simply adds the further terror of madness itself – and then on top of that the horrible surmise that those whom the rest call mad have, all along, been the only people who see the world as it really is.

C.S. LEWIS, *Perelandra*

I

She kicked the door furiously, over and over.

It didn't budge.

She could hear the whimpers and calling from inside and wanted more than anything else to break into the room and kill everyone inside.

She needed to.

The clouds had turned into a tempest with streaks of lightning, dredging large gashes into the edges of her mind

Get in there, it bellowed. The calm voice was calm no more.

It was angry.

Kill them, it thundered. *Kill them.*

She thrust her foot against the door again and again, emitting a loud cry of frustration.

Lifting the Beretta, she took aim at the door again. She was about to squeeze the trigger when something caught in the corner of her eye.

Movement.

Turning, Kirstin saw at least nine students dart out of a doorway farther along the corridor. They bolted for the stairwell in the north-west corner as fast as they could.

One boy slipped on the wet floor and went sprawling. A girl quickly turned to help him but saw Kirstin looking towards her, holding the pistol in her hands.

Kirstin recognized her. She was the girl in braids that was sitting with Donny in the cafeteria.

Making a rash decision, the braided girl left the boy on the floor in favor of the escape route.

Kirstin turned and pointed the gun towards the girl, firing three shots that barely missed the escapee as she disappeared down the steps, screaming hysterically all the way.

Get them, the calm voice instructed her.

Kirstin looked at the door beside her. She still wanted to get inside and kill the people in there.

She needed to.

Focus, said the voice. *Go and get them.*

The fallen boy attempted to get back onto his feet. His old sneakers kept slipping, unable to find the traction to assist him in his desperate attempt to flee.

Kirstin pursed her lips, not wanting to leave her intended prey, but for the sake of the calm voice. She moved away from the classroom door and started towards the north-west corner of the passageway.

The boy looked over his shoulder towards his pursuer. He was pushing up with his arms and kicking his legs in desperation. His sneakers kept squeaking against the wet floor.

He was going nowhere.

She raised the pistol and aimed as she approached, firing twice.

The first bullet hit him in the shoulder, sending him sprawling onto his back.

The second hit him in the center of his chest.

By the time she reached his side, his breathing had stopped and his face had relaxed. He was roughly her age. She recognized him from a couple of her classes, but didn't know his name.

Nor did she care for it.

She kicked him gently in the ribs, checking to see if any of him remained in there.

The boy remained silent and still.

The sound of water falling down the stairs filled her senses. The flow was slowing as she descended to the lower floor.

Holding the pistol out in front of her, she stepped onto the lower floor and peered down the corridor towards the cafeteria first before moving her eyes in the direction of the administration office.

The eight students could be anywhere.

Kirstin headed towards the front doors of the school. By her reckoning, it was the most obvious escape option.

She stepped carefully and slowly, attempting to not disturb the inch-thick water at her feet too much. Cocking her head now and then, Kirstin trained her hearing on the area in front of her.

The sound of falling water was overwhelming.

Not only did it resonate from the stairwell behind her, it was also reverberating along the hallways as it spilled down the other steps throughout the building.

There was no way she could hear the footfalls of her quarry.

She could only hope they would make a mistake.

She listened for a murmur, a cry, a sob or a sniffle.

Slowly, deliberately, she planted one foot in front of the other as she crept along the western corridor towards the intersection to the center passageway.

The rattle of a chain and rumble of the front doors pricked at her ears.

Could be someone trying to get in, she thought. *Could be the cops.*

She moved as close as she could to the wall on her left, keeping her eyes on the opening into the intersection to the right. The administration office was down the passage in that direction. Beyond it were the front doors to the school.

Her backpack slid across the wall as she angled herself to see farther and farther down the hallway as she drew closer and closer to the corner.

The small window of the reception area appeared in her view. The door to the little office was open.

As she moved a little farther, she could see shadows dancing on the wall.

There was someone partially blocking the light emitting through the glass panels on the doors.

Kirstin pointed the Beretta into the passageway as she tilted her head around the corner.

There were no police officers at the door, just two boys a little older than her trying to pry the door open by their own strength. Stepping carefully into the intersection, she looked to the center corridor behind her, towards the stairwell she usually took to get to her locker.

There was no one there.

Returning her attention to the two boys at the door, she stepped forward slowly, keeping the barrel of her gun trained on the boy to the left.

They hadn't noticed her. They were too engrossed with trying to break through the door.

"We should break the glass," one of them whispered. His voice carried to her, filling her ears with clarity.

"There's metal mesh on the outside," the other pointed out.

"We'll kick it out," the first suggested. "Someone will hear and come and get us."

"Shhh." The other shook his head as he reached up to release the sliding bolt. "She'll hear you."

His forehead split open. A bullet hole appeared before the boy's face in the glass panel of the door. A fine spray of blood filled the view before him, before his body dropped listlessly upon the wet floor.

Speechless, the other boy stared wide-eyed. His hands trembled at the sight of his friend lying on the ground.

Clouds of blood appeared in the water around the open wounds in the front and back of the boy's head before slowly streaking away under the doors with the escaping water.

The second boy felt something sting his neck.

He raised his hand to the area of pain and pressed his palm against a spot just behind his jaw. He felt a warm flow run between his fingers.

Curiosity suddenly overwhelmed him. He pulled his hand back into view and peered down towards his fingers.

Thick blood covered his entire hand.

The warm flow spread from his neck and down his chest.

He dropped to his knees, a feeling of lethargy overwhelming him.

His eyes moved to a figure standing by the door to the reception area.

Increasingly blurring, he could make out the form of a girl staring down at him. She held a gun at her side and cocked her head to the side as he fell prostrate onto the floor beside his friend.

Darker and darker, she grew as he became more and more drowsy.

He closed his eyes and drifted away, wishing the bad dream to be over.

II

"Cheese and crackers," Plasket shouted, peering across the road towards the school. The sound of gunfire coming from the direction of the front doors made him jump inside his skin.

He and Morris had been escorting the students and three staff members across the road and through the gate of the elementary school.

Richardson had stopped by the gate to make sure all the students made it into the grounds safely. Now she crouched alongside several students, the last to arrive, as they waited for more shots to be fired.

None came.

"Get them around the back," Plasket barked at her, pointing towards Morris who stood at the western corner of the building.

The other officer beckoned to them with his hand before pointing to an unseen area behind the structure.

Keeping low, the principal and the students raced along the front of the school, passing closed windows with their blinds pulled down before rounding the corner to see an open play area with colorful climbing equipment and painted games on a cement quadrangle.

The other students sat upon low benches, intended for smaller children, that lined the edge of an area underneath a large shade cloth. Both receptionists were standing to the side, watching and waiting for Richardson to arrive.

There was a sense of relief amongst everyone when the remaining students and the principal arrived safely.

Morris observed them all for a moment as students exchanged hugs.

As far as he was concerned, they were out of danger.

"Stay here," he called to all of them. "Wait until we tell you it's safe to leave."

Richardson nodded.

Her face wore the appearance of distress.

Morris, upon reflection of how she looked, couldn't imagine how the people inside the high school must be coping.

He darted back around the building to see Plasket waiting for him by the gate.

"We should check it out," the other called over.

Morris nodded, making his way out of the school grounds and towards the road.

Both officers briskly walked by the media van where the young reporter was standing in front of the camera giving a run-down of what was occurring.

"And I can see the two police officers making their way towards the school right now, Phil," she was saying as they stepped across the road. "We can't see too much from our current location, but we have been able to hear gunfire coming from the upper level of the building and, to repeat, shots coming from the front door most recently. We are unsure whether the shooter is trying to hit anything out here at this time."

Her voice trailed off as the two officers reached the other side of the road, heading in a northerly direction to get parallel to the front door of the building. They reached the curbside where the path leading to the entrance met the street.

From their point of view, they could see water spilling over the steps that led up to the front platform. Plasket peered up to the stars and stripes waving lazily in the gentle breeze.

"Just another day in the USA," he mumbled.

Morris glanced over at the other police officer. He understood the meaning behind the statement.

"There's too much of this kind of shit."

Plasket nodded, dragging the corners of his mouth downward.

"What do you see?" he asked Morris.

"Not much," he answered. He trained his eyes on the doors and saw something pressed against the glass panel on the left. "There's some blood, I think, coming under the door. The water looks a little pink."

Plasket squinted, peering towards the doors.

"That's a kid," he said. "There's a kid there."

"Where?"

"Against the door," Plasket pointed. "That's a kid for sure."

"We need to get closer," Morris told him. "Stay low and follow me."

Plasket nodded, taking his P229 out of its holster.

Both men ducked down and ran along the path as fast as they could. They crouched on the left side of the steps, ducking for cover by the edge of the platform.

Carefully, keeping their bulk below the level of the platform, they peered towards the door.

They could clearly see a red tinge in the falling water.

The sight of a boy's body pressed up against the glass panel of the door informed both police officers that what they were seeing was blood. The open wound on the boy's forehead told them he was beyond help.

From their position, they saw a second boy with a lot of blood over his neck lying nearby.

Morris took a deep, shaky breath.

Neither of them was his son.

He felt some relief that he wasn't looking at the body of his own boy. Somewhere deep inside, there was a glimmer of hope that his boy was still alive.

Shame swept over him as he considered the fathers of these two boys.

They're all somebody's sons, he considered.

A sudden barrage of bullets burst through the glass panels, sending a spray of glass shards into the air and striking the edge of the platform near the two officers' heads.

"Fuck!" Plasket dropped to his rump onto the wet ground.

Morris ducked his head as pieces of chipped cement went flying over him.

Firing back, Plasket pointed his weapon towards the doors and fired randomly into the entrance. He got five shots off before Morris grabbed his arms.

"Stop," he bellowed. "We don't know where anyone is in there."

"Shit." Plasket lowered his gun. Morris was right. He couldn't see the shooter and there could be innocent people just beyond the door for all he knew.

"We need to get back," Morris said to him.

Both men ran to the north-west towards the road, away from the door and, they hoped, out of the shooter's range of view.

More shots rang out behind them as they increased their pace.

By the time they reached the roadside, the shooting had stopped, and they were out of breath.

Morris peered back to the building as he placed his hands on his hips, his chest rising and falling in rapid sequence.

"Fuck!" Plasket wheezed as he placed his pistol back into its holster. "Fuck! Fuck!" He placed his hands on his knees and continued to whisper the word over and over with each breath.

Morris looked at the reporter and her cameraman. The lens was pointing straight at them.

"Shit," he whispered. "We just made national television."

III

Kirstin remained pressed against the wall inside the open doorway of the administration office. She extended her arm into the corridor, directing the Beretta towards the entryway into the school building.

She couldn't see the police officers any longer. They had moved beyond her view.

The gun's magazine was empty.

She had fired every round that she had remaining in the clip out through the doors to the intruding cops.

Hoping they got the message to leave her alone, she moved over to the reception counter and ejected the magazine into her awaiting hand. After placing both pistol and clip onto the counter, she slid her backpack off and placed it beside the weapon.

She took the P229 she had taken from the dead police officer upstairs and sat it next to her dad's Beretta. She took a box of bullets she had brought from home and reloaded the empty clip.

Her skills were improving. She was getting faster.

The bell rang again.

Time to move to class, she thought, allowing herself to smirk.

Before long, she had a fully loaded 92 Compact and P229 sticking out of the back of her jeans. She placed a spare clip for the Beretta in her left back pocket, and a spare magazine for the P229 in the pocket on the right.

After carefully reloading everything else into her backpack, she zipped it up and slung it over her shoulders again. She checked the utility knife still sitting in the front right pocket of her jeans, sliding the blade in and out before stuffing the device back in place.

By the time the clang of the second bell that signaled the commencement of lessons resounded, she was ready to resume the hunt.

At least six more students hid somewhere downstairs in the building. She needed to find them and kill them.

Focus, the calm voice reminded her. *They can't escape. You already made sure of that. All they can do is hide.*

She stepped back into the corridor and headed back into the building, turning right at the cross intersection in order to move along the southern passageway.

Each step she took was deliberate, slow, silent.

Her effort to remain silent had paid off before. She could only hope the other students were as stupid and noisy as their two friends lying by the front doors.

Their own selfish ambitions for freedom distracted them. So distracted, they didn't even realize that she was right there.

Not until it was too late.

She felt proud of the outcome.

It couldn't have come off any better.

If only she could do the same thing again.

Finding each of the doors to the classrooms lining the passage open, she peered into each, crisscrossing the hallway as she carefully searched for anyone cowering inside. Eventually, she rounded the corner into the southern corridor.

More open doors, more empty rooms.

Kirstin stood outside the library door. The area beyond the glass paneled doors with thick timber frames was dark.

Almost pitch black.

The only light emitted from small emergency lighting posted in each of the corners, partially blocked by tall bookshelves and casting strong, dark shadows throughout the room.

She pushed the door open.

A loud squeak filled the silent room, along with a gentle swish of water being pushed away from the entrance.

Cautiously, she stepped inside as she reached around behind her and pulled both handguns out of the waistband of her jeans.

Someone is in here, the calm voice told her.

She silently agreed.

She could sense it.

The hairs on the back of her neck stood on end.

Someone was watching her.

Someone hidden in the darkness.

IV

"What the hell is going on out there?" Lindsay Merrick whispered.

Her eyes, along with everyone else's in the cafeteria, were staring towards the locked doors that led back into the corridor. Many of them had frozen in place in fear after hearing gunshots above them. They remained in place after hearing more shots that sounded closer.

"She's moving around out there," one of the male students blurted. "She's coming for us."

"Shuttup," Donny snapped at the other, tightening his arms around Stephanie's shoulders. She sat by a table near the northern wall, as far away from Kirstin as she could get. A large towel draped over her shoulders.

Donny sat behind her, slightly to the side. He kept his hands on her arms or embraced her when he noticed her getting upset.

He really felt useless in his current role as consoler to the girl, but whenever he offered to assist someone else, she would fret and reach for him.

Understanding why she adhered to him in such a way, he stayed with her. He was one of the first people she spoke to every morning before riding the bus to school. He was also one of the last she saw before returning home each afternoon.

He was familiar to her.

Although she attempted to elevate herself in his presence by bragging about her exploitive weekend adventures, something that he didn't enjoy hearing about, he saw her now as nothing more than a scared little girl. The many times she had boasted about how grown up she was because she engaged in intimate relations with this guy or that guy meant nothing now.

Besides, he didn't believe a single word that came from her mouth when she started talking that way. He knew most of the guys she mentioned in her stories, and none of them had ever mentioned her in theirs.

He felt sorry for her on most days.

Today, he felt the need to be protective.

She reached out through the thick towel that was wrapped tightly around her and gripped her fingers around his elbow that was resting against her breast. He could feel each of her shaking breaths beneath his arms.

"It's okay," he told her. "She can't get to you. I won't let her."

She nodded.

She believed him.

Donny glanced towards the kitchen area. He could see McFarlan talking into her walkie-talkie.

Even though the expanse of cafeteria was silent, mostly, a few murmurs and sobs here and there emitted from around the room, he wasn't able to hear the police officer's conversation. He guessed she was trying to get the answers they all wanted.

What was going on?

When would they be rescued?

His eyes moved around the room to see groups of four, five or even six people huddled under blankets. Some larger students had smaller ones on their laps, positioning their chairs in tight, compact clusters before draping covers around themselves.

Some concerns and wicked thoughts filled Donny's mind when he first saw this happening around the room. The idea that some boys might take advantage of the situation and suffer from wandering hand syndrome occurred to him.

But he watched them, ready to say something if he needed to, and saw no such thing. Some girls huddled up with the boys and, as blankets draped around them, the lads simply wrapped their arms around them, just as he was doing with Stephanie.

The thought of doing what he envisioned probably crossed their minds. If he could think of it, then surely they could as well.

The reason they didn't was very apparent. He could see that in all the students' eyes.

They were too afraid.

They were too upset.

"She just fired upon two officers outside," McFarlan said, finally answering Lindsay Merrick's query. "They're both fine. The students who made it out are across the road and safe."

"Thank God," Merrick replied. "Thank God."

"What about upstairs?" the student Donny had rebuked earlier, asked. "What was that?"

"You just don't get when to keep your mouth shut, do you?" Freddie Morris, seated next to Donny, shook his head.

"I think we deserve to know what's going on," the boy argued.

"You can't work it out on your own?" Freddie glared at him. "What do you think she's doing out there? Party games and pony rides?"

"Fuck you, Freddie," the boy spat.

"Hey!" Aiden Fisk called from the kitchen. "That was uncalled for."

The students moved their eyes over to the teacher, who approached the serving counter. The boy lowered his head as the sounds of whimpers and sobbing increased throughout the room.

"I get that you're upset," the teacher continued. "I really do. I'm upset too. But we don't need to upset ourselves any more than we already are.

"We need to think about the others in this room and be a little sensitive to what they need. Some of us here don't really need to know what is happening upstairs. Even those of us who are curious, don't really need to know.

"I'm sure we'll find out more than enough when we get out of here. I'm sure you'll see this on the news for days to come and I'm sure that the people in this school and this town will talk about it forever.

"Right now, we just need to think about how we can keep safe until someone comes to get us. Got it?"

"And what if they don't?" the boy snapped back. "What if she gets in here first?"

Fisk glared at the boy. He didn't know how to respond.

"She won't," Donny replied. "Freddie and I locked the doors. They won't open unless we unlock them for her."

"She could shoot her way in," a girl suggested, her voice frantic and shaking with fear.

"No," McFarlan assured her. "She was shooting at me before. None of her bullets could get through those panels. They're too thick. We are all perfectly safe in here. We have food and water. We can last for days in here."

"Days?" The girl raised her eyebrows. McFarlan suddenly wished she had kept her mouth shut.

"She didn't mean it like that," Donny told her. "They'll come and get us out before then. Won't they?"

He turned to McFarlan.

"You'll all be in your own homes tonight," she told them, hoping her words were true.

Captain Julia Reece was stepping out of the vehicle as Officer Summer Florez was still applying the handbrake. The older woman slammed the door behind her and jogged over to the two officers standing by the edge of the road parallel to the entrance into the high school.

"Shouldn't you two be standing somewhere else?" she called to them as she approached from the direction of the driveway into the school grounds.

Florez had parked next to Morris' vehicle, pointing the right front corner of the sedan towards the footpath that ran along the front of the schoolyard.

"She's gone," Plasket called back. "She could be anywhere."

"She could point that gun of hers right at you, for all you know," the captain said, looking towards the doors.

"She'd want to be one hell of a shot from that distance," Morris told her. "I don't know too many people who could hit their mark this far away with a handgun."

"Ever heard of stray bullets, Randy?" quipped Reece, scanning the windows along the upper level. "Any movement from up there?"

"Nothing," Morris replied. "We haven't seen anything since she was near that door. Before that, the only thing we saw was smoke coming from somewhere to the back."

"You didn't have time to check it out?"

"I had people out here on the lawn and these guys across the road," he told her.

She turned her head to see the television reporter and her cameraman. The lens pointed towards the police captain, a bright light beaming towards her from atop of the camera, while the young reporter spoke into a hand-held microphone.

"Watch how you perform," she said to the two officers. "They're going out live right now. Interest in this has sparked some since the shooting you heard coming from upstairs."

"They waited that long?" Plasket asked. "I guess an officer down and a handful of dead kids isn't enough to grab media attention these days."

"There are too many stories like this, these days," Reece said. "Kids with guns. Mass killings. Every damn day it's something. I just didn't expect it to happen in this town."

"Teachers should carry guns," Morris blurted.

"What?" Florez said, catching up to the captain finally.

"Nothing," he replied. "Just something I heard a senator say on TV back when Obama was trying to get the gun laws changed."

"Makes sense," Plasket said sarcastically. "It's not as if teachers have a highly stressful job. There's no chance one of them would go *postal* and do this kind of shit in any school themselves."

Morris pursed his lips and nodded. He secretly yearned for a day when no guns would be needed. Especially within any community that he was a part of. But he couldn't see it happening anytime soon. Especially in his home state, where the law allowed people to wear their holstered weapons in public areas.

The idea of escalation always rested in his thoughts. Some asshole brings a pop-gun, so the next asshole brings a semi-automatic to destroy the first. And so on it would go until someone pulls the trigger on a machinegun or, even worse, some form of military hardware.

He didn't know why the girl inside was doing what she was doing.

It didn't matter why.

But he knew that if the powers-that-be allowed guns inside that building after today's events, armed teachers protecting students, then it would only be a matter of time before someone with one of those guns had a bad day and acted upon it.

Plasket was right.

Schools were the one place guns did not belong.

"I need to get around the back," Reece told them. "The chopper is inbound and will land on the football field. I want you to come with me."

"Me?" Morris pointed to himself.

"You've been here the longest," she told him. "I think a change in scenery might be needed. Plasket!"

"Yes, Ma'am," the other officer replied.

"You and Florez will stand on the line out here," she ordered. "Do not approach the building again. Just keep any onlookers and media away. Got it?"

"Yes, Ma'am." He pointed. "They're the only media here and they've been pretty cooperative."

"So far," she interjected. "And there will be more on the way. This story has gone national. It'll be only a matter of time before more vans or helicopters appear."

"We'll need more people out here," he said, peering towards the young woman he was being posted with.

"I've already recalled Jaye and Roselia from the crime scene out of Jackson," she told him. "Brandon and Jolee will come as soon as forensics finish with everything they need to do."

He nodded compliantly. It was only another four officers, but it was the best they could do.

Morris started along the path towards the south, making for the driveway where his vehicle sat.

"Where are you going, Randy?" Reece asked.

"I thought you wanted to get around to the football field," he pointed to the vehicle access. "We can follow that right around."

"I want to go this way." She pointed to the northern edge of the building. The student carpark and delivery access lane for the cafeteria were on that side of the building.

"That driveway doesn't go all the way around," Morris told her.

"I know," she replied. "But I'm not interested in the driveway. I want to look at the doors to the cafeteria."

"You want to see if we can break in?" he asked.

"I think we should try to get those people out of there as soon as we can."

He nodded and glanced towards the front doors of the school.

"Might I suggest we stick to the path and not take any short-cuts across the lawn?" he said. "Just in case she is sitting in there pointing that gun towards us."

VI

Three of senior students, two boys and one girl, crouched behind a tall bookshelf. Two of them pressed themselves as close to
the wall as they could, shivering from the damp clothing that had
covered their skin for too long.

One boy peered through the books of a stand-alone shelf that
partially obstructed the view of the entry into the library and the
counter beside it. By moving his eyes through the gaps between
books and shelf, he could see the dark silhouette of a girl with a
ponytail and a backpack slung over her shoulders.

He watched her as she stepped quietly towards the middle of
the large room. Her head turned to her left, looking away from
their hiding place. There were more bookshelves in a section near
the far wall, just past a large area with tables and chairs set out
for study groups.

Go that way, he silently prayed. *God, make her go that way,
please.*

He hoped that if she ventured to the furthest side of the library, he might have time to find a better place for himself and
the two that had followed him.

A loud chattering caused him to turn around suddenly.

"Shhh." He held a finger up to his mouth.

The girl covered her mouth, her jaw quivering uncontrollably
from a combination of chill and fear.

The other boy placed his arms around her, rubbing her arms
to warm her skin.

The first boy peered back through the gaps in the books towards the counter by the door.

The girl with the backpack was gone.

His eyes scanned the room, peering intently into the darker places, hoping to find her moving in the shadows.

He tried to focus his hearing on any sounds of water sloshing. He looked for any light rippling through the liquid covering the floor.

It was as if she had disappeared.

Turning back to the other two, he put his finger to his lips before pointing to the edge of the stand-alone bookshelf. He signaled them to follow him as he eased towards the end of the shelving they hid behind.

The girl shook her head.

She didn't want to go anywhere.

The first boy mouthed the words, *Come on.* He wasn't able to tell if she had seen his lips move, so he beckoned with his hand, waving towards himself.

She shook her head defiantly. Her face turned towards the other boy, silently pleading with him to stay.

"We need to go," he whispered as quietly as he could.

She continued shaking her head.

The first boy was struggling with feelings of fear and frustration. In his opinion, they needed to move before the girl with the backpack found them.

"We need to stay together," the other boy told her, keeping his voice to the volume of a quiet breath.

Her chin quivered and her eyes darted around, momentarily locking onto every dark shadow they could find.

She nodded nervously, clinging onto the boy's shirt as he kept his arms around her. He guided her slowly and cautiously towards the first boy, who was standing at the end of the bookshelf.

The first boy had been looking around the edge of the shelving, peering back towards the place where he had seen the silhouette of the girl. She was still nowhere in sight.

He turned to see the others slowly approaching, drawing nearer and nearer.

Good, he thought. *She has finally come to her senses.*

As he turned to look back around the edge of the bookshelf, he felt a strange sensation move across his face. It was sudden and silent. He experienced a little pain, but it was more of a surprise.

As a warm flow spread down his skin, over his neck and across his chest, he still wasn't able to discern what had happened.

He stopped in place, feeling an odd throbbing pulsation through his lips and left eye.

The dark shadows throughout the library grew larger and darker.

A loud sloshing sound filled his ears as he felt a new pain against the side of his head.

He had fallen, and he didn't know why.

There was no gunshot.

There was no sound at all.

Am I dying?

He couldn't tell as the darkness covered all.

He heard a girl screaming in the distance, as if she was at the far end of a long tunnel drifting farther and farther away.

VII

Thinking quickly and steering the girl in the other direction, the second boy moved towards the other end of the bookshelf. She continued to scream as he moved her into the open area between the shelves and the counter by the door.

They raced as fast as they could, sending a flurry of water splashing up all around them.

"Come on," the boy hollered, urging her forward. "Move faster."

Kirstin backtracked along the bookshelf, slipping the freshly stained utility knife back into her right pocket.

"She's coming," he shouted. "Move. Move."

The girl kept screaming, propelled forward only by the boy pushing her onwards.

Kirstin lifted the P229 from the waistband of her jeans with her left hand as she finished stuffing the blade into her pocket with her right. By the time she had both hands on the pistol, she had reached the end of the shelving area and took aim.

"Come on," the boy cried, edging closer and closer to the counter near the door.

It was only a few more paces to the hallway. From there, they could flee to another room and hide again. "Move it."

The girl continued to scream as the shot rang out.

The boy sloshed against the wet floor. His leg twitched slightly, sending tiny waves across the library.

The girl stopped running, frozen with fear.

Her wide eyes stared down at the fallen boy.

Her screams became silent.

The sound of soft splashes approaching filled her senses as some elements of reality came back to her.

The girl realized at that moment, the only other person alive in the room with her wanted to see her die.

Kirstin didn't hesitate. She simply walked up to the girl and placed the muzzle against her head.

The girl fell onto the boy, spilling blood and brain matter across his shirt.

The storm raged, and the lightning flared brightly as the blood rain fell.

Such a shame, she thought as she peered down at the bodies at her feet. *I would have liked some light to see that better.*

The thunder softened.

Focus, it said. *You're not finished yet.*

Kirstin stepped over the bodies and made her way past the counter, through the door and back into the southern corridor. She turned to her left and continued heading towards the southeast corner.

Her pace was a little faster. Each footfall splashed a little, sending ripples and echoing sounds of disturbed water along the length of the passageway.

She no longer cared if they heard her coming. The gunshots were loud and still ringing in her ears.

Her prey knew she was coming for them.

VIII

Florez cursed as she instinctively moved her bandaged hand to her holster.

"Where did that come from?" she asked nervously.

"Down there somewhere." Plasket pointed to the southern end of the building.

"Could she have gotten out?"

"That came from inside," he told her, lifting his walkie-talkie from his belt. "She's moved further inside," he assured the young officer. "Believe me. You'll know it if she shoots at you."

"Are you sure?" she asked.

"Oh yeah," he said, reflecting upon his experience by the front doors as he lifted the radio to his mouth. "Morris, come in."

"Morris here," a voice replied through the speaker.

"She's moved to the southern end of the building," Plasket informed the other. "We just heard shooting coming from inside."

"Understood," Morris replied.

Morris hooked his walkie-talkie back onto his belt. He was crouching by one of the external doors that separated him from the people inside the cafeteria. Water was trickling from underneath, spilling across the path that ran alongside the building and onto the sopping lawn between his position and the students' car park.

"I can't see a way to open these from out here," he told Reece. "Not without some kind of cutting tool."

She was peering over his shoulder, moving her eyes over the door for any sign of weakness or grip-hold. There was nothing. The doors were designed to be opened from the inside.

She stepped forward and pounded on the door.

Several students seated by the door screamed at the sudden sound. Frightened eyes turned, expecting the worst.

"She's coming," Stephanie gasped. "She's coming."

"It's not her," Donny assured her, pulling the girl closer to him. "She's still inside somewhere. You're all right."

She rested her head against his chest, hearing his heart pounding. He was scared, too.

McFarlan moved hastily across the room towards the door.

"Police," a woman's voice called from outside. "Are you okay? Is anyone injured?"

"Is that you, Captain?"

"Kimmie?" the voice called back.

"Yes, Ma'am," she replied. "We don't have any injured, but we have a lot of scared people in here. Any news on when we might be able to get out of here?"

"We're limited on staff at the moment," the captain said through the door. "But we have a chopper heading in from Houston."

"How long, Ma'am?"

"I can't say exactly. Maybe ten minutes max."

Some people clapped upon hearing the news. Others gave a quick cheer. A few of the staff members exchanged embraces, allowing themselves to laugh and smile at the prospect of escaping.

"Shut up," Freddie Morris suddenly snapped.

"What's your problem?" a girl asked. "They're coming to save us."

"And she might just hear how happy you are about it and find a way in here before they get to us," he replied. "She's still has ten minutes. Maybe more."

Delight returned to fear as they realized that they may have signaled Kirstin into speeding up her assault.

"He's right," McFarlan told them. "The captain said they will arrive in ten minutes. They'll need to assess the situation and look for the best way in before these doors come anywhere near to being opened. Until then, we sit tight."

The captain listened to the exchange inside. She turned to Morris, who stood upright, wearing a concerned expression.

"Hang in there, guys," she said through the door. "We're doing everything we can."

"Captain?" McFarlan's called.

"Yeah," Reece placed a hand on the door, wishing that she could simply tear it from its hinges.

"The radio seems to have gone quiet."

"We're communicating on a different channel," she replied. "I want you to stay tuned to the one you're on. That girl might try to contact you again. I don't want to imagine what she might try to do if there isn't anyone there to respond."

"Understood," the young officer replied.

The captain was proud of the woman inside. She was holding up far better than expected.

Reece couldn't imagine what was going on through the young officer's head. She had just lost a colleague and seen things that nobody should ever see.

"Kimmie!" the officer called out. "Randy Morris. Have you seen my son? Freddie?"

"He's right –"

"Dad," the boy called out. "Dad, I'm here. I'm all right."

Morris cried, resting his palm against the door.

"Thank God," he said, as the captain placed a comforting hand on his shoulder. "You hang in there, Freddie. You'll be out soon enough. I promise."

"Okay," the boy answered. "The sooner the better."

"I hear ya!" Morris wiped his eyes.

"We've got to keep moving," Reece told McFarlan. "You keep focused. Okay? We're all thinking of you out here."

"Thanks, Ma'am," came the response.

Reece and Morris continued along the path, heading towards the rear of the building.

"We need to get them out of there," she told him. "I don't know how much longer she can keep this up."

Morris frowned, glancing over his shoulder at the door they had just come from.

"She's tough," he said. "I know I wouldn't have been able to last this long." His mind was more so on his son than it was the young police officer. He knew she had been trained and would do her best. But his boy was only a boy and didn't have the coping mechanisms to make it through something like this.

"Your son's alive, Randy," she said, presuming his thoughts. "He's alive and safe."

"He won't be safe until I get him back home," Morris told her. "I need to call Chantelle so that she knows that he's okay."

Reece nodded. If she was the boy's mother sitting at home, possibly seeing this unfold on the news, she would want to know that her son was all right, too.

"Call her," she told him.

As they continued towards the north- western corner of the building, Morris lifted his phone from his shirt pocket to call his wife.

IX

"E-T-A three minutes," the pilot of the UH-1 Huey helicopter announced through the headset.

The sergeant tapped his wrist where his watch was strapped before holding up three fingers. The others, clad in black tactical gear with HK MP5/10 submachine guns slung onto their chests, nodded to acknowledge the message.

Each of them checked their gear. Flash grenades, smoke bombs, tear gas, spare magazines, side arm and knife. All of this stored in a variety of pockets and pouches on their flak jackets.

Pointing to one of the team members seated beside the open door, the sergeant touched his radio receiver, showing that he wanted to talk to the man. The other responded by switching his radio on.

"Yeah, Sergeant," he called into his mouthpiece, attached to his helmet.

"Leave the pop-gun, Kibble." The leader pointed to a long carry-case resting on the floor of the chopper. "The target is inside the building, moving about. We wouldn't know where to put you."

"No sniper, Sarge?" one of the other men asked.

"I don't remember signaling you to turn your radio on, Garcia," the sergeant remarked.

"Sorry," Garcia replied. "It's just that we don't usually get called to one of these unless we're needed."

"All I know," the sergeant said, "is that there is one lone shooter moving around the school. I also know that the shooter is a sixteen-year-old girl."

The looks shock exchanged between all four men informed the sergeant that they were all listening into the conversation.

"Considering that the school is filled with other students who may appear similar in size and shape," the leader continued, "I would prefer it if we confronted her in closer proximity than required with a sniper rifle."

"Sixteen?" another gasped, shaking his head.

"That's right, Reynes," the sergeant nodded. "Which is also why I would prefer it if we didn't touch triggers during this one. If we can take her alive, I will be a happy man. Understood?"

The men nodded.

Kibble looked out of the door to the ground sweeping by below them. There were paddocks filled with tilled soil, crops, and livestock. Several clusters of houses passed by, showing their closing proximity to the town of Edwards Hill.

"Fine with me, Sarge," he said. "One less thing for me to carry. Garcia's just upset that he won't get to play with his new binoculars."

"They got a new laser sight I want to try," the other replied defensively. "I haven't used them in the field before."

"You're like a fucking kid," Reynes chuckled.

"Like you never wanted to play with new toys," Garcia said.

The sergeant smiled, shaking his head.

"Just remember what we're here to do," he told all of them. "Rescue is priority. We still have people in that building who need to get out alive."

"Do you want me to circle the school before we land?" the pilot asked.

"That would be great," the sergeant replied. "Can you take it wide? I want to see as many windows and doors as we can."

"Sure thing."

X

She stood in the doorway peering into the metal shop room. Benches and large machines lined the walls. There were six large work tables neatly positioned into two columns in the middle of the room with wide spaces between each for people to move between safely.

Industrial-style drill-press machines, lathes, saws sat neatly between bench spaces along the far wall, overlooking a view of the teachers' carpark. Thick bars covered the outside of the windows.

It was there, standing next to a drill-press, that she found two petrified boys, one holding a ball-peen hammer, the other with a long file with a sharpened point.

She cocked her head, eyeing the tools in their hands.

They held them up defensively, shaking uncontrollably from the damp, cold clothes they wore and the fear that gripped them so harshly.

Kirstin lifted P229 and waved it towards them.

The boy with the file broke down, relaxing his arms.

He knew he didn't have a chance.

The other was more defiant. He continued to hold the hammer in front of him.

She took aim and squeezed the trigger.

The boy dropped the file as his chest exploded in a fine spray of red mist.

The second boy's jaw fell open in a silent scream as his friend fell on the wet floor.

Suddenly, his stomach felt as if received a hard, heavy punch.

He looked down to see an expanding flow of red moving from beneath his shirt, over his pants and onto the floor.

Letting the hammer go, he dropped to his knees, clutching his hands over the wound in his gut.

His eyes moved to the girl with the gun. She was tucking it back into her jeans as she moved around the benches in the room, making her way towards the two young men.

She crouched beside the fallen boy with the chest wound.

His face was white, and his lips were turning blue.

He was still alive.

For the moment.

Kirstin reached for the long, sharp file he had dropped, holding it in front of his face tauntingly, swinging it by the handle so that the point passed closely by his right eye.

"Please don't," the one on his knees pleaded.

She gripped the handle tightly, staring coldly into the kneeling boy's eyes as she plunged the file hard into the other one's face.

A loud sickening crunch emitted from the boy's skull as the file slid through his eye and deep into his brain.

The kneeling boy cried, his face contorting into a foul shape that Kirstin found disgusting to look at.

Leaving the other on the floor, file sticking out of his head and legs twitching in spasm, she moved around the kneeling boy and retrieved the hammer from the floor.

The boy closed his eyes.

He knew what was about to happen.

He prepared himself for the impact as she raised the hammer over her head.

A distant sound, like a rapid deep thumping, built.

Growing louder and louder.

His eyes opened and looked up to the face of the girl. She was peering out through the window, searching for the origin of the noise.

The frames holding the glass in place rattled.

She ducked in order to look higher into the sky.

It was crystal blue outside.

Inside, the storm was raging.

They're coming for me, her mind screamed. *I'm out of time.*

The blood rain fell, and the thunder roared.

Focus, the lightning told her calmly.

The large helicopter, painted white and blue with *HOUSTON POLICE* inscribed on the side, flew into view. It swept across the sky just over the staff parking area, lowering slowly towards the road.

"Shit." She ducked, hiding her body below the windowsill, keeping her eyes on the chopper.

"Help me," the kneeling boy tried to call. He was weak. Too much blood had seeped from him and the muscles in his abdomen wouldn't contract in order to help project his voice. "Help me, please." He dropped his head against his chest as tears streamed down his face.

The chopper flew out of view. The terrible sound of pounding continued to thump inside the metal shop classroom.

Kirstin raised herself back up and leaned over to watch the flying mass move away.

"Help me," the boy slurred, barely audible.

She raised the ball-peen hammer over her head before bringing it down with all of her strength towards the kneeling boy.

SEPTIMUS INTERLUDIUM

"THE CALM VOICE MADE ME DO IT"
By Reg Polinski
THE INTERNATIONAL REVIEW
ONLINE BLOG ARTICLE
FRIDAY FEBRUARY 12 2016

On 11th September 2001, one lone gunman went on a rampage at a Washington State Elementary school. He injured five individuals, including two young children. Because of the bravery of one of the male staff members, he was crash tackled to the ground and apprehended by the police. He was sentenced to life imprisonment and now sits in a cell. When asked why he committed such a heinous crime, he simply replied, "The Calm Voice made me do it."

During the terrible winter of 2014-15, another individual mowed through a park in Toledo where he hit and killed two elderly ladies who were drinking coffee and injured a further twelve individuals who were using the grounds as a thoroughfare from a bus station to an office building on the opposite side. His reason for driving his SUV through the park was, "The Calm Voice told me to."

There are many other accounts of such behavior occurring, not only in the USA, but also all over the globe. Dismissed as mere cases of paranoia and schizophrenia, the men deemed guilty for these terrible crimes have been isolated and exposed to treatment for a sickness that they may never truly be cured of.

Nor will they ever be.

Clumped with countless other cases where the perpetrators have claimed the voices made them do it, these particular cases will simply disappear over time and vanish from our memories if they haven't done so already.

Why?

Because they weren't newsworthy.

Other more pressing news stories made the front pages on each of these days when the crimes of the Calm Voice were committed.

The Bali Bombings in 2002; the Boxing Day Tsunami in 2004; Hurricane Katrina in 2005; The Execution of Saddam Hussein in 2006; The Mumbai attacks in 2008. Even the death of Michael Jackson in 2009 achieved precedence over any of the cases involving the Calm Voice.

It's almost as if the acts of the Calm Voice herald an event that would spark the interest of the populous. An event that would knowingly overshadow anything else appearing in the media. An event far more memorable.

How many victims, how many injured, how many slain?

How many can we attribute to the Calm Voice?

Officially, none.

They were all cases, are all cases of mental instability. Open and shut.

No one, either in authority or in the general public, is interested in the crimes of the Calm Voice. None, except the families of the victims.

After extensive research, we can state that none of these crimes are directly related in any way, shape, or form.

None of the victims knew their attackers. None of the attackers knew each other.

There is no Calm Voice Club where people sit around and discuss their intended assaults. If anything, it could be said that the perpetrators are as far removed from each other as anyone could possibly be.

One sanitation worker, a bunch of lawyers, bankers, mechanics, teachers, homemakers, and one reporter for a foreign newspaper, the spectrum and range is as wide as it is deep. And it is not only confined to occupation, but racial variation and cultural diversity.

There appears to be no pattern.

The only commonality is that all those arrested claimed that the same individual instructed them to perform the attacks.

The Calm Voice.

So, who is the Calm Voice?

As mentioned before, some have suggested that it is a product of schizophrenic disorders. A malfunction of the mind.

Others have hinted that it is a mere excuse or justification created by the perpetrators for their acts.

Some would say that the Calm Voice is an entity, or group of individual entities that influence certain individuals at their lowest point.

In any case, I expect that more cases involving the Calm Voice will eventuate. The biggest fear we should concern ourselves with is the one case that won't be overridden by bigger news stories on the day.

In this reporter's opinion, it's only inevitable, a matter of time before we read about the Calm Voice in headline news.

Sadly, as a society, we simply overlook these things and move on with our lives without questioning the deeper meaning behind why these kinds of things happen in our world.

It has become the norm, and we have become numb to it.

DEMENS : SENSELESS

Great wits are sure to madness near allied;
And thin partitions do their bonds divide.

JOHN DRYDEN, *Absalom and Achitophel*

I

"What are they doing?" Florez shouted over the din. She held onto her hat, pressing it against her scalp as the aircraft passed overhead.

"No idea," Plasket replied as dust clouds burst into the surrounding air.

"What?" the young woman called, covering her eyes and turning around to face away from the onslaught of fine debris and leaves being tossed from the surrounding trees.

"No idea," the other repeated, hollering louder.

Florez glimpsed the reporter across the road holding her skirt with one hand as she continued to give a running commentary into the microphone that she held in the other. Her eyes were all but squeezed shut as her hair waved violently in all directions.

The camera tilted upwards, following the helicopter as it circumnavigated the school building. As it moved away to the northern edge of the yard, the wind subsided, allowing the dust and leaves to resettle upon the ground.

"Shit." Florez started spitting onto the ground. "I think I swallowed half of Texas."

"Shit." Plasket's eyes fixed on a vehicle approaching from down the road. He was half expecting parents of school children or more media to turn up. But what he saw was far worse. "Shit! Shit!"

"What?" Florez spun around to see a large black SUV approaching. "Shit!"

The Huey continued along the northern face of the high school building, making its way towards the football field behind the school. Both Captain Julia Reece and Officer Randy Morris were standing by the bleachers, waiting for it to land.

"Captain, you there?" a voice called from Morris' walkie-talkie.

"Give me that," she said to the officer, reaching her hand out to him. He lifted the radio from his belt and handed it over promptly. "Reece here."

"We got trouble out here," Plasket told her. "The mayor just showed up."

"Shit," she said to Morris. The sound of the helicopter grew louder as it reached an area parallel to the north-east corner of the building.

"You want me to..." Plasket's voice disappeared in the aircraft's sound passing over the bleachers to hover above the field.

"I can't hear you," she yelled into the walkie-talkie. "Hold him there until I return. I'll be there as soon as I can."

Both Morris and Reece watched the chopper land gently on the fifty-yard line. Within moments, five men loaded with a variety of equipment had jumped down from the Huey and started across the football field towards them.

The chopper's engine changed tone as the pilot relaxed the throttle and prepared to cut the engines. One of the approaching men pointed over his shoulder with his thumb as he drew closer to the two awaiting people.

"You don't mind if we park here, do you?" he asked.

"Not at all," Reece replied, shaking her head.

"Sergeant Phillips," the man announced, extending his hand.

She took it and smiled politely. "Captain Reece," she replied before turning to the man beside her. "This is Officer Morris."

The sergeant shook the man's hand and looked past the bleachers towards the school building.

"Where do you want us to call home base?" Phillips asked.

"Ah..." She looked at Morris for an answer. His face appeared just as confused as she felt. "I really don't know. I've got two more officers standing on the line out the front. Local media has been out there most of the time and the mayor just showed up."

"We have someone inside," Morris told him.

The sergeant's ears perked up. "Where?"

"In the cafeteria," the officer replied.

"Where's that?"

"Just along the side over here." Morris pointed towards the northern wall.

"Have you been in contact with him?"

"Her," Reece told him. "We just spoke to her before you arrived. She got quite a few people in there before locking the shooter out of the room."

"Why haven't they tried to get out themselves?"

"The shooter padlocked the external doors shut," the captain informed him.

Phillips signaled his men to follow him as he started walking towards the school building.

"Do you know if she locked all of them?" He peered towards the doors that were positioned along the eastern wall that led into the gymnasium. "These for example. Are they locked?"

"We don't know," Morris told him. "We haven't investigated the scene. You've got three uniformed cops on the scene and two more in the field."

"I've got four more on their way as soon as they are available," Reece told him.

"Where are they?" Phillips asked as they moved towards the corner of the school.

"They were on the phones when I left them," she replied.

"Please don't presume that I'm making some statement about country police or about your capabilities as a captain when I say this," he said as he stopped in his tracks right beside the corner. "I'm sure you earned your position, Ma'am, and you have my full respect and I'm at your command while I am here. But I have seen a few of these kinds of things throughout my career and sometimes they go balls-up.

"Some of those balls-up times aren't because the unsub has acted out. They're already doing that, anyway. Sometimes it's because of the families of victims who gather on the line and overrun the officers positioned there. You'll need more than three uniformed cops here for crowd control before this is over."

She nodded, taking his words as sound advice as she lifted her cell phone from her jacket pocket. Taking a few steps towards the delivery access lane nearby, she ran her finger through her contacts list and pressed to dial the station.

"I think we'll set up there," Phillips told his men, pointing to a dry patch of concrete path between the two doors that led into the cafeteria.

II

Kirstin wheeled a trolley laden with a two gas tanks and welding equipment attached to it. One tank labeled O2, the other C2H2.

They clinked together occasionally as she pushed it slowly before her. The water on the floor was still deep enough to leave an expanding wake around her as the trolley broke the surface of the liquid.

She moved towards the north-east corner of the corridor, passing the center corridor. Her eyes moved into the long passage to her left, seeing the two boys lying by the front doors in the distance.

She paused at the end of the passage, scanning the doors on either side of the room.

There are still two more, she thought.

Standing the trolley upright, she lifted the Beretta from behind her and stepped into the corridor.

One by one, she opened the classroom doors, finding the first four rooms empty. She wondered if the last two students who had escaped from upstairs might have returned to the upper level. Perhaps they had discovered a new place to hide.

The next room on the right was a science laboratory classroom.

She pushed the door open and entered the room.

To her right were work benches set up for the students to work at. To her left was the demonstration counter. She moved beside the counter, passing the large whiteboard on the wall as she peered along the aisles on either side of the working benches.

The room was empty.

A door leading to the preparation room sat on the far side of the wall behind her. The room was a small space where teachers could store equipment and set up class experiments. It sat neatly between two labs and serviced both classrooms with doors leading to both.

A small window beside the door leading to the prep room allowed her to peer inside.

She could see drawers and shelves, cabinets and trolleys laden with a variety of equipment and supplies.

Carefully, quietly, she turned the knob on the door and stepped into the room. It smelled like a cross between a chlorine pool and a hospital.

She moved around a bench positioned in the middle of the room, making her way for the door on the opposite wall that would take her into the lab next door.

Peering through the window by the door, she scanned the room with her eyes, hunting for the two escapees.

The two girls sat on the wet floor behind the last workbench on the farthest side of the room from the door. The two girls were exposed to the elements of water and cool air. Their almost bare backs pressed against the cold bricks of the back wall as they wrapped their arms tightly around each other, sobbing, sniffling and shivering together.

"D-d-do you th-th-think sh-sh-sh-sh-she's c-c-c-coming?" one with her hair in braids managed.

"I d-d-d-don't kn-n-n-know," the other replied, sitting to the braid-wearer's left. Her upper body shook uncontrollably as it tried to warm itself.

A soft, long squeak came from the front of the room.

"W-w-w-what was that?" the girl in braids asked, whispering as quietly as she could.

The other shook her head.

I don't know.

"T-t-t-take a l-l-l-look," the braided girl suggested.

The other shook her head more sternly.

No frigging way.

"G-g-go on," the girl with braids urged.

Staring at her friend with wide eyes, her chin quivering and her hands shaking, she took a deep breath to muster all the courage she could.

It didn't come too quickly.

She removed her arms from the braided girl's shoulders and leaned over to her left.

From her place of perspective, she could see the door leading into the prep room.

It was wide open.

She couldn't remember if it was open when they had first entered the room. She was too busy running for her life and trying to find a place to hide.

I don't think it was;; she thought. *I think it was shut.*

She leaned back into her friend.

"W-w-was the p-p-prep room d-d-door open w-w-when we first came in h-h-here?"

"I d-d-d-didn't see," the girl in braids replied.

There was a quiet sloshing in the thin layer of water covering the floor, emitting from somewhere in front of them.

Small waves rippled from the front of the room, along the aisles between the work benches to collide softly against the back wall of the science lab.

The girls' hearts seemed to stop beating.

The world around them fell silent except for the sound of water moving around the room.

With all of their might, they tried desperately to silence every snivel, every sob, every chatter of their teeth.

SHLOSH!

The water splashed softly, sending another group of fresh ripples towards them.

The braided girl put her hand over her own mouth, hoping that it would muffle the sounds she was making.

It didn't.

SHLOSH!

More ripples rolled across the thin layer of water.

The girls both closed their eyes; an instinctive reaction they had shared watching scary movies. If you don't see the monster, the monster won't hurt you.

SLOSH!

The sound was close.

Too close.

The braided girl knew the monster was here.

This wasn't a movie she could hide under the covers from.

The monster wasn't going to simply leave her alone.

She opened her eyes and peered up at the sweet face of a young girl wearing a t-shirt and jeans, standing on the opposite side of the working bench they were hiding behind. The girl wore her hair in a neat ponytail and didn't appear that much younger than herself.

This is the monster?

Kirstin stood with both hands behind her back, smiling down at the braided girl.

The girl with braided hair furrowed her brow. She didn't understand why she was being hunted by such a person.

It made little sense.

Kirstin's smile turned to a dark grimace as she raised her right arm. Her hand held a glass bottle containing a clear, yellowish tinged liquid. The braided girl's eyes fell upon a white label with letters and numbers stenciled on it.

H2SO4.

The girl in braids screamed. She knew exactly what the glass bottle held.

The second girl opened her eyes and turned just in time to see the container leave Kirstin's hand.

It flung through the air at an intense velocity, heading directly for her head.

The girl felt her stomach tighten into a knot as her friend continued to scream and she attempted to move out of the way of the bottle.

It was too late.

The glass broke apart as it hit the side of her head.

She saw stars dance around her as the clear liquid splashed over her skin.

The contents of the bottle sprayed over the girl in braids, splashing in her screaming mouth, spraying into her wide-open eyes.

Kirstin stepped back and moved to the side of the bench so that she could watch what happened next.

The first girl's head lolled against her chest. The impact of the glass bottle striking her head was enough to knock her out.

The second girl, still screaming, frantically splashed water from the floor onto her face, on her eyes, into her mouth.

"Does it burn?" Kirstin asked her curiously, lifting herself onto the workbench to observe the occurrence. "What does it feel like?"

The girl in braids screamed shrilly as the sulfuric acid ate into the nerves inside her eyelids.

Thunder and lightning played loudly in Kirstin's head as the crimson clouds danced wildly.

She didn't like these girls.

Her eyes ran along their long legs that extended from beneath tiny shorts. More skin appeared above the hem, vanishing once again under tiny singlet tops that barely covered their chests.

She remembered the girl with braids in her hair from the morning and in the cafeteria. She had been trying to flirt with Donny, rather unsuccessfully.

"Slut," Kirstin said. "You're just like Stephanie and her bitches."

The girl in braids screamed louder as the pain became unbearable.

Kirstin was becoming bored.

She lifted the Beretta and fired a round into the unconscious girl's head.

The girl in braids stopped her shattering cries. She tried to look about her, but her eyes were half closed, red and swelling. She began wiping her eyes with shaking hands, whimpering loudly.

"Wavz abbening?" she grunted.

Kirstin pictured her tongue acting similar to her eyes, swelling and burning as the acid laced her skin.

She smiled at the sight and sound of the girl struggling with her words.

"Elb me." She reached out around her with outstretched arms and open fingers. There were no tears, but the girl was crying. "Bleeze elb me."

Focus, said the calm voice. *There is still work to be done.*

"Bleeze." The girl almost seemed to choke on her words. Her hands fell upon her friend. Upon realizing that there was no longer any life there, she bawled.

"Donny is mine," Kirstin said coldly.

She raised the Beretta again and fired.

III

"What's going on?" Martin Saunders asked the young female officer quietly. They were standing in the kitchen area of the cafeteria, out of earshot of the students and most of the other teaching staff in the room. Only Aiden Fisk could hear their conversation as he stood by the sink, opening a box of granola bars he had found in the pantry.

"I don't know," McFarlan replied, shaking her head.

"We heard the helicopter some time ago," he continued. "Don't they usually break the door down by now?"

"This is my first time doing this too," she told him. "I have no idea how long it could take them. I'm scared too."

He locked eyes with her and felt ashamed. She held herself extremely well and deserved better treatment than he had given her.

"I'm sorry," he said, frowning. "I'm really sorry."

She placed her hand on his shoulder. "It's okay."

They held their gaze, communicating silently, neither knowing exactly what was transpiring.

"It's only been five minutes," Fisk interjected as he ripped the top from the cardboard box.

"What?" McFarlan turned to him, breaking the moment passing between Saunders and herself.

"I said it's only been five minutes," he repeated. "Or thereabouts. Since the helicopter landed, I mean."

"Seems longer," Saunders said, looking at his watch. It might have been helpful if he had been keeping an eye on the time, but he hadn't.

"I saw two more boxes of these in there," Fisk informed them. "I think we should distribute these and get some water out to the kids. I noticed some cases of bottled water in the cool room."

"That's a good idea," the cop replied.

"I'll get the water," Saunders offered, making his way towards the passage to the side of the kitchen.

"I'll get another box," the other teacher said, leaving the one he had just opened on the bench by the sink.

McFarlan picked up the carton of granola bars and carried them into the eatery. She walked over to the serving counter and placed them on a table next to Lindsay Merrick, the English teacher.

"Hey," the officer announced herself to the other.

"Hi." Merrick smiled politely, sitting in a seat, holding tightly onto a towel that was wrapped around her shoulders.

"How are you holding up?" McFarlan asked.

"I'm okay," she replied. "A little scared."

"Then you're doing better than me," she said before leaning in close and whispering, "I'm scared shitless."

Merrick smiled and nodded. "Me too."

"Do you feel up to doing something for me?"

The teacher nodded.

"I need these handed out." McFarlan pointed to the granola bars. "Could you organize the other teachers and get these out to the students first?"

"Will there be enough?" she quizzed, eyeing the size of the box.

"We have more on their way and some bottled water," the cop informed her.

"Okay." The teacher stood up before calling softly across the table to another teacher. "Sandra, can you help me, please?"

The other woman nodded and lifted herself from her seat.

McFarlan placed a gentle hand on Merrick's shoulder and gave it a reassuring squeeze. She then retreated to the kitchen, where another open box of granola bars waited to be delivered.

Before long, they had provided all students and staff members in the room with sustenance. It wasn't enough to ease the fear that continued to invade their thoughts, but it was a temporary relief as they focused their attention on something else for a moment in time.

That was until the large wooden door panel on the south-western side of the room rumbled.

Something outside the room in the corridor thumped against the door.

There were some gentle knocks and more rumbles that immediately followed, building tension and fear again.

"She's back." Stephanie cried.

Donny put his granola bar down and wrapped his arms around her again. Her body was shaking, almost convulsing as her nerves seemed to lose all control.

"She's back. She's back. She's back."

"Shhh. It's okay," Donny whispered into her ear. "We're safe."

"Hey," a boy called from behind them. All eyes turned to see the student thumping his fist against the door that led to the student carpark. "Are you cops still out there? Hey?"

"We're here," a man's voice replied. "I'm Sergeant Phillips. We're working as fast as we can to get you out, son."

A loud scraping noise emitted from outside the cafeteria from the hallway beyond the large wooden panel door.

"I think she's working as fast as she can to get in here, man," the boy hollered back.

Suddenly, the sounds coming from within the school stopped.

"Shhh," someone hissed to the boy. "I think she hears you."

The cafeteria fell silent.

All ears strained to hear if there was any sound of movement from the passageway.

Nothing.

"What's your name, son?" Phillips' voice called from the other door.

Several people jumped at the sudden intrusion.

"Naw, man." The boy pressed his face to the crack where door met building, whispering to the man outside. "She's here, listening to us. You gotta get us out now."

"Okay," Phillips replied in a lower volume. "Hang in there. You'll be out here with us soon."

The room remained quiet, except a few people sobbing here and there.

Without warning, the scraping noise started again. It sounded like something grating across the linoleum, slowly being dragged along the floor.

Several people winced at the noise. It reminded a few teachers of educators in their past, scraping fingernails over a chalkboard. Others imagined a dentist drill boring a deep hole into the enamel casing of their teeth before moving through bone and nerve.

It seemed to go on forever and ever.

Each of them was silently willing it to stop.

The screeching continued for a moment longer, ceasing at last with a final thud against the large wooden panel.

The rumble emitted loudly through the cafeteria, met with a mix of relieved sighs and fearful shrieks.

McFarlan felt her chest tighten as silence ensued. Although she was glad the terrible noise had stopped, she knew it had some significance to the girl outside the doors.

Kirstin was busying herself with something.

The cop figured the girl must have a plan.

And the plan would not be of any benefit to those within the room.

IV

"What the hell is going on?" a large man with gray hair wearing a dark suit hollered as he rounded the corner of the school building, marching angrily towards the SWAT team huddled near the door to the cafeteria.

Morris held his finger to his lips and a hand up to quieten to approaching man.

"Don't shush me, Officer Morris," he barked as he hurried along the path that ran alongside the building. He moved his eyes to Reece, who was standing beside the door, trying to listen to what was transpiring inside. "Why did I have to find out about this from the TV news and not from you, Captain? Shouldn't I have been apprised of what is going on?"

"Mister Mayor," she said, "the incident unfolded rather rapid—"

"I should have been notified the very moment when the first shot was fired." He started turning red in the face. "Instead, I hear that we may have... *May have*, they said on the news, a dead cop in there, and who knows how many teachers and kids."

"As I was saying," Reece said, "this unfolded rather rapidly. We don't know what is happening in there. All we know is that there are a bunch of people inside this room right here who need to get out. We know there is a student who is shooting at people."

"Killing people in a school that is occupied by people in my constituency, Captain," the mayor interjected angrily.

"We're doing the best we can with what we have," she argued.

"And what's with the fucking chopper?" he snapped. "You scared half the town with that shit."

"We called Houston for more people," she replied.

"You can find time to call Houston, but not the mayor of the town you're in?"

Running a hand-held wall scanner along the edge of the door, Garcia showed signs of irritation.

"Shut the fuck up," he hissed.

"What did you say to me?" There was more than a hint of anger and arrogance in the mayor's voice.

Garcia lowered the scanner to his side, turning to lock eyes with the old man, wanting so much to knock his face in.

"I said, shut the fuck up. We're trying to do our job."

"And who the hell are you?"

Phillips quickly lifted himself to his feet and stepped between his observer and the mayor.

"He's mine," the sergeant interjected. "And if you want to speak to any of my men, you need to speak to me first."

"And you are?"

"Sergeant Phillips," he replied. "Or you can call me the guy who's going to knock you on your ass and drag you back across the line of police tape out there."

"How dare—" the mayor said.

"Shuttup," Phillips interrupted. "I haven't finished. I'm also the guy who's going to arrest you for obstruction to a police operation, which is what you are doing right now."

"I'll have your job, Reece," the big man snapped.

The color drained from her face.

Phillips stepped closer to the mayor, almost touching.

"Don't threaten her," he said. "She doesn't work for you. She works for the state. The state appointed her. You are just some town suit and tie realtor who got all of his friends to choose him over some local farmer. You're nothing compared to her.

"On top of all of this, I plan on reporting your conduct to the authorities. You're preventing me from doing my job right now. And if there's one thing I really find annoying, it's when assholes who think they're the big cheese try to inject their authority into situations where they have none.

"Now!" Phillips pointed over the mayor's shoulder. "Keith Owens, mayor of Edwards Hill, fuck off back to the line with the rest of the civilians before I put you in cuffs and lock you in one of the police vehicles out there for the national media to see."

The mayor pursed his lips and stood his ground defiantly.

His eyes darted from Phillips to Reece, back and forth, as he considered his options.

Phillips reached for a pocket on his vest, lifting the Velcro tab with a loud ripping sound. The glint of metal flashed in the mayor's eyes, and he realized the sergeant was retrieving his handcuffs.

Without a word, the big man turned and stormed away, reaching into his jacket pocket and pulling out his cell phone.

"Thank you," Reece said.

"It's all right," Phillips replied. "You don't need to be worried about people like him. They're all talk and all bullshit."

"You must have done a bit of research before coming here," she said.

"What?" he said, crouching beside his men again. "Knowing his name and job? I always make some mental notes about the place I'm about to work in. Mayor's name and background. Captain's name and background. Unsub's name and background. Number of hostages. That kind of thing."

"Where do you get that information?" Morris asked. "There's no way they could get files together quick enough."

"Home base relays it all to me over the radio on the way out," he explained as he opened a black gym bag by his feet. "Most guys take notes, but I've always had a great memory."

"Sergeant's got a steel-trap mind," Reynes quipped. "You don't ever want to lie to him. He'll catch if you ever slip up with your stories."

The other men smiled and nodded, knowing this to be true through experience.

"Take this one time," Reynes continued. "I told the guys that I got with this girl in Baytown. That part was true. But when I told them she could bend her leg over her neck like a pretzel..."

"That's enough," Philips interjected as he lifted a small, hand-held blow torch from the bag. "Let's keep our heads on what we're doing."

"Sergeant." The other nodded, accepting the slight rebuke as the other men around him snickered and smiled.

Garcia had used a thick black permanent marker to draw three circles on the door and frame; one near the top, one in the middle and the last near the bottom.

"I've marked the hinges, Sarge," he informed the team leader.

Phillips ignited the blowtorch with a small, chrome flint striker that was clipped to the side of the device. With one quick squeeze of the striker, a bright yellow flame burst from the spout of the torch. The sergeant reattached the flint striker to the clip on the side before turning a dial set above the nozzle, turning the flame from yellow to blue.

"Who's got the CO2?" the sergeant asked.

"I have," answered the last man in the team, holding up a small red tank with a hose sticking from its top.

"Get ready, Juarez." Phillips moved into position so that he could start cutting near the bottom of the door. "I'm doing this blind, so there's a good chance the timber will catch before we cut through the hinges. Don't open on me with that thing unless I tell you to. Got it?"

"Sure thing, Sarge," Juarez replied, standing at his leader's side at the ready with the extinguisher.

Phillips pushed the tip of the flame into the line where the door met the doorframe. The paint turned black first before the timber splintered little by little, opening the gap slightly.

V

"I can smell something burning," a girl sitting by the door announced.

McFarlan made her way through the groups seated around tables, pushing past some who had stood to see what the girl was talking about.

Though the light in the room was dim, the officer could see smoke rising from the door. She could smell the unmistakable scent of burning wood and metal as a sharp, bright, blue flame burst through the edge of the lowest hinge.

"Move back," she ordered the groups gathered about. "Move away from the door. They're cutting through."

The sound of scraping chairs erupted as many students moved, lifting themselves from their seats to create an open space by the door.

A fine red glow grew brighter and brighter on the metal that joined the wooden panel in the doorframe.

It was slow going as the flame gradually moved into the hinge, casting a thin line of dark smoke along the edge of the door.

"This is going to take a while," said a boy. "Isn't it?"

"Move your chairs and find a new place to sit," McFarlan told them.

Stephanie shivered, her feet on the edge of her chair as she hugged her knees against her chest. Donny kept his arms around her, rubbing her shoulders to keep her warm.

"You hear that?" he said to her. "They're coming to get us out of here, Steph. You'll be home soon."

She was crying as she felt some relief, but there was still a strong sense that she still needed to fear what moved about the school on the other side of the room from her.

Kirstin was in the teachers' lounge, taking a breakfast bowl from a cupboard near the sink before grabbing a bag of powdered sugar from the bench top where a pot of coffee was steaming away. She placed the sugar bag into the bowl and returned to the passageway.

Focus.

With a quick look towards the front door, checking to see that she was clear to move, she started towards the science labs farther along the corridor. Glancing over her shoulder now and then, she continued to search through the glass panels of the front doors for any sign of the police attempting another approach.

Only the bodies of the two dead boys were any sign of human existence. She couldn't even see the cops guarding the area outside the taped line far in the distance near the road.

Her feet slapped against the wet surface of the floor. Most of the water had run out of the building, or to lower sections of the ground floor.

She wasn't concerned about the noise her feet made anymore. Although there were still people upstairs she could pursue, it was the group inside the cafeteria that had her full attention.

The arrival of the helicopter presented an untimely urgency to see her task fulfilled. The cop hadn't handed Stephanie over to her. So she needed to take the bitch instead.

The thunder was distant, and the clouds were gently moving in circles. The storm had subsided for now. But she wanted it back.

She needed it back.

She ached for the lightning and the blood rain.

Carrying the bowl with the sugar bag, Kirstin entered the science lab and made her way directly to the preparation area between the two classrooms. She put the bowl on the counter and lifted the bag of sugar out before resting it beside the dish.

She slid open a door to a cabinet positioned above her on the wall and reached inside to retrieve a jar of white powder. It had a label made of masking tape with letters and numbers written in thick magic marker, *KCIO3*. In brackets beneath the large letters were the words *Potassium Chlorate*.

Removing the lid, she tilted the contents into the bowl. She took a glass rod from a drawer nearby and stirred the powder about, removing lumps that had formed.

She then opened the bag of sugar and added the contents to the white powder. Again, using the glass rod, she mixed the ingredients carefully until she felt satisfied with her efforts.

Moving across the room, she returned to a cupboard where she had discovered the last component during her earlier visit into the room. She reached in and lifted out another glass bottle of H2SO4, Sulfuric Acid.

Carrying the bottle in one hand, she lifted the bowl carefully in with the other and returned through the science lab, back into the passageway. She moved along the hallway towards the eastern end before turning left, making her way towards the cafeteria. She passed the maintenance office, gymnasium and stairwell in the north-eastern corner before turning left again to walk by the first large wooden panel that led into the eatery.

The next large door was her destination. There, she had placed a table she had dragged from a classroom just down the hallway. Next to it, pressed against the large panel, was the trolley with the welding rig attached.

Kirstin placed the bowl of combined white powder and bottle of sulfuric acid carefully on the table, lifted the utility knife out of her pocket and extended the blade as she approached the welding rig.

She started sawing into the long rubber tubing, connecting the welding torch to the tanks, near the valve attached to the top of the oxygen bottle. It was slow going, but she was determined to see it through, adhering to the voice inside that guided her on.

Focus.
Focus.
Focus.

VI

A cable was fixed to a portable power supply sitting near the rear hatch of the van. It snaked along the ground, up one leg of the tripod where it was jacked into the camera. Dwyers had angled the lens just so to keep both cops and one of their cars in shot before locking the mount in place so he could get some coffee.

He sat in the back of the vehicle, next to the power supply, with his feet on the ground as he drained a cup of the hot, bitter liquid from his Thermos. Peterson continued to stand by the camera, monitoring the mayor as he paced back and forth along the police tape, talking on his cell phone.

She had noticed the old man on the device since reappearing from the side of the high school several minutes earlier. He had made numerous calls in that time, chatting briefly, only to hang up and dial again for another brief conversation.

"Mister Mayor," she called, crossing the road towards him. He didn't hear her, continuing to look towards the school as he talked on his phone. "Mister Mayor."

He turned and held a finger up to her. *Wait*.

"Did you get all that?" he said before waiting for the other to reply. "Good."

He pressed the phone's screen and turned his attention to the reporter.

"Mister Mayor, I'm Samantha Peterson from Edwards Hill News. We're an associate of Harwell Corporation. Channel thirty-six in Dallas and Houston."

"I know who you are, Miss Peterson," he interjected abruptly. "I know what you're after. In my opinion, all news reporters, like yourself, are nothing more than vultures waiting for the lions to leave the carcass so you can get your share.

"Is that what you're here for, Miss Peterson?" He pointed to the school. "Are you waiting for your share of the carcass?"

"This is news, Mister Mayor," she replied, a lump forming in her throat.

"Then you should go back over there," he said, pointing to the news van, "and report your news."

"You don't want to go on record?" she asked him. "You don't want to make a statement at all?"

"You want a statement?" he said, lifting his phone in front of him so he could start pressing and swiping the screen again. "I have two words. No comment."

With that, he turned away from her and placed the phone against his ear.

Who are you calling? she wondered as she returned to the vehicle.

He pulled his phone away from his ear and pressed something, ending the call. Swiping across the screen once, twice, he pressed his finger down and returned the device to his ear.

Her phone played *Wild Thing* by the Troggs.

I hope he's not calling me;; she joked to herself.

"Phone's ringing," Dwyers called from the back of the van, stating the obvious.

She quickly opened the passenger door and reached up to the dash console and retrieved the apparatus. It was working its way through the instrumental introduction of the song and was almost about to let Reg Presley sing the opening line when she pressed the green *ANSWER* button on the screen.

"Yeah," she said.

"Sam, it's Jerry," the voice on the other end of the line announced. "You've got choppers inbound from CNN and Fox."

"Choppers are coming, Wayne," she called over her shoulder.

"You might need to get a little dirty," Jerry continued. "Tell Wayne to get mobile so you can get right up on that line. Do what you got to do to get the story. Okay?"

"Got it, Jerry," she said. The phone line was dead before she finished replying. It didn't matter. She had an idea. "Get the camera ready to move. I gotta do something."

She started across the street to the two cops standing on the line.

"Where are you going?" Dwyers called after her as he rounded the vehicle to stand by the tripod.

The camera caught her engaging in conversation with the two officers. There were several fingers pointed in the school's direction by both parties before Peterson pointed to the sky.

The officer lifted his radio from his belt and walked a few paces away to hold a discussion. As he did so, Peterson kept talking to the female cop, pointing towards the north of the high school building and back to the van several times.

Within moments, the male police officer returned and pointed to the van before swinging his arm around to point to the student carpark. Dwyers furrowed his brow at Peterson's reaction. She clasped her hands and gave a little bend in the knees as a great smile spread across her face.

She moved briskly back towards the camera operator, a small hop in her step.

"What did you do?" he asked.

"You haven't packed the gear yet?"

"Samantha?"

"We're going to move the van around to the access lane for delivery vehicles," she told him. "We'll set up the camera where the SWAT team is cutting into one door. The police will tape the driveway shut behind us. We'll be the only mobile news team with permission to be right there when people are released from the building."

He stared at to her, wide-eyed and shocked.

"Pack the gear, Wayne!" She clapped her hands. "We need to move now."

VII

It wasn't long before the news van parked in the access road that led to the back door of the cafeteria's kitchen. Morris had directed Dwyers to park on a section of the driveway parallel to where the SWAT team was working.

After parking the vehicle, the camera operator set his equipment up on an angle so he could watch the police officers work over their right shoulders. He locked the tripod off and ran the cable back to the portable power unit in the back of the van.

A thin line of black smoke wafted across the face of the door as the camera captured one of the SWAT team members cutting into the side of the panel, near to the ground, with a blowtorch.

Behind them, back along the access lane, Plasket stretched a fresh roll of police tape across the driveway. He had tied one end around a telegraph post on one side of the lane, and the other wrapped around a tree, effectively placing an elevated line across the vehicle access.

He tied it off as best he could and dropped the rest of the spooled tape on the ground by the trunk of the tree. Satisfied with his efforts, he walked back along the street towards Florez. She was eyeing the mayor, who had crossed the road after making several phone calls, and was now standing with his arms folded over his enlarged middle as he stared back at her.

"You okay?" Plasket asked her as he stepped to her side.

"That old bastard keeps looking at me," she replied, nodding towards the observer across the road. "He hasn't taken his eyes off me since he moved over there."

"Maybe he likes you," the other joked.

"He's up to something," she said.

Two vehicles rounded the corner at the far end of the street. They made their way along the road, pulling up near the two police vehicles parked at the entrance to the school staff car park.

Moments later, eight police officers in full uniform made their way towards Florez and Plasket. They were a mixed bunch of three women and five men, varying in ages from experienced officers to young boys and girls.

"Hey Cory," one of the older men called.

"Charlie," Plasket called back. "I thought you weren't back on shift until tonight."

"Captain called us all back on duty," the older man replied. "I've only had four hours of sleep. Hope there's coffee."

"No such luck," the other informed him before gesturing to the younger officer standing with him. "This is Summer Florez."

"Rookie?" the older man asked.

"Yessir." She held her left hand out to him, consciously keeping her bandaged hand by her side. He took it with a smile and shook it sternly.

"Lieutenant Charlie Sedgewick," he replied. "How did I never notice you?"

"I'm still on probation, sir," she told him. "The captain keeps me pretty close."

"Of course she does," Sedgewick nodded, letting her hand go. "Bet she only has you on day shift and working the office. Right?"

"Yessir."

"Then that's why I've never noticed you." He scanned the building slowly. "What do we know, Summer?"

"Sir?"

"Inside there." He pointed with his chin as he placed his hands on his hips.

"One shooter, we think," she said. "At least one police officer dead and an unknown number of other victims, sir."

"Doug Borden, right?" he looked over to Plasket.

"Yeah," the other replied. "Kimmie McFarlan's in there too."

"In the cafeteria, I hear," Sedgewick remarked.

"The captain is around the side with Randy and the SWAT team," Plasket told him. "They're cutting through the door now."

"Good." The lieutenant nodded. "Media?"

"Local have been given access to observe the SWAT team rescuing the people in the cafeteria."

Sedgewick shot a look to the other officers gathered around.

"That's a little unorthodox," he remarked, shaking his head before thrusting his thumb over his shoulder towards the mayor. "What about this asshole?"

"He's been on the phone since the captain ordered him out of the taped area."

"I bet he didn't take that too well." Sedgewick looked around the lawn. "Where are all the other kids that made it out?"

"Across the street." Plasket pointed. "Randy and I moved them around back of the elementary school a while back."

"They probably need food and water." He turned to the group. "Rhonda, Dennis, check on them and then order pizza and a shitload of drinks from Pontrelli's. Put it on the station's tab."

The two officers darted across the road, passing the mayor, who maintained his posture, crossing his arms and glaring towards the police officers.

"Francis," the lieutenant called.

A young female officer stepped forward. "Lieutenant."

"I want you to do a coffee run," he told her. "Keep it basic. Black for everyone. Grab a shitload of satchels of sugar and that fake sweetener stuff. Get some cream to go around and those stirring sticks. Take Paul with you. We'll need..." he started moving his lips as he counted with his fingers. "There are five in the SWAT team, right?" he asked Plasket.

"Yeah." The other furrowed his brow. "Why?"

"Seventeen large cups," he continued telling Francis. "Get them from Fisher's Diner and tell them the situation, and that I'll fix him up when I get the chance."

The lieutenant turned back towards Plasket, his eyes moving across the building's façade.

"I guess that takes care of that," the younger officer remarked, looking sideways to Florez, who was staring disbelievingly at the older man.

The authority in his voice and the speed he used to administer it was encouraging. He placed his hands back on his hips, looping his thumbs over his belt.

"So," he said to both Florez and Plasket. "Where do you want us?"

"You outrank us," the young female cop replied.

"Yeah," he nodded, locking his eyes with hers. "But you have been here longer. You've seen things and heard things we haven't."

"Captain just said to hold the line," Plasket told him.

"Then that's what we'll do." The lieutenant smiled before turning to the three remaining officers standing behind him and pointing towards the students' car park. "Spread out along the tape that way. I want one of you at the entrance of the driveway. I'll stay here and you two can stand near the cars. There's some shade there. You deserve a little relief after being out here for so long."

The five officers moved off to their designated areas.

Sedgewick turned to face the mayor, who was still standing across the road with his arms folded and an impressive scowl on his face.

The lieutenant gave a polite wave, knowing it would reinforce the mayor's current mood.

"Afternoon, Mayor Owens," he smiled.

VIII

Samuel Redman had placed his jacket over the face and torso of the boy wearing glasses. With the help of the other two boys, they had moved him to the floor by the opposite wall to the classroom's doorway.

Posadas remained in the corner with the four girls. They had stopped crying, but their shivering had intensified.

The female teacher tried to keep them as warm as she could by rubbing their backs and hugging them tightly. Her attempts were not so successful as she, too, was struggling with how cold she felt.

Their clothing was all wet through to the skin. The air in the room seemed to drop in temperature.

"Why is it so cold?" one boy asked, wrapping his arms around his chest and jumping up and down on the spot.

"This room is always cold," the other boy replied. "Maybe it's because there are no windows."

"You should really get up and move about," Redman told the girls in the corner.

"She might hear us," one of them said. "She might come back."

"I think she's gone for now." The teacher reached his hand out to her. "Come on. Miss Posadas deserves the chance to stretch her legs a little."

The girl took his hand, allowing him to help her to her feet. She let out a soft moan as a sharp pain moved through her muscles.

"You gotta stretch it out," a boy said, pointing to her leg. "That's elastic acid building up in there."

"Lactic acid, stupid," the other boy chided.

The girl grinned as she bent one knee and extended the other leg in front of her, stretching the hamstring.

"I know," the first boy replied. "I just wanted to make her smile."

The other girls slowly lifted themselves off the floor and took the first boy's advice, stretching their muscles after sitting for so long.

"I can't move," Posadas whispered. She almost laughed at her predicament until she tried to bend her knee. She winced and wrapped both hands around her right knee.

"Charlie horse," the second boy suggested, nodding to himself. "You need someone to massage it. I can help with that."

She shot the boy a look, cocking her head to one side as she pursed her lips.

"In your dreams, son," Redman said, crouching by his colleague. "Where exactly?"

"Just below the knee," she replied.

He started rubbing her calf muscles. "Move your foot up and down."

She winced each time that she extended her foot. Redman continued to rub the lower section of her leg as her movement became more and more rapid.

"I think it's loosening up," she told him.

"Try to stand," he told her, reaching his hand out to her as he lifted himself upright.

She let out a loud grunt as he pulled her to her feet.

"The kid's right," he said, tilting his head towards the first boy. "You need to stretch your muscles. You've had these girls resting on your legs and they've seized up some."

"Here, Miss Posadas." The boy placed his hands against the wall at shoulder height and lifted himself onto his tip-toes and back down again. He repeated the movement again. "Do this. It'll stretch your calf muscles."

The teacher copied the boy, wincing each time she rose.

"Should we try to move to another room?" a girl asked, her eyes locked onto the body of the boy wearing glasses.

"Why would we do that?" another girl quipped. "She's still out there somewhere."

"We're not going anywhere yet," Redman told them. We're as safe here as we would be in any room. Besides, we have a barricade here which is giving us a little protection."

"It didn't protect him," another girl said, pointing with her chin to the body on the floor.

"It could have been worse," the second boy told her. "We were lucky. Imagine what this room would look like without that barricade."

Redman didn't want any of them to think about that, let alone think of it himself.

"It's very sad that so many have been taken from us today," the teacher told all of them. "But we are still alive. I'd like to keep it that way. We'll stay here until help comes. We'll support each other through this and help each other as much as we can. Okay?"

The students nodded.

"We'll get out of here, guys," he continued. "I don't know when, but I plan to go home and I need to make sure you're all safe before I do."

IX

The sound of an approaching helicopter drew Plasket's eyes to the sky. He scanned the area above the center of town to the south-west and saw the chopper heading in his direction.

It had to be the news.

If it were another aircraft carrying police personnel, he would have noticed it.

"Dammit." He shook his head.

"That's nothing," Florez said, gazing down the road. "Look."

He turned his head to see three vehicles, two sedans and one pickup truck, heading their way.

"Goddammit," he spat as he lifted his walkie-talkie from his belt. "Captain, you there?"

"Morris here," a voice replied. "I'll just get her."

There was a moment of crackle over the speaker as Plasket waited for the captain to talk.

"Reece," she finally said.

"Captain," he started. "It's Cory. We got a chopper heading inbound and three civilian vehicles coming along the road."

There was another moment of silence.

"Chopper has got to be media," she told him. "Civilians are probably parents who have seen the news."

Plasket moved his eyes to the old man standing across the road. His arms still crossed and his stare upon the approaching vehicles as a broad smile spread from ear to ear.

"The mayor seems pretty pleased at the moment," the officer informed her. "You don't think he might have had something to do with any of it?"

"The news choppers would have come anyway," she said. "People from town might be another story. We know something like this was going to happen. It was just a matter of time. Just do your best to keep them back from the school."

"Will do, Captain," Plasket replied as the vehicles passed him by, pulling up to a stop directly in front of the school.

Two large men wearing baseball caps jumped out of the pickup and hastily made their way towards Lieutenant Sedgewick, who was eyeing the mayor until the vehicles arrived.

"My kid's in there," one man bellowed angrily as seven more men emerged from the two sedans. His chest puffed out and his approach told Sedgewick they were in for trouble.

The helicopter moved to a position high above the staff carpark and hovered there. Plasket knew the camera in the aircraft was most probably filming the men getting out of their vehicles. He and Florez started along the road to assist the lieutenant.

Sedgewick moved to stop the approaching men's advance.

"I'm going in there to get my little girl," the first man said defiantly.

"If I were in your shoes," the lieutenant replied. "I'd want to do the same. But I can't let you go in there."

"Fuck you," the man blurted, moving his face within inches from Sedgewick's. "I'd like to see you stop me, motherfucker."

"I understand that you're upset right now," the lieutenant said calmly. "Don't put me in a position where I might need to arrest you for your own safet—"

"Arrest me?" The man held his arms out wide and came within an inch of touching his chest against the police officer. "Arrest me for what? Arrest me for wanting to get my kid. You can't stop all of us. Go ahead. Arrest me, dipshit."

The man pushed by Sedgewick, making his way to the police tape.

The lieutenant grabbed the man by the arm and, with a twist of the wrist, caused the man to buckle to his knees.

Plasket was amazed at what he saw. Never in his whole life had he seen a man take down another individual so easily with just one hand.

Within one swift motion, Sedgewick had his cuffs out with his free hand and over the wrists of the man before placing him face down on the road.

"You asshole," the man hollered. "I just want to get my kid outta there."

"I know," the officer acknowledged. Plasket started increasing his pace as the second man, followed by another, ducked under the tape and bolted across the lawn towards the front doors.

"You better let him go," one of the other men said to Sedgewick as the remaining six newcomers gathered in a semicircle around the lieutenant and his captive.

"This man is being detained so I can protect him from the danger inside that police tape," he told them. "My advice to you, gentlemen, is to back the hell away so I can do my job."

"You need assistance, Lieutenant?" Plasket called as he drew near.

"I might," Sedgewick told him, eyeing the angry faces of the six crowding around him.

"Should I go and get them?" Florez asked, looking towards the two men nearing the front steps of the high school building.

"No," Plasket told her, remembering the earlier incident when he and Morris approached the building. "Just call out to them to come back. Don't go anywhere near there."

She ducked under the tape and cupped her hands around her mouth.

"Hey," she yelled as loudly as she could. "Come back. It's dangerous."

"Captain?" Plasket called into his walkie-talkie.

"Reece here," she replied, almost immediately.

"Lieutenant Sedgewick has had to detain one of the fathers out here. We have six more crowding him at the moment and two that have breached the line."

"Where are the two that have breached the line?" she asked.

"One is thumping on the door right now," he told her. "The other is standing at the bottom of the stairs."

"Don't approach the building," she ordered. "Stay where you are. One of the SWAT guys is on his way around."

"Let me in right now," the man bellowed through the door. Even though the bodies of two dead boys were clearly in view, he ignored them and continued to bash against the door as loudly as he could. "Let me in right now. Let me in right now," he called over and over.

Further inside the building, through the corridors and near the cafeteria, Kirstin's ears heard the calls.

She had just finished cutting through the rubber hoses attached to the two tanks of the welding kit and stuffed the utility knife back into her hip pocket.

Turning to the west, she pulled the P229 from behind her with her left hand and jogged along the passageway.

"Let me in right now," the man's voice shouted. "Let me in right now."

The chanting reminded her of a protester at a rally.

Extremely annoying.

"Stop that," Florez pleaded. "You don't know what you're doing."

"His boy is in there, stupid bitch," one of the six men behind her remarked. "All of our kids are."

"Don't call me a stupid bitch, sir," she replied calmly. "My IQ score is one hundred and thirty-two. There are some kids across the road behind the elementary school. If you had half a cell inside your brain, you might check over there first before causing trouble out here."

The six stared back at her dumbly.

"Go and check." She pointed to the building across the street.

"Let me in right now," the man at the door continued to yell, thumping on the door in rhythm to his words. "Let me in right now."

"Sir," Florez called across the front lawn to the man.

"Just stay over there, hot stuff," the man at the base of the stair called back. "Let the big boys handle this. Okay?"

BLAM!

The man at the door collapsed in a lifeless heap.

"Shit," the second man cried as he half crouched as he ran back towards the female police officer.

BLAM!

A fine spray of pink burst from the second man's head as his legs buckled, sending him sprawling across the path that stretched between the road and the school.

"Holy fuck," one of the six called out as they all squatted in fear.

"What happened?" the man under Sedgewick called.

"Dwayne and Steve are dead," the other replied. "Fuck!"

The man in handcuffs considered the words for a moment.

"That could have been me," he whispered.

Sedgewick moved his eyes to the body lying on the path. It was a good thirty yards from the doors of the high school.

"Shit, she can shoot," he gasped.

Plasket eyed the helicopter high above the carpark. He knew that what had just transpired had surely been televised on one network. Turning, he saw Mayor Keith Owens staring at the air-craft. His arms were dangling by his sides and the color had drained from his face.

Kibble bolted along the front of the building with his HK sub-machine gun at the ready. He pulled up quickly beside the steps to the platform, keeping himself shielded by the protruding wall of the building.

The man on the steps had a hole dead center in his forehead. From his point of view, it was a clean shot. There was no suffering.

Peering into the glass panels of the doors, he could see the two boys, but no shooter.

She was gone.

He relaxed his posture and pressed the talk button on his radio.

"No sign of the girl, Sarge," Kibble said. "Two dead inside the door and two fresh kills outside."

"I only heard two shots," Phillips replied.

"The girl's good, I think," the sniper answered. "You want me to stay here?"

"No," his sergeant told him. "I'll need you with me when we go in. I'm cutting the top hinge now."

"Officer McFarlan," Kirstin's voice warbled through the walkie-talkie attached to the female cop's belt, "are you there?"

She was standing between the door and some students who were watching the flame as it continued to cut through the door hinges. Glancing around, she saw Stephanie stiffen in her chair. Donnie immediately talked to her, trying his best to keep her calm as he had been all day.

It was clear to McFarlan that the girl's nerves had set on edge so much that some long-term damage may have occurred. Even in her relaxed state, Stephanie's eyes continued to dart around the room, peering into the shadows for signs of the girl in the corridor.

"Watch them," the officer said to Lindsay Merrick, pointing to the group of observers. The teacher, like many of the students gathered about, was more interested in seeing the door open than she was in supervising kids.

"Officer McFarlan," the girl's voice sang into the radio.

"How can I help you, Kirstin?" She hurried to the kitchen, taking the walkie-talkie out of the students' earshot and into the small passage where the pantry and cold room were situated.

"Give me Stephanie Granger," the girl ordered. "I've lost count of how many are dead. There are still some more I haven't touched yet. But I will stop, if you give her to me. I promise."

The assurance did not sound as if Kirstin had any plan to see it through. McFarlan's gut feeling told her that Kirstin had the full intention to continue to kill as many as she could before she could be stopped.

She closed her eyes and shook her head.

This day would have only one conclusion.

You're sixteen-years-old, McFarlan thought. *How could life be so terrible that you're willing to throw it all away at sixteen?*

That's what she felt like saying. Instead, she said six simple words.

"Why are you doing this, Kirstin?"

"Because I was told to," she answered. "Now, give me Stephanie."

"Who told you to, Kirstin?

"Give me Stephanie Granger," the girl repeated, ignoring McFarlan's question.

"You know I can't do that," the police officer replied. "And I wouldn't even if I could. Please Kirstin, just give yourself up."

"You know I can't do that," the girl repeated McFarlan's words. "And I couldn't even if I wanted to."

The words frightened McFarlan a little. She didn't quite understand what was meant by them. There was a hint that Kirstin didn't believe she was in control anymore.

"They're through," one of the boys called.

Several people cheered.

"What's happening in there, Officer McFarlan?" Kirstin's voice warbled through the speaker.

Shit! She can hear us.

McFarlan turned to see Aiden Fisk standing in the kitchen.

"Tell them to be quiet," she instructed him. "She can hear them."

"Shit," he spat before turning on his heels and moving into the eatery.

"I don't know what's going on," the cop told the girl.

"Hey," Fisk shouted, pointing towards the doors that led to the corridor. "Keep it down."

The din dropped to an immediate murmur as the students remembered why they were trapped in the cafeteria.

"Don't lie to me," Kirstin said to the cop. "It sounds like a party in there."

"Just a lot of scared people who really want to go home," McFarlan replied.

"I think I heard some cheering," claimed the girl. "Why don't you unlock the door and let me in to see? Then I can take Stephanie out myself."

"I won't be opening the door for you, Kirstin," McFarlan assured the other.

"You won't?"

"I'm sorry, but there's no way."

"Then I'll huff," she said. "And I'll puff. And I'll blow the door away."

OCTAVUS INTERLUDIUM

Extract from the Diary of Kirstin Matthews

Monday April 24 2017

Steph, Nancy and Angela are going to die today.
I've got my daddy's gun.
Soon, those bitches will be dead.
Then my work is done.

Calm Voice loves me.
I am Calm Voice.

Bye Bye!

IGNIS : FIRE

The world is becoming like a lunatic asylum run by lunatics.

DAVID LLOYD GEORGE

I

"As you can see, right now Phil, the special weapons and tactics team is removing the door to where several students and teachers have been hiding throughout this ordeal," Samantha Peterson said into the camera.

Wayne Dwyers had framed the reporter on the left of the screen so he could view the officers in action behind her. Two of the darkly clad men were moving the black gym bags full of equipment to the left side of the door and placing them against the wall of the building. The others were carefully maneuvering the door away from its position, lifting it as they prepared to carry it off.

"We should see people coming out any moment now," Peterson continued.

The door fell outwards, towards them. Within moments, all three had the door in their grasp and were moving it to the right side of the access. The two SWAT members who had moved the gym bags were now moving into the darkroom with their MP5 submachine guns at the ready, beyond the view of the camera.

"Do we know of any injured amongst this group, Samantha?" Phil Gouldman, the anchorman sitting in the studio, asked.

"From what I've been told, Phil, we have no physical injuries," she replied. "But I suspect we will see quite several traumatized faces and people in desperate need of consoling. We just saw two of the special weapons and tactics team members enter the building. They have assured me that the shooter is not in this area of the school."

"They went in with their weapons raised," the anchorman said into her earpiece.

"I would assume when I say this," she answered. "But they are possibly following a set procedure. Taking precautions before moving people out of the building."

"Where will they evacuate them to, Samantha?"

"The immediate rally area is on the northern side of the student carpark to my right," the reporter said, pointing to an area off to the left of the camera. "Afterwards, they'll take them across the road and to the grounds behind the elementary school. There are already a number of students who escaped earlier in the day, waiting over there with the principal of the high school and a few staff members."

The camera recorded Captain Julia Reece and Officer Randy Morris move towards the car park. The other three SWAT members, after leaving the door on its side against the wall, positioned themselves on either side of the opening.

A face appeared from the darkness.

It was a woman, shielding her eyes from the sunlight with a raised hand. She stretched her other arm behind her, reaching into the unseen room.

Gradually, cautiously, she stepped into the light. A young girl was gripping her hand tightly, following her into the open.

"We can see the first of the people coming out," Peterson commented. "It appears to be a woman, possibly a teacher, here at Edwards Hill State High School. She's holding onto a girl's hand."

The SWAT team urged them out with gesturing, pointing towards the car park where the police captain and the uniformed officer were awaiting them.

The woman and the girl moved with more haste as they found their courage, realizing they were safe. Both cried before they made two steps from the door.

"I couldn't even begin to imagine what must be going through their minds right now," Peterson said.

Dwyers zoomed in on them, staying with them until they reached Reece and Morris. He then opened the lens back out to a wide shot to frame both the reporter and the door in view as another person emerged through the door. Another girl appeared, followed by another.

"Here, come some more," the reporter remarked.

More girls moved through the doorway, following the others as they made their way towards the student car park. Quite a number of female students and teachers had come through the opening before Peterson made another comment.

"It would appear that only the women and girls are being guided out at the moment," she reported. "Hold on. I think I can see someone being carried out."

II

Donny carried Stephanie carefully through the doorway. She had her arms around his neck and head on his shoulder. She was breathing heavily and rapidly, causing quick gasps of hot breath to sweep over his neck.

At any other time, he might have been happy to have a pretty girl panting just so on his skin, but at this moment, he had concerns. He followed the gestures of the SWAT team members and headed straight for the car park.

"She's not looking too good," Freddie Morris said, running by his side.

"What can you see?" Donny asked.

"She's turning green, man."

"Freddie," a voice called from ahead of them.

"Dad," the boy called and ran ahead to embrace his father.

"Thank God," the police officer cried as he wrapped his arms around his son. "It's good to see you, boy."

"You too, Dad," Freddie replied, his voice muffled by his father's shoulder.

Donny continued past them.

"Are you hurt?" Morris asked, holding the boy at arm's length.

"No," Freddie told him before pointing to Stephanie. "But the girl. There's something wrong with her."

"Where?"

"With Donny there," he replied.

Morris started after the boy carrying Stephanie. "Put her on the grass over there, Donny."

Donny turned to see Morris pointing to a patch of grass just to the north of the car park. He carried the girl past the stationary vehicles and lowered her onto the lawn.

"What's wrong with her?" he asked the police officer.

"Shock," Morris replied. "Fear. Sickness. A bunch of things."

"Kirstin wants her," Freddie told his father. "That's what she's been telling that lady cop over the radio."

"Usually we'd lay someone down for shock," Morris told Donny. "But I got a feeling she might puke. Put her on her side facing downhill and elevate her legs."

Donny complied, placing himself at Stephanie's feet where he intended to sit her feet on his lap. She fretted, reaching out to him and calling for him.

"Freddie." Morris pointed to Stephanie's feet. "I need you to sit there instead. Donny, she needs you where she can see you."

The boys acted fast.

Freddie was sitting cross-legged with her feet in his lap within seconds. Donny sat just beside Stephanie's, where he could stroke her hair and hold her hand.

She settled down almost immediately. Her breathing slowed and her skin color returned to normal.

"You're outside now, Steph," Donny told her. "There are cops everywhere. She can't get to you now."

Morris crouched in front of the girl.

"try to relax, Steph," he said. "That's your name? Steph?"

"Stephanie," she said in a hoarse whisper.

"Okay, Stephanie," he smiled. "I've gotta help the others. I need you to stay here and look after Donny and Freddie for me. Can you do that?"

She smiled and nodded.

"That-a girl." He touched her shoulder reassuringly before moving his attention to the boys. "Stay here until I come back. I don't think we should move her right now. I'll call the paramedics to come for her. She may want you to go with her."

Donny nodded. "I can do that."

"Do you have a phone on you?" Morris asked.

"It's in my bag," he replied. "In my locker."

The cop moved his eyes to his son.

"The same thing," he said. "Teachers don't like us having them in class."

"You picked a great time to listen to your teachers," remarked Morris.

He looked at Stephanie and couldn't see anywhere in her clothing that she could keep a cell phone.

"Okay." The cop nodded before looking to his son as he reached into his pocket for his own cellphone. "I want you to use my phone and call Stephanie's parents first. After that, let Donny call his mom so he can tell her he'll be taking Steph to the hospital."

"You want me to go with them?"

"No way," Morris replied. "You wait here for me. I'm not letting you out of my sight for the rest of the year."

III

"They're letting people out," a girl shouted. She was standing with a small group huddled around a boy who was watching the news on his smartphone.

"They're what?" Frieda Richardson questioned, looking over at the group of students a few feet away from her. She rose to her feet and moved away from the small bench where she and the two receptionists waited.

"Take a look." The boy offered her the phone.

Instead of taking it, she craned her neck to see to see the image of Samantha Peterson talking to the camera. She couldn't hear the reporter's words, but she could see people moving from the school building in the background, across the screen from right to left.

"I think that's the cafeteria," one girl said.

"Are they going to kill Kirstin?" another asked.

Richardson pursed her lips and shook her head.

"I don't know," she replied, almost a whisper. "I think they'll try to arrest her. I hope they try to arrest her."

"But she shot a lot of people," another student put in.

Richardson nodded. "I know."

The principal felt the corners of her mouth droop as tears welled in her eyes. A part of her wanted Kirstin to be taken down by the police for what she had done. The frequent sound of gunshots coming from across the road had set all of them on edge, students and adults alike.

Another part of her wanted the girl to be rescued. This part of her saw Kirstin as a confused little girl who was acting out according to some strange misunderstanding that had triggered in her head.

She needs help, Richardson thought. *She needs to be put in a psychiatric facility where she can be treated.*

Torn between the two feelings, she didn't know what she wanted exactly. She was a principal of a high school and she had high expectations of Kirstin Matthews. A part of her wanted the girl dead, and this made her feel ashamed.

One student noticed the tears rolling down Richardson's cheeks. She moved to her principal silently and wrapped her arms around the adult.

It was too much.

Frieda Richardson couldn't contain herself and broke down.

For the whole day, she had been the perfect role model. She had held her head high and played the part of the responsible adult.

Now, she was a blubbering mess.

The boy lowered the smartphone, his chin quivering. He peered at the principal for a moment as his brain processed and equated that teachers are human, too.

Before long, his arms wrapped around the woman as well.

As students and adult shed more tears, more arms embraced her.

The small group of students that were huddled about the small screen, watching the news, were now clustered around their principal.

Other students seated about the play area of the elementary school watched the event transpire. A silent, empathetic understanding circulated between them that, until this moment, this one woman had been carrying the weight of the entire world on her shoulders.

She had not only concerned herself with their immediate well-being, but her thoughts had also been upon those still trapped inside Edwards Hill State High School.

Every shot that rang through the air had been another piece added to the load. Every minute, every second, had been an eternity as she waited for some information to come and receiving none.

It was too much.

Way too much.

And now it had finally taken its toll.

The deep, dark, crimson clouds swirled inside her head like a tumultuous tempest. Inside her mind, she imagined a gale-force wind tearing through the sky as the blood rain teemed down.

Focus, the lightning rumbled.

She had managed to cut through the rubber hoses attached to the welding torch, and dropped the apparatus to the floor.

With a twist of her wrists, she opened the valves on both the oxygen and acetylene tanks, twisting the taps until they would not move any farther.

Lifting the glass bottle of sulfuric acid, she moved towards the north-east corner of the passageway, ducking around the corner of the eastern hallway, preparing to run as fast as she could towards the center corridor.

Focus, the calm voice told her again.

She closed her eyes and took a deep breath, lifting the bottle over her shoulder. She opened her eyes and peered at the bowl of white powder, the mixture of powdered sugar and potassium chlorate, her intended target.

"That's all of them?" Phillips asked, standing in the middle of the room.

"None back here," Martin Saunders called from the kitchen.

"Then I need to thank you all for staying back to make sure everyone got out safely," the sergeant said to those in the room, "but I need all of you out of here."

"Come on," McFarlan said to the two teachers who remained behind. "I'll walk you out."

"You'll need to go with them, Officer McFarlan," Phillips told her.

"I thought you might need me here," she replied. "Kirstin has been in contact with *me* throughout the day. Not anyone else."

"I understand that," the SWAT leader assured her. "But she may not want to comply or put her weapon down."

"Don't kill her," the officer pleaded.

"Trust me." he placed a hand on her shoulder. "We will try to arrest her and bring her in unharmed. You have my word."

Reluctantly, McFarlan nodded.

"Come on," Aiden Fisk stretched his hand out to her. "I'll walk *you* out."

She smiled and took his hand.

The three of them moved to the open doorway as Phillips pressed the talk button on his radio.

"Okay guys," he said. "Come on in."

As McFarlan and the two teachers stepped into the bright light of the mid-afternoon, the three SWAT team members standing outside advanced past them and into the darkroom.

Phillips was releasing the upper sliding bolt as Reynes crouched to do the same to the lower device.

Kibble raised his MP5, directing it towards the door and placing his thumb at the ready to switch off the safety lever.

The other two stood on either side of him, guns up and waiting.

Phillips signaled his men using hand gestures.

Kibble, Garcia, Juarez, watch the sides.

The men nodded, understanding their responsibility.

Reynes, open the door.

The man reached for the handle and prepared to pull the large wooden panel open.

V

Kirstin threw the glass bottle through the air.

It spun and twisted a little as it floated high, almost striking the ceiling.

But her aim was true.

She was already running as it smashed high against the brick wall just to the side of the door where the table had stood.

Her legs had carried her about halfway across the distance from the north-west corner to the center corridor when the clear, corrosive liquid sprayed over the white powder in the bowl.

As the instant chemical reaction occurred, and a jet of flame erupted from the mixture, she bolted into the passageway to her right and pressed herself against the wall as hard as she could.

The flame ignited the gas that had escaped from the tanks, mixing in the air to create a lethal combination.

The large wooden panel splintered into countless shards of timber as a brilliant ball of flame burst with magnificent force into the cafeteria.

The five darkly clad men flung across the room at an incredible velocity.

Phillips felt something smack him on the back of his helmet. It took him a moment to realize that it was the wall on the northern side of the cafeteria.

Lifting himself from his side to lean against the wall, sitting with his legs pointing awkwardly into the room, he tried to get his bearings. Blackness surrounded him like a thick, tangible blanket.

A few light spots appeared as his eyes regained focus. Small pieces of flaming timber dotted the room like stars. The sun streaked like torchlight through the dark clouds of smoke funneling through the open door to his left.

"Shit," he spat, looking around the smoke-filled room for his men. "Phillips," he called his own name out loudly.

"Garcia," he heard from somewhere in the murkiness.

"Kibble," came another reply.

"Juarez," another voice resounded.

Then silence.

"Reynes?" Phillips hollered. He winced as a sharp pain stabbed him in his left side. "Anyone see Reynes?"

Phillips moved his hand down to a spot just above his hip. There was a large sliver of wood sticking from his flesh.

"Oh shit," Garcia hissed.

"What is it?" Phillips asked, feeling a throbbing in the tissue around the invading protrusion.

"Reynes is gone, Sarge," the other replied.

"Are you sure?"

"He's got no fucking face."

VI

"Oh, my god!" Samantha Peterson gasped. The camera zoomed in, enlarging the doorway in the frame. Thick, black smoke poured from within the room, wafting into the sky.

Two men and a uniformed female police officer were in the vision, lying on the ground a few feet from the plume of smoke.

Dwyers focused on the three people, a part of him wanting to see if they were moving or not.

They were.

The female cop rolled over onto her back before slowly sitting up. One man was on his hands and knees, crawling away from the door.

The last man remained on his back. He moved his head, turning it towards the uniformed woman. She reached her hand out to him and he took it.

The cop rose to her feet, stumbled a little before widening her stance. Her free hand went to her ear before she shook her head a little.

"There seems to have been an explosion from inside the building, Phil," Peterson commented. "I'm not sure if you're seeing this. My earpiece has fallen out. But it was an enormous explosion. We could feel the heat from way back here.

"You might be able to see three people on the ground. They appear to be okay. But I don't know what condition of the special weapons and tactics officers are in. They entered the building only moments before."

The camera zoomed in further, tightening the shot of the three people who had escaped the blast.

There was an exchange of words between one man and the police officer. She was pointing to the open doorway as he continued to hold her hand in his. He lifted himself to his feet and placed his hands around her waist, and kissed her.

Her arms embraced him around his neck, holding him there for a moment.

"I, ah…" Peterson couldn't find the words. "Are you getting any of this Phil?"

The cop and the man released one another.

She disappeared into the smoke, returning to the cafeteria.

He helped the other man, still crawling on his hands and knees, to his feet and moved towards the student car park.

Dwyers followed the men until they met Julia Reece, who escorted them the rest of the way. The camera operator swung the lens back to the smoke-filled door, where he locked off the tripod so he could take his hands away from the camera for a moment or two.

"Phil?" Peterson called. "I think my earpiece is busted. I'll just continue on then."

"What the hell was that?" one boy yelled. "Are they trying to blow up the school now?"

"What?" the other boy called back, sticking a finger in his ear.

Samuel Redman heard a constant high-pitched whistle moving through his head.

The sound was extremely loud, and the floor seemed to lift and fall dramatically. They all lied on the wet linoleum, scrambling to get back up, confused as to what had just occurred.

"Is everybody okay?" Redman called. Dust had fallen from the ceiling and covered them from head to foot, clinging thickly to their wet clothing.

"I'm all right," Rosina Posadas replied, her legs sprawled apart as she rested at in an awkward position on the floor. The four girls helped her to her feet, one of them trying to brush the dust off the teacher, smearing it over her blouse instead.

"Shouldn't we get out of here?" one girl suggested.

Redman shook his head.

"We still don't know what's going on out there," he told them. "We should wait here until the police come for us."

"I really need to go to the bathroom," another girl told them.

"Yeah," one boy agreed. "Me too, Mister Redman."

The teacher looked to Posadas. She appeared disheveled and in desperate need of a hot shower, but immensely beautiful underneath it all.

She looked at him with her deep brown eyes and simply shrugged.

After glancing around the classroom, he could see no way for the two sexes to separate and be able to have any privacy in order to relieve themselves.

There was a bathroom across the hall and a little to the east of their position, only a few paces away. He was in two minds, but the fact that his bladder was pushing so hard against his skin presented the winning argument for the inner conflict.

"Okay, boys," he said. "Help me move this furniture."

Within moments, they moved the barricade aside.

Redman signaled everyone to move to the back wall of the classroom as he placed his hand on the doorknob.

When he was sure that they were out of sight from anybody in the corridor, he slowly opened the door. Cautiously, he tilted his head into the passageway and looked both left then right.

The hallway was empty.

He signaled for the others to follow him out the door.

"Straight into the girls' bathroom," he told them before directing his attention to the boys. "All of us. No arguments."

They silently agreed, nodding as they exited the classroom.

Redman kept his eyes moving as they crossed the passage, making a direct beeline for the facilities.

Smoke was rising from the stairwell at the eastern end of the corridor, filling the passageway.

He remained outside, making sure that all seven others with him entered the bathroom together.

With one last look in each direction, believing they were relatively safe for now, he followed them in.

By the time he entered the bathroom, passing several shallow basins before entering an area lined with cubicles, the others were already behind closed doors.

He thought about waiting until they were back in his sight before allowing himself a moment of release, but his bladder was all but screaming at him to let it go.

He quickly dashed into a stall and shut the door behind him. His zipper couldn't come down faster.

The feeling of elation and freedom was overpowering, and he almost let out a sigh of relief. Closing his eyes, he let his body liberate what it had been holding.

Sheer ecstasy.

She ran as fast as she could around the side of the elementary school. The first thing she saw was the plume of black smoke billowing from the northern side of the building.

"Missus Richardson," Karly Childers called behind her, frantically trying to keep up with her boss. "Where are you going? It's not safe out there."

"I want to know what the hell is happening to my school," she replied.

"They're burning it down," Mayor Keith Owens remarked.

"Shut up, Keith," one man standing by the road called out.

"Look for yourself." The old man pointed.

The man shook his head and turned to face the worried principal.

"Don't listen to him, Frieda," he told her. "This prick just got two people killed."

"Excuse me," the mayor snapped. "I got them killed, how?"

"You got us all worked up," the man hollered. "You phoned us and told us that our kids were being shot."

"All I did was inform you of what was going on," Owens interjected. "I saw it as my responsibility to make my constituents aware of what's happening in their community."

"You put us in danger, you dumb bastard!" The man started forward, suddenly held back by another two, who stood on either side of him.

"I put you...?" The old man pointed to himself before directing his finger to the building across the road. "The shooter is over there. I didn't put the gun in their hand. I didn't make them pull the trigger. They're the one who's doing this. Not me."

"Shut the fuck up, Keith," Richardson shouted. All eyes suddenly widened with surprise. None more so than Owens, as he felt belittled yet again. "No one wants to hear your voice right now except for you. There are kids and teachers dead over there. People I know and respect and love. So just keep your goddamn mouth closed for once in your life."

The mayor turned red in the face. He bit his lip and walked away, towards the awaiting man he'd just argued with. When he realized where his feet were about to take him, he changed direction and headed the other way.

"Are you okay?" Childers placed her hands on the principal's shoulders.

Richardson frowned and moved her tear-filled eyes over the façade of Edwards Hill State High School. Her eyes landed on the body on the path and the man lying near the door.

Broken windows and shattered glass lied at the base of the building. Her arms instinctively went for her receptionist, wrapping themselves around the young woman as she wept.

VII

She leaned against the wall with both hands flat against the bricks. Her head was swimming in wide circles, moving faster than the clouds.

Her eyes were closed, and her knees were on the floor.

Everything seemed to move up and down, side to side.

She thought the wall and rooms between her and the cafeteria weren't enough to protect her from the shock wave of the blast.

Taking a few slow, deep breaths, she opened her eyes and peered to her left, towards the front doors of the school building. She could see the light breaking through the thick cloud of dust and smoke.

Carefully, keeping low, she edged around the corner and back into the eastern corridor as she lifted the Beretta from her jeans with her right hand, and the P229 with her left.

Crouching, duck-walking below the smoke that filled the top half of the passageway, she crept towards the north-eastern corner, darting her eyes to the right where the open door to the gymnasium was situated.

Focus, the calm voice told her again. *Not too long now.*

Kirstin felt her heart racing in her chest as she drew closer and closer to the corner. She could see the black smoke lifting into the stairwell and moving swiftly like an upside-down dirty river flowing against gravity.

Her hands were shaking with anticipation.

Her ears were ringing from the loud explosion.

Each breath burned her lungs and throat.

She needed to get outside and take in some fresh air.

Focus, the thunder told her. *Keep your mind on what matters.*

Duck-walking, she reached the corner and peered around the corner towards the cafeteria.

What little remained of the welding equipment was a tangled metal mess of shrapnel and twisted iron. The table and bowl she had placed against the door were simply gone. The door had been torn away from the rails it once rested upon.

There were no flames, just smoke covering the ceiling and char and ash on the floor and walls.

She was about to move forward, towards the opening into the cafeteria, but stopped abruptly.

The high-pitched ringing in her ears was immensely loud. But beneath it, she could hear voices coming from inside the eatery.

"Are you okay?" she heard a woman calling.

Is she talking to me? Kirstin wondered, cocking her head to the side and peering towards the dark doorway.

"I've been injured," a man replied. "Took some shrapnel in the side. Damn it hurts."

"I'm all right," another man called.

"Me too," said another. "You want us to go on, Sarge?"

"Yeah," the first man's voice answered. "In a minute."

Shit!

Kirstin felt a knot tighten in her stomach.

She quickly rose to her feet, pointing the Beretta at the smoking opening into the cafeteria as she backed across the passageway into the gymnasium, vanishing into the darkness.

VIII

Crouching by Phillips' side, McFarlan placed a rolled-up towel carefully around the protruding piece of timber, as thick as her wrist, sticking from his side. As delicate as she was, he still winced and let out a groan or two.

"Charlie, are you on?" Garcia said into his radio.

"I'm here," a reply came through his earpiece. "What just happened?"

McFarlan suddenly felt out of the loop. She wasn't able to hear the other party, but it was clear the other SWAT members could.

"We need the med kit," Garcia said to the unseen person. "The Sarge is injured. Reynes is down."

"Dead?" the other asked.

"Yeah," the SWAT member replied. "You better come quick."

"On my way."

McFarlan looked at each one of them.

"Charlie?"

"Our pilot," Phillips told her. "Also our medic."

"Every time you talk," said Kibble, "you move your abdominal muscles, which means that thing sticking out of you moves too. So shut up."

"Yes, dear," he replied.

"I'll take point," Garcia said to the other two men. "Juarez?"

"My usual," he answered

"I guess I'm in the middle." Kibble adjusted the strap on his submachine gun, shifting the stock closer to his right shoulder.

"Where do you want me?" McFarlan asked.

"No way." Garcia turned to face her. "You stay back here. I can't risk you in there."

"She's been talking to me," the female cop argued. "She might listen to me."

"Have you seen what's left of this door?" Juarez pointed to the opening into the corridor. "Do you see my friend here? She ain't listening to anyone, sweetheart."

"I don't need any of you storming in there with itchy trigger fingers, looking for some pay-back," McFarlan contended. "She killed my friend, too. My job isn't to put a bullet in her for that. My job is to take her in alive."

"Listen, lady." Juarez stepped towards her. "She's the one going around with the itchy trigger finger. She's the one dropping people left, right and center. She's the one blowing the fucking building apart. And while I don't intend to blow her away, I will put a bullet in her if she leaves me with no option. Kid or not."

"Simmer down," Phillips grunted. The others moved their eyes to him. "Go for the arrest. No more dead kids today. Please."

Juarez frowned as he locked his eyes with his leader's. Reluctantly, but understandingly, he nodded.

"No more kids," he agreed.

"The lady takes the rear," Phillips added. "If she can talk the girl down, let her."

"Sarge, stop talking," Kibble ordered, pointing to the injury, noticing a red stain expanding over the towel.

Phillips nodded.

"Let's go and get her," said Garcia, making his way to the door. "Stay close. Stay low."

IX

Stepping through the remains of the door, Garcia looked to his right into an empty corridor. He turned towards the left and walked slowly, cautiously towards the eastern end of the passageway. He placed his feet carefully, navigating a clear path through the twisted metal remains of the welding equipment.

"Careful here," he whispered to Kibble, following closely.

The marksman looked down to the charred ground, eyeing the portions of tank and frame that had once rested against the door. There was barely anything left.

Still, if his boot was to come in contact, it would no doubt make a loud metallic noise that would warn the girl of their approach.

"Watch this shit," he said, turning to Juarez, who was making his way through the opening.

"I see it," the other replied.

As McFarlan entered the corridor, Juarez tapped her shoulder and pointed to the debris. She nodded, understanding his concern, and stepped exactly where he stepped, placing her feet where he placed his as he followed his team members.

With his machinegun pointed towards the open doorway into the gymnasium, Garcia continued to edge forwards deliberately, gradually, trying to see into the darkness beyond. His eyes could make out a line of objects deeper in the room, lying along the center of the wet floor.

To him, they appeared dark, rough, and irregular in form. As he drew closer to the door, his eyes adjusted to the dimness of the room. The shapes on the ground became clearer and clearer.

It wasn't until he was standing in the doorway that he was able to fully comprehend what he was looking at.

A line of charred bodies stretched across the middle of the basketball court. He could determine that most of them were only kids.

A lump formed in his throat.

His feet carried him through the doorway and into the room. His eyes fixated on the dead children.

"What the hell?" Juarez hissed as he entered the gymnasium.

BLAM!
BLAM!
BLAM!

They dropped onto the ground, landing hard on their stomachs.

"Where the fuck did that come from?" Kibble hollered.

Juarez turned his head and saw McFarlan disappear from view behind the wall. She was still in the corridor and out of immediate danger.

"I think I'm hit," Garcia called, moving his hand to his hip. There was a throbbing pain just above his thigh.

BLAM!

Garcia's head snapped backwards as the bone above his nose shattered.

"Jesus." Kibble swung his machine gun towards the bleachers to his left and opened up.

The noise was terrifyingly loud, booming, and reverberating throughout the large auditorium as splinters of timber exploded from the seating area.

As he fired, he rose to his feet, stepping towards the direction the fatal shot had come from.

He continued to shoot until the magazine was empty.

With a quick press on the release button, the empty clip fell loudly onto the floor as he reached into a compartment on his vest for a replacement.

BLAM!
BLAM!

Both bullets hit their mark.

One in his neck.

One through his cheek.

The sight of Kibble falling to the floor was sickening. Juarez felt his stomach tighten as he watched his friend crash down.

"Shit," he spat.

This girl is fucking good.

In the corner of his eye, he saw McFarlan poke her head around the edge of the door.

"Get back," he yelled, waving with his left hand as he directed his gun towards the bleachers.

"Somebody," he heard Phillips say in his earpiece. "Talk to me."

The rear guard pressed the talk button as he moved his gaze over the bleachers, particularly to the deep shadows beneath them. She was in there somewhere.

Hiding.

Watching.

Lining up her next shot.

"I'm all that's left, Sarge," he replied. His voice was raspy from inhaling smoke and shaking with a heightened adrenalin rush. "I don't think I'm going to make it out."

"Don't talk like that," Phillips told him. "Try to get out and lob some tear gas in there."

"She'll have me before I get the chance," he informed the other, reaching for a canister on his belt. "She's got me. I know it."

He quickly popped the pin on the cylinder and rolled the small metal container across the floor towards the seats. A light colored smoke billowed out of the canister as it bounced at the base of the bleachers.

"Get back," Juarez shouted to McFarlan.

BLAM!
BLAM!
BLAM!

The first two bullets plowed through the SWAT member's head. The third thudded into the wet floorboards by his body.

McFarlan watched as Juarez's body went limp, lifeless.

The smoke built around the bleachers and expanded throughout the room.

As its gray mass grew, spreading over the seats, engulfing the fallen SWAT team, the young police officer could hear the girl coughing.

X

Each intake of air felt as if fire were spreading through her lungs. Her vision blurred as stinging pain flared in her eyeballs.

The crimson clouds churning in her head replicated, white ones expanding all around her.

She couldn't see.

She couldn't breathe.

She needed to move.

Clumsily, she stretched her arms out, feeling for the underside of the bleachers. The knuckles of her left hand smacked against an iron support beam, knocking the P229 out of her grasp. It clunked noisily onto the floor and slid away from her.

"Shit." She crouched and felt around for the weapon.

It was gone.

It doesn't matter, the calm voice told her. *You still have the other gun.*

Another coughing fit started again as she reached for her backpack. She had taken it off so she could fit under the seats when moving beneath them into her hiding place.

Her hand smacked against the wet surface of the floor. Her bag wasn't there.

Somehow, in the mess of expanding cloud, burning lungs and stinging eyes, she had gotten turned around. She wasn't where she thought she was.

She had moved away from where she placed her backpack.

The spare magazines for the Beretta were in the backpack.

Her diary was in there too.

Overwhelming panic flooded her.

Focus.

"I can't," she whispered in a hoarse, barely audible voice.

Saliva and snot dangled from her nose and mouth as she crawled on her belly under the lowest bench. As she emerged from beneath the bleachers, she lifted herself slowly upon her hands and knees.

With her left hand, she pulled the front of her shirt up and over her nose to wipe the mucus away.

"McFarlan?" she called. Her voice was raspy. "McFarlan? You there?"

She continued crawling away from the bleachers; the Beretta gripped tightly in her right hand.

The crimson clouds turned and turned.

The lightning flashed, and the thunder roared.

She couldn't remember how many bullets remained in the clip.

Fear.

Anxiety.

Pain.

All manner of feelings flowed through her, over her, instantaneously.

Focus, the calm voice ordered her.

"I'm trying." She gritted her teeth as the coughing started again.

Crawling.

Crawling.

She wiped her eyes and nose on the back of her left hand and along her arm. Loud wheezing escaped her throat with each flame-filled breath.

The pain was intolerable.

"Turn yourself in, Kirstin," called the police woman. McFarlan's voice came from her right, from the direction of the door.

Kirstin lifted herself upon her knees and pointed the pistol in that direction. She wasn't able to see anything anymore.

"Give me Stephanie Grange—"

"Stephanie is outside," the cop interjected. "She's safe and far away from where you can't get to her. I'm the only one left in here."

"She's outside?" Kirstin couldn't believe it. She felt betrayed all over again.

Her parents had betrayed her when they wouldn't allow her to go out with her friends and be a regular teenage girl.

Her friends betrayed her when they treated her like an infectious, diseased castaway because she wasn't able to join them in their social gatherings and moments of debauchery.

Her teachers betrayed her when they tore shreds away with each spiteful remark about her comments, replies and reflections in the classroom.

They had all betrayed her.

They had all hated her.

They had all feared her.

They should have all died.

"She's outside and safe," McFarlan answered. "You're cornered and hurt. Please, Kirstin. Put the gun down and turn yourself in."

The girl sobbed as the storm inside of her raged.

She saw herself standing on the bodies of all those she had liberated from the physical. A hill of twisted corpses under the torrential tempest.

Wind howling.

Clouds churning.

Lightning blinding.

Thunder roaring.

The blood rain pouring.

Washing.

Washing.

Washing her dirty, naked body clean.

She hadn't liberated Posadas, the lesbian pedophile wannabe.

She hadn't liberated Stephanie Granger, the once trusted friend who had turned on her like a venomous asp.

There was so much more that she could have done. So much more work to accomplish.

"Kirstin," the cop called. "Please put the gun down."

Focus, the gentle thunder told her.

"They won't just put me behind bars for this," the girl sobbed, dangling the pistol by her side as she kneeled on the floor. "They'll give me the chair or whatever it is that they do."

"They can find you help," McFarlan replied. "They'll treat you. Please."

"I've killed too many for that." She lowered her head and wiped her face with her left hand again. "They'll never ever let me walk free. You know that."

"Kirstin," the officer pleaded, "I don't know what the decision will be after this. But I know they can get you help."

She couldn't see the floor below her. Her only sense of place was because of her hearing the police woman talking to her from the doorway.

Focus, the calm voice said. *There's nothing more to do here.*

Kirstin nodded as she lifted the Beretta and placed the muzzle against her temple.

"Kirstin, don't," McFarlan said. The girl heard the cop step into the room as her boot smacked against the wet timber floor by the door. "Don't do that."

"I had all the help I needed." The girl smiled as she pointed across the room to her left and tightened her finger on the trigger. "I left a message over there so that you would know."

"Know what, Kirstin?"

"Goodbye, Officer McFarlan."

XI

The sound of the gunshot was loud.

Kirstin slumped onto her left side.

Lifeless.

McFarlan stood only a few feet away, peering down at the body of the girl. She had tried to reach her before the girl could pull the trigger, but she was too slow.

Just a two more steps and maybe...

The girl stared towards the door as an expanding pool of blood spread out around her head.

Kirstin was dead.

McFarlan wasn't sure whether to be glad that the ordeal was over or upset that the child before her had killed herself right there.

There was anger towards the girl for everything she had done, and there was confusion as to the reason she did it.

Was there a reason?

McFarlan noticed the Beretta resting on the floor by Kirstin's hand. Some part of her training resurfaced, and she kicked it across the floor back towards the bleachers.

As the smoke cleared, rising high into the rafters of the roof, the cop recalled the girl's words.

I left a message over there so that you would know;; she had said.

McFarlan moved her eyes over the fallen SWAT team, to the charred remains of children lying in the middle of the floor.

She made her way towards them, taking a wide detour around the victims to not disturb the scene.

As she drew nearer to the burned bodies, McFarlan noticed great cavities created in their stomachs.

The taste of bile stung the back of her throat as she pictured Kirstin performing the act of disemboweling each of them.

For what purpose? The cop wondered. *This couldn't be the message, surely.*

She looked farther to the other side of the room and noticed something else on the floor.

Crossing the wet timber, the items became clearer and clearer.

Small groupings of intestinal organs.

Deliberately positioned.

Meticulously placed.

McFarlan felt her mouth frowning as the urge to vomit became overwhelming.

Closer and closer she drew.

Clearer and clearer the scene became.

The organs resembled letters. The letters organized into four words.

The four words formed a Latin phrase.

EGO SUM PLACIDO VOX

"I am Calm Voice," McFarlan interpreted quietly. She stared at the macabre message for a long time, saying the words over and over in her head, mouthing them in both Latin and English. "I don't understand," she said, shaking her head.

She turned and absorbed the scene of bodies around her. Her mind was racing with a million thoughts at once.

None of it made sense.

Who the fuck is Calm Voice?

NONUS INTERLUDIUM

SCHOOL COUNSELOR STUDENT EVALUATION

Sections Intentionally Omitted Under Fourteenth Amendment—Rights Guaranteed: Privileges and Immunities of Citizenship, Due Process, and Equal Protection

NAME: Kirstin Jane Matthews
ADDRESS: XXXXXXXX
PHONE: XXXXXXX
BIRTHDATE: 02/15/2001
AGE: 12 Years 4 Months
GRADE: Sixth grade completed
SCHOOL: XXXXXXX
EXAMINER: Dr. Hilary Allen Ph.D.

Kirstin is a 12-year-old girl who was referred to me by her English teacher, Mrs. XXXXX, regarding some erratic behavior that has been observed recently during class. Academically, Kirstin is a high achiever with outstanding results in all subjects. Kirstin is withdrawn and doesn't socialize with the other students during break times. She has also proved to be reluctant when group work activities are conducted during class time.

Kirstin's mother admitted that some of these arising concerns didn't occur until Kirstin's menstrual cycle begun. According to her mother, Kirstin had her first period at the age of nine. At first, my reaction was to regard Kirstin's problem as an ingrained reaction brought on because of embarrassment. Her inability to relate to her peers may have been caused by the early developmental issues she faced at such a young age.

Furthermore, Kirstin's mother informed me that the concerns had escalated when they told Kirstin they were moving from Nebraska to Texas. Taking this into account, I applied anxiety as a primary factor to Kirstin's condition.

Upon meeting Kirstin, my first impressions were that she is a well-mannered girl who is much more mature than her parents gave her credit for. A young girl who is beyond her years.

Her immediate responses to my prompts demonstrated a deeper understanding of the world and social structures. When asked why she doesn't interact with students her own age, she claimed she doesn't relate to people her own age. She further claimed to not relate to anyone at all and that she found people to be strange.

I asked her if she ever suffers from persistent headaches, to which she claimed she did not, but that she saw flashes of light in the corner of her eyes at night. Sometimes red. Sometimes white.

I further questioned about these flashes, and whether they appear when she is feeling a certain way. She informed me they come when she is angry or sad and that they come often.

I probed further and inquired what she does to make the flashes go away. Kirstin told me she doesn't want them to go away, that she likes the flashes. She told me that all she usually does is close her eyes and listen to the rain in her head.

It is my recommendation that Kirstin proceed to a more intense psychological evaluation and further treatment for possible schizophrenia and depression. I further advise that Kirstin be kept from social interactions with her peers, as there is room for aggressive and perhaps violent behavior to surface.

A referral form to the Nebraska Wesleyan University Psychology Department for Kirstin to undergo a thorough examination has been mailed out to Mr. and Mrs. Matthews.

I am still awaiting a response.

EPILOGUS

You know, a long time ago being crazy meant something.
Nowadays everybody's crazy.

CHARLES MANSON

Standing on the side of the road just outside of the Edwards Hill Elementary School, Richardson watched a long string of emergency vehicles with flashing lights pass her by as she held her cell phone against her ear.

"No," she said to the person on the other end of the line. "Don't worry about me. Stay there with the kids. I'll need to be here for a while, I think."

The high school students and two receptionists had made their way around to the front of the school, where they observed the mustering of vehicles with flashing lights and multitude of people who were appearing from nowhere. Above them, news helicopters circled like vultures in search of carrion.

It was surreal.

Many adults gathered near the fence line of the school. There were police officers escorting young, upset and confused students through the door of the building into the awaiting arms of sobbing and thankful parents.

Richardson couldn't help letting a tear or two fall over her cheeks. She considered how she might have reacted if it was her coming to gather her two children after a long ordeal such as today had brought.

"I'm fine, Frederick," she assured her husband. "I've been behind the elementary school for most of the day. Are Andrew and Terri okay?"

She wiped her eyes as a young mother cradled a young boy, carrying him out the gate.

Officer Summer Florez watched transfixed as both Captain Reece and Lieutenant Sedgewick quickly paced across the road, making a beeline for Mayor Keith Owens. The two senior officers navigated the street, moving between loaded police cars and other emergency vehicles as they closed in on Owens.

"Guess that support from Houston finally showed up," Sedgewick said to his commander.

The old man was spouting claims that the police were to blame for the day's occurrences. Most of the gathering parents and citizens ignored his claims as they pushed by in order to collect their children and get away from the scene as quickly as they could. He was in the middle of such a rant when he turned his head and noticed the approaching law enforcers.

"There she is!" He pointed to Reece. "She's the one who should be accountable for all of this. She should have demanded that our precious town have more of a police presence in our streets. Edwards Hill can now be named an unsafe community because of her. Captain Julia Reece."

"Shut the fuck up, Keith," a parent hollered to him. "Those poor bastards on the grass over there would still be alive if it weren't for you."

"Precisely why we're here, Mister Mayor," Reece said as they approached.

He moved away from the approaching captain and lieutenant.

"I have the community's best wishes at heart," he proclaimed.

"Keith Owens," Reece called out, loud enough for all to hear. "I'm placing you under arrest for endangering the lives of community members, resulting in the deaths of two individuals. Dwayne Forrester and Steven Tulley. You have the right to remain silent. Anything you say can and will be used against you in a court of law. You have the right to an attorney. If you cannot afford an attorney, one will be provided for you."

Copious applause drowned out the reading of the Miranda rights.

Sedgewick grabbed the older man forcefully by the elbow.

"Don't touch me," the mayor protested, trying to wriggle his way free.

The lieutenant ignored Owens, snapping his handcuffs tightly over the mayor's wrists.

"I'm going to sue all of you for this," the mayor promised them. "This is defamation at its best."

"Put him in the car, Lieutenant," Reece commanded.

"With pleasure," Sedgewick replied, forcing the older man to walk onto the road towards an awaiting police vehicle.

As he shoved the mayor into the backseat of the sedan, he looked over the roof towards Florez and Plasket, who were still standing near the police tape line.

"How are you holding up, rookie?" the lieutenant asked as he slammed the car door shut.

"Fine, sir," she replied with a smile.

"It's been a long day, huh?"

"It's had its moments," she answered.

He moved around the vehicle to the driver's side.

"How would you like a few shifts on the night crew?" he said as he opened the door. "It'll free up your days and give you time to work on that tan of yours."

"I don't know if the captain would be too pleased with that, sir."

"I'll talk to the captain," he told the young officer. "I can be rather persuasive."

She shrugged and held her bandaged hand up for him to see.

"I still got this for a while," she said.

"Come on," he urged her. "The nights are mostly poker and pizza around here."

She pursed her lips and grinned, nodding.

"Okay," she said. "Why not?"

"Good." Sedgewick smiled. "What about you, Cory? Come and join the dark side for a while."

"Thanks Charlie," the officer replied. "But you and your band of vampires will have to survive without me."

"Your loss," the lieutenant said, lowering himself into the driver's seat and shutting the door.

Florez turned to Plasket as Sedgewick drove away with the mayor in the backseat.

"Night shift," she gasped, an enormous smile invading her face.

"You'll be bored in less than ten minutes," he told her. "I guarantee."

III

He held onto her hand, crouching beside her as the para-medics strapped her onto the gurney. She was looking into his eyes affectionately as he listened to the ambulance officer next to him.

"She may be suffering from hypothermia and shock," the woman in uniform told him. "We'll take her back for observation. Will you be riding with us?"

"Do you think we could ever have a chance?" she asked him halfheartedly.

"What?" He looked at her, confused.

She lowered her head. "I just thought, because you stayed with me, you might..."

He shook his head disbelievingly. "Don't mistake my compassion for affection," he told her. "I stayed with you because no one else would, Stephanie. You have made more enemies in this school than you have friends. And I'm sorry to say that you have probably lost all of your friends today."

She sobbed. It made little sense to her he would hold her so closely all day long if he didn't love her in the slightest.

"I have always liked Kirstin," he told her. "Always. She was smarter than all of us. Prettier than you and all of your friends put together. She didn't do all the terrible things that you and your friends did to everyone and to each other."

"What about all of this?" She pointed to the school building.

"This isn't her," he replied. "I don't understand why she did this. This wasn't the Kirstin I knew. Something snapped. How else could this have happened? Something inside of her had enough.

"All I know is that you are a very nasty girl, Stephanie Granger, and I have spent way too much of my time with you today.

"These guys are here to look after you now. I don't think I need to escort you to the hospital after all. You're a big girl. You can look after yourself."

He nodded to the paramedics and rose to his feet, pulling his hand away from hers. She tried desperately to hold onto him, but her fingers slipped from his grasp.

"Donny," she wept. "Please don't."

"Goodbye, Stephanie," he said as the ambulance officers lifted her into the back of the emergency vehicle. "Take care."

The doors closed with a hefty slam before the ambulance rolled away.

Crouching beside Phillips, the last remaining SWAT member, she held his hand as Charlie the helicopter pilot packed gauze against the wound on the sergeant's side. Two ambulance officers wheeled a gurney in through the door at that moment.

"I'm so sorry," McFarlan told him again, her eyes wet with tears.

"Stop blaming yourself," Phillips replied. "None of it was your fault. It was all her."

"I know," the young police officer said. "But I still feel like shit. I couldn't even talk her out of it."

"She wasn't going to be talked out of it, Kimmie," the older man assured her. "This was only ever going to end with her in a body bag. I'm sad to say it, but it's true."

"We need to get him out of here," one paramedic insisted as they lowered the gurney to floor level.

"He's got a protrusion just above his hip here," the pilot informed them. "I've packed it as best I could."

"It's as good as we could do," the other ambulance officer said. "You a medic?"

"I was a pilot in Afghanistan," Charlie replied. "Weren't we all medics?"

"Time to go," Phillips told McFarlan. "You should get out of here. Take a vacation."

"What about you?" she asked as she let his hand go.

"I don't know," he said as the three men lifted him from the floor and onto the stretcher. "I might just lie around for a week or two."

She smiled. What else was he going to do?

Several uniformed officers passed through the door, heading into the building. There had been steady traffic flowing into the school for some time. Mostly, police and firefighters in search of survivors.

"You really should get out of here," he said again. "Don't stay in here. This isn't a good place to be right now."

She nodded as the paramedics raised the gurney back to full height.

"Catch you around, Officer McFarlan, he said as they wheeled him through the door.

"Catch you around, Sergeant Phillips," she replied with a weak smile.

"I should go too," Charlie told her. "I need to get the Huey back to Houston."

"Thanks for what you did for him," she said, shaking his hand.

"That's my job," he replied. "You take care."

And with that, the pilot followed the gurney through the door and left her on her own in the dark cafeteria.

Peering around the room, she saw overturned tables and chairs, all pushed away from the broken door that had blown open from the explosion. It was hard to believe that one little girl had caused so much damage to just this room alone, let alone the rest of the school.

McFarlan wondered how far this damage would reach.

Would it venture further than the immediate families and friends of the victims? Would people from across the nation pay attention? Across the globe?

She hadn't seen the complete picture, the masterpiece Kirstin had created. She had only seen a little piece.

Still, it was enough.

The macabre shaping of letters and words, formed by the innards of children.

It was enough.

As more uniformed people moved through the door and into the room, passing through to enter the corridor beyond the broken door, she closed her eyes.

The words were there.

EGO SUM PLACIDO VOX

She opened her eyes again, knowing that when they inevitably closed, they would return. Branded into the insides of her eyelids, they would always be there.

"Hello?"

A woman's voice called from beyond the door to the passageway.

"Is anyone there?"

McFarlan wiped her eyes with the palms of her hands and tried to compose herself as best she could.

"Hello?" the voice called again.

"Yes," the police officer replied. "I'm here."

"The fireman said to come this way," a young woman said as she stepped over the rubble and into the room. "Is it over?"

"It's over," McFarlan said assuredly as she stepped towards the approaching woman. "Are you okay?"

"I'm a little cold and wet," she replied as some more people emerged behind her. "I'm Rosina Posadas. I'm a teacher here. These are some students that were hiding with me and another teacher."

"Samuel Redman," a man said as he followed the last of the six students into the room. "There are more people upstairs."

"I'm sure the firefighters and police already inside will find them," McFarlan told them. "Please come this way. There are emergency vehicles outside. I'm sure they'll be able to help you."

Emerging from the building, McFarlan noticed a triage of sorts set up in the carpark behind several emergency vehicles.

Flashing lights and the rumbling sound of gas generators invaded her senses as the cool evening air swept over her.

Some police officers hastily came to their sides and escorted her and the eight others towards a canvas gazebo where a large stack of blankets and some camping chairs waited. She noticed the students and teachers that from the cafeteria with her, sitting around in groups with fresh coverings over their shoulders. Some were gripping foam cups of steaming liquid, while others simply stared blankly at the ground, silently thankful to be alive.

"You're all right now, Kimmie," a voice said on her left. She turned her face to see who it was that was holding her around the shoulders, moving her towards the gazebo.

"Roselia?" McFarlan furrowed her brow. "Is that you?"

"It's me," the other young police officer replied. "Are you hurt?"

"No," she replied. "Just cold and wet."

"What about what you saw?" DeLong questioned, sensing that there was more under her the surface of her friend than she was letting on.

McFarlan suddenly burst into tears. Her knees buckled as fatigue suddenly made itself known to her.

Delong wrapped her arms tightly around the other, pulling her tightly against her frame.

"It's all right," she assured her friend. "You're all right."

Her vision blurred as tears flowed from her eyes. She could only make out forms among the bright flashing lights.

The shape of a man emerged before her.

"Kimmie?" the man said.

DeLong released her hold a little to turn and see who was there.

McFarlan wiped her eyes and blinked, trying to regain some clarity.

"It's Aiden," the man told her, sensing that she was having difficulty seeing him. She let go of DeLong and threw herself into the arms of the teacher.

Without hesitation, he wrapped his enormous arms around her and kissed her forehead.

"You're safe now," he whispered into her ear. "It's all over."

She placed her head against his chest and let out a soft cry.

"It's all over," he said again as he hugged her tightly.

She relished his words and tried to take them to heart. But she wasn't so sure they were entirely true.

Was it over?

Was she truly safe?

Even now, as she closed her eyes and listened to his heart beating against her ear, she saw the message Kirstin had left on the gymnasium floor.

Written with internal organs of dead children.

EGO SUM PLACIDO VOX

I Am Calm Voice.

How could she ever be safe with this in her head?

How could it ever be truly over when this awaited her whenever she closed her eyes?

VII

"We have been informed that there are over seventy victims inside the school building behind me, Phil," Samantha Peterson reported into the camera. Behind her, against the brickwork of the high school, was the rapid blue and red glow of flashing lights as ambulances and police vehicles from neighboring towns pulled into the carpark off camera to her right.

"Several survivors have been discovered by the police in the upstairs classrooms and are being escorted out through the cafeteria as I speak," she continued. "We have seen quite a number of emergency vehicles arriving and a large crowd has been gathering outside the front of the school as family members of students and staff come looking for answers. There is a large forensics team inside the building at the moment who should be able to provide some further information when they have completed their examination of the scene."

"Have the police been able to share any details, Sam?" Phil Gouldman asked her, his image appearing in a small window at the top left of the screen.

"All we know so far is that the police believe this to be the work of one individual," Peterson replied. "A young female student who allegedly shot both of her parents in cold blood this morning before attending school.

"As far as a reason for her murderous rampage, the police are remaining close-lipped for the time being. We can say that the girl has sustained a self-inflicted gunshot wound, resulting in her death. They were unwilling to share any details of her name or age. Phil?"

"Thank you, Samantha Peterson, reporting live from Edwards Hill State High School," the anchorman said as his image enlarged, filling the entire screen. "To recap. Over seventy people, including students and school staff, have been killed by a lone perpetrator in what is being labeled as the worse mass shooting in our nation's history. The murderer was a young girl who ended her own life, bringing this five-hour ordeal to a resolution.

"In further news, the CDC has announced the mysterious outbreak in northern Washington, Idaho and Montana to be of an epidemic category. Teams have been deployed along with the national guard to help bring the..."

VIII

The television screen went dark as he pressed the power off on the remote control.

Placing it on the small side table, he swung his legs over the edge of his bed and planted his feet squarely on the dorm room floor. A large banner with the word *COMETS* stretched across it in orange letters hung lopsided on the wall above his bed.

Already dressed in his jeans and a gray T-shirt, he pulled on a pair of socks before slipping into his hiking boots. As he laced them up, he glanced across to his roommate, who was lying on his own bed facing the television. The roommate's eyes were staring blankly at the television, which might have looked normal if the screen was still on.

A deep gash that ran through the roommate's throat had stopped spilling blood over his shirt and bedspread. Now it just glistened in the light emitting from the globe on the ceiling.

He admired his handiwork as he finished looping his laces, reaching for the assault rifle and backpack loaded with spare magazines lying on the floor under his bed.

Dark, ominous clouds twisted and churned in his mind as distant thunder rumbled from deep within.

Lightning flashed, illuminating from beneath the clouds' surface, causing a deep crimson light to fill his head.

Underneath it all, submerged deep within, a soft voice whispered.

Focus.

IX

Focus.

AFTERWORD &
ACKNOWLEDGEMENTS

The Calm Voice came about in 2016, when I heard a news report about a shooting in San Bernardino on the 2nd of December. With 38 victims, 22 injured and 16 dead, I waited for the inevitable response from both media and politicians. Should there be gun reform in the USA?

Admittedly, I sway slightly to the left, so my immediate reaction was and still is with a definite affirmative. Yes.

Considering I'm a citizen of Australia and not the United States of America, I didn't necessarily believe I had a place to express my opinion. In Australia, we've had very few cases of mass shootings that match any experiences in the USA. That said, I don't know of many other nations that have experienced mass shootings like that of the USA.

However, we had them.

Strathfield, New South Wales 17 August 1991.

Wade Frankum, aged 33, went on a rampage injuring six people and killing 8, including himself and a student who attended my high school. She was in her final year, one year ahead of me.

The following is from an article; from https://www.sydney-criminallawyers.com.au/ title; Remembering the Impact of the Strathfield Massacre.

Two months following the Strathfield massacre, the Australian cabinet agreed to a series of national gun controls, which included bans on Lithgow manufactured self-loading military style rifles, as well as repealing the 1903 Australian Rifle Club regulations.

Then Australian justice minister Michael Tate told his fellow ministers that the federal government had to take a lead on a national gun control strategy. According to Tate, underlying the reforms was the principle that "the possession of firearms is not a right, but a conditional privilege."

And in late October 1991, the Australian Police Ministers' Council pushed through national uniform gun laws. But despite these measures, the gun controls in Tasmania and Queensland remained lax.

Port Arthur, Tasmania 28 April 1996.

Martin Bryant, aged 28, killed 35 people and wounded another 28 victims. After the shooting, the Australian government issued The National Firearms Agreement in 1996, effectively banning the sale and ownership of automatic and semi-automatic rifles, with exceptional circumstances where the prohibition doesn't apply. Because of these gun control reforms, Port Arthur was the mass shooting on such a large scale Australia has experienced.

Port Arthur, in this writer's opinion, was Australia's wake-up call. We acted immediately. We're not perfect down under. Gun crimes still exist, but nothing in the same vein as Port Arthur or Strathfield.

Since 2016, according to statista.com, and as I write this, the United States of America has experienced 47 mass shootings. This number doesn't account for every gun crime and isn't inclusive of every school shooting in the USA. Since 2016, there have been 24 school shooting incidents in America where the total injured number 86 and the deceased 45.

The land of the free.

The home of the brave.

Still, the debate about gun regulation in the USA is yet to begin.

I wrote **The Calm Voice**, originally released as *I Am Calm Voice*, to be a grotesque slasher-type story with the perpetrator able to get their hands on a firearm with ease. It isn't a political statement regarding gun control, but I couldn't resist making a comment about something so elemental when, for a time, the television and radio seemed to spout a new report about a school shooting every week or even within a couple of days.

As I mentioned previously, we're not perfect in Australia but, I'm so glad we'll never experience the gun violence statistics suffered by the United States because of our reforms.

For this, I am thankful.

Thanks to my family for their loving support. It's always good to get an encouraging word to help me along. There are times I really needed it.

A shout out to my editor, the best editor ever, Sally Odgers. You are greatly appreciated for your hard work. Especially, considering that my work is so jam-packed full of things that need editing. I'm so glad I found you.

Special thanks to The CS Lewis Company Ltd for granting me the permission to use a small extract from, PERELANDRA by CS Lewis © copyright CS Lewis Pte Ltd 1944. This was the first time that I ever sought permission to use another author's work. Needless to say, I literally jumped for joy when I read your reply.

To the good people at Whitekeep Books and Ingram Spark. Without you, this book would not have made it to print, or into the hands of readers everywhere. I'm eternally grateful for that.

More thanks to the writing and reading community on social media. Without your reposts, retweets, likes, pokes, smiley face emojis and kind words; others may have missed the news of these books. You are a very tight community and I love all of you for your enthusiasm, inspiration, encouragement and patronage towards books. You're all exceptional!

Last, but not least, I'd like to acknowledge the many sources of inspiration for my embarking on this journey. The obvious writers (in no particular order); Stephen King, Margaret Atwood, George R. R. Martin, James Patterson, J. R. R. Tolkien, Dan Brown, C. S. Lewis, J. K. Rowling, R. L. Stine, Matthew Reilly, Tara Moss, Jane Caro, Neil Gaiman, John Flanagan, Ahn Do, Oliver Phommavanh and Nathan M. Farrugia. Some of these folks have shared a wealth of knowledge with me and I could not be more grateful for their help.

Warm wishes to all,
Robert E Kreig

ABOUT THE AUTHOR

Robert E Kreig was born in Newcastle, Australia and grew up in its outer suburbs.

He has always had a love for books, particularly well-told stories involving action, adventure and fear.

Some of Robert's favourite authors as a young reader included J. R. R. Tolkien, Stephen King, Orson Scott Card, Ray Bradbury and Frank Herbert. As he grew into adulthood, the list continued to lengthen, adding more influential writers such as George R. R. Martin, Matthew Reilly, Nathan M. Farrugia, Dan Brown, James Patterson, Michael Connelly and Lee Child just to name a few.

Inspired by movies like Star Wars, King Kong, Jaws, Jason and the Argonauts and other great adventure pieces, Robert listened to the voices in his head and entertained the strange visions dancing through his mind to assist him with writing his fantasy series The Woodmyst Chronicles.

Robert has penned ten books for the series which follow the lives of many characters, particularly focussing upon a family who must face many trials before the epic conclusion. Clashing swords, strange creatures, flying dragons and sorcery inhabit the world surrounding Woodmyst.

Robert has also written a standalone book, Long Valley.

Robert currently lives in Canberra, Australia where he hopes to one day become a full-time writer.

ABOUT THE AUTHOR

OTHER BOOKS BY THIS AUTHOR

THE WOODMYST CHRONICLES

From a faraway land...
...comes a new adventure.
The Woodmyst Chronicles is the story of a small community that faces the hardest of trials in a world filled with darkness, violence and magic.

Books In This Series...
THE WALLS OF WOODMYST
THE SONS OF WOODMYST
THE HEIR OF WOODMYST
THE WARLORDS OF WOODMYST
THE HUNTRESS OF WOODMYST
THE SHADOW OF WOODMYST
THE BRIDES OF WOODMYST
THE GODS OF WOODMYST
THE WEAPONS OF WOODMYST
A FAREWELL TO WOODMYST

LONG VALLEY

In the small community of Long Valley, nestled comfortably beneath snow-capped mountains, people quietly go about their business. Everybody knows everybody and there are no worries to give mind to.

But something has awakened.

A tragic accident near the valley's army base sparks a number of terrifying events, placing the local civilians in mortal danger.

A contagion is subsequently released into Long Valley, infecting pets, livestock, wildlife and people.

It's up to the local law enforcement and a small band of citizens to try to keep the town safe.

In the end, it becomes a struggle for survival as the people of Long Valley are overcome by the urge to feed.

www.robertekreig.com

www.whitekeepbooks.com

www.ingramcontent.com/pod-product-compliance
Lightning Source LLC
Chambersburg PA
CBHW020245120726
47904CB00001B/92